T0195090

CROSSING BORDERS

ILMARINEN G. VOGEL

BALBOA.
PRESS

A DIVISION OF HAY HOUSE

Copyright © 2019 Ilmarinen G. Vogel.

All rights reserved. No part of this book may be used or reproduced by any means, graphic, electronic, or mechanical, including photocopying, recording, taping or by any information storage retrieval system without the written permission of the author except in the case of brief quotations embodied in critical articles and reviews.

Balboa Press books may be ordered through booksellers or by contacting:

Balboa Press
A Division of Hay House
1663 Liberty Drive
Bloomington, IN 47403
www.balboapress.com
1 (877) 407-4847

Because of the dynamic nature of the Internet, any web addresses or links contained in this book may have changed since publication and may no longer be valid. The views expressed in this work are solely those of the author and do not necessarily reflect the views of the publisher, and the publisher hereby disclaims any responsibility for them.

The author of this book does not dispense medical advice or prescribe the use of any technique as a form of treatment for physical, emotional, or medical problems without the advice of a physician, either directly or indirectly. The intent of the author is only to offer information of a general nature to help you in your quest for emotional and spiritual well-being. In the event you use any of the information in this book for yourself, which is your constitutional right, the author and the publisher assume no responsibility for your actions.

Any people depicted in stock imagery provided by Getty Images are models, and such images are being used for illustrative purposes only.
Certain stock imagery © Getty Images.

Print information available on the last page.

ISBN: 978-1-9822-3360-0 (sc)
ISBN: 978-1-9822-3361-7 (e)

Balboa Press rev. date: 08/28/2019

CONTENTS

PART ONE

PART TWO
WORLDS AT WAR

PART THREE
ALMOST HOME

PART ONE

CHAPTER ONE
THE TRAIN

It was the fall of 1942. Georg's commanders believed that their Hospital train was on its way to battlefields near Leningrad and Moscow.

Since June of 1941 when Hitler broke the non-aggression treaty with Stalin, new challenges of modern warfare became visible. Military command structures had proven to be insufficient to serve the logistics needs of the war economy and the war itself.

At the time the railways were the most efficient transport mode for long distance deliveries. To move just one battalion to the front in Russia by railroad took eighty to one hundred trains. Scheduling these trains required knowledge the army command did not have:

They had no personnel trained in the operation of this complex system of machinery, tracks, switches, depots, service stations for locomotives and centers for repairs and maintenance. Scheduling trains running through a grid system with signals and communications systems was not a matter of simply ordering desired moves. Without understanding the components and how they interact rail service cannot function.

Rail systems were known only to railroaders. Army commanders tried to force freight down the tracks. When another train was in the way, a locomotive had seized or a depot was out of coal or water, that branch of the system came to a halt. Such failures were answered by Hitler's military by executing people who were assigned to schedule such trains.

Russia used longer trains with stronger engines running them at lower speeds over larger distances and were able to maintain rail service despite their adverse climate. Distances from headquarters to battlefields in Russia were not comparable to the Poland and France campaigns. Hitler's high command had no choice but to turn railroad operations over to the Reichsbahn. This was a public organization that knew how to run trains. This is how they avoided the breakdown of Operation Barbarossa, the war on Russia.

According to the Treaty of Versailles, medical trains were not permitted to be run under the Red Cross by the German government. This hospital train was running under the disguise of a freight train.

Doctor Georg Hofmeister served on this train as the assistant to Doctor Wilhelm von Wallenstein. His rank was second lieutenant which came with his medical degree. He had received his basic military training with the cavalry. He had participated in short assignments of mounted campaigns in France.

This story is leaning on circumstances and episodes remembered by people who were present at the time and on records available to the public now. It covers the time during the years of 1942- 1946. Operation Barbarossa and the war on Russia and travel under the command of the medical corps. It is telling his Return from Russia and a last deployment in Italy towards the end of the war.

The survival of our protagonist depended on complete secrecy and a journey by all means available to a person with knowledge of medicine and an ability to connect with people of different national, ethnic and religious backgrounds. It is the story that was never told.

All names of persons are invented, and poetic license was used to invent encounters and episodes of this story of personal choices during the complete breakdown of humanity.

CHAPTER TWO
TO THE FRONT

Georg stretched his toes and dropped his legs over the side of his bunk. The sound of the moving train had sent him into a deep restful sleep. He inhaled the smell of early autumn wafting in through the cracked windows of the sleeping compartment he shared with his commanding officer and medical mentor Dr. Wilhelm von Wallenstein.

It took Georg a while to remember that he was on the way to the front. The smell of disinfectants and soap reminded him. Georg and Dr. von Wallenstein usually woke up before first light. Both enjoyed the quiet time when the rest of the hospital staff was still asleep, and the night shift was eating breakfast.

Under the direction of Dr. von Wallenstein the hospital was open to serve civilians and anyone in need of medical attention or emergency services along the track whenever the train was side railed. This happened when military supply trains moved past. The engine crew switched locomotives at rail depots. They stayed with the train. Running a mobile hospital was a specialty. They maintained the hospital's hot water and potable water systems. The crew worked under the supervision of their head engineer.

This morning Georg looked out of the window and watched as the world woke up. Nature was reacting to the rising sun. Rivers were running. The world was peeling out of the early morning mist looking pristine. No signs of war. The train moved at a steady pace. Wheels were squealing as it snaked its way alongside a river one long sweeping curve after another making everyone feel a little drunk. The smell of the coal fire from the locomotive mingled with the steam and gave the air an unmistakable sweet scent.

This was Georg's first deployment on a mobile hospital. Freight cars had been altered for service as a hospital, equipped for medical services and the performance of complex operations as war injuries required.

This day they were being side railed again to let combat supply trains move past. The arrival of a second train on an adjacent rail was raising curiosity. It looked like another hospital train moving in the opposite direction. Georg went to find out. He decided to ask Hans, the head engineer of his train.

"What do we have there? This is the first hospital train we have seen travelling away from the front."

"Yes, it is." Said Hans. "This train comes from the Russia front near Moscow. They need help. They have wounded on board and not enough medical personnel. Their head surgeon was wounded in an ambush and the head nurse appears to be shell shocked. You might want to see the doctor and the nurse. Maybe you can help them."

"Would you be kind enough to send for their commander? I think we should speak with them on our train and inspect their train after we have learned more of what they might need?"

"Right away doctor. I will do it myself." Promised Hans.

An hour later a meeting took place at the dining car of Georg's train. The room had a long narrow table bolted to the floor with benches on either side. Along the outside walls were benches and small fold down tables for patients who could not climb over the benches. At the side of the room near the kitchen was a counter where food was laid out for those who could serve themselves.

Georg introduced himself to Dr. Friedrich, the heavily bandaged head surgeon. He greeted Sister Anne, the head nurse and introduced Dr. von Wallenstein. Georg asked the kitchen staff for water and hot tea. He stood by the food counter and served plates of the food the cooks had prepared. He seated the surgeons at the head of the table and seated himself across from the head nurse. He was facing Dr. Friedrich and Sister Anne who sat across from Dr. von Wallenstein. Dr. Friedrich spoke with a soft and friendly voice:

"Thank you for your hospitality. We are feeling lucky that we were able to meet up with you and we appreciate any support you can offer. We are returning with wounded from the front near Moscow. Patients on our train are mostly victims of frost. They have not received any winter gear. Temperatures suddenly dropped. We were returning our wounded to Berlin but were ambushed at a depot. We lost patients; I took several bullets myself. Sister Anne was right beside me when it happened. I owe it to her great skills and stamina that I am still alive."

The nurse nodded but did not speak; Georg noticed her discomfort when Von Wallenstein asked questions about losses of staff and patients during the ambush. Dr. Friedrich answered all the questions even ones that were directed at Sister Anne. Georg looked at her as she nervously shifted in her seat and looked away. Dr. Friedrich spoke for her:

"We lost three of our nurses, two medics and many patients." While the doctor spoke, Georg observed sister Anne. She was tall, her blonde hair was combed back into a tight bun and she wore light green scrubs. Her fingernails were cut short and expertly manicured. Her hands were narrow with long fingers. She moved hands frequently from lacing her fingers tightly to crossing her arms in front of her chest. Her light complexion and pronounced cheekbones looked similar to Dr. von Wallenstein's features. Her blue eyes were set wide under a pronounced forehead and nose. Her lips were full, and she had very white teeth. Had she claimed to be his daughter, no one would have questioned it. She picked at her food but did not eat much.

While questions were asked and answered von Wallenstein's mind had wandered off.

In his mind he began to describe his situation for a letter he was composing to send to his wife. He was a good delegator and had to be personally addressed to stay focused.

He composed:

> *Our doctors and nurses are confronted with injuries so horrific that letting the wounded bleed out seems like an act of mercy. Yet we work tirelessly to stop the bleeding and give medications to reduce pain. We act with stoicism seemingly unable to feel empathy. Conversations are short and*

contain few words of comfort. They go straight to the task at hand. Thoughts of home and family are suppressed to avoid depression and heartbreak. Our first responders are the real heroes of this war. They are also the casualties no one can see. Our care providers serve all humans, no questions asked. We treat medical issues and ask no questions. We do not linger on our own needs. That must wait until we return home.

His mind returned to the present.

"How can we help?" he heard himself ask. "We are outward bound. We have supplies. Dr. Hofmeister will make a list of what you need to get your patients home."

Georg turned his attention to the team from the other train:

"We will come to your train and bring burn dressings and pain medications for frost injuries. Expect us at 14:00 hours. We will find out what we can share of our supplies and what personnel you need. We will replace personnel you have lost."

Von Wallenstein who had not been listening, turned to Georg:

"Take your team over to their train and see the patients. Let me know if we need to make any personnel changes. I understand they are shorthanded."

"Yes Doctor. I just made an appointment to take our team over at 14:00 hours." Georg affirmed.

"Excellent; I expect your report at 18:00 hours," von Wallenstein said.

Georg was concerned about the condition Sister Anne was in. When the meeting was over, he took her aside and said:

"Sister Anne, you have been through an extremely difficult and shocking experience. You should not have to shoulder this alone. If you like, I will be happy see you for an examination and for a consult. A debriefing might make you feel better. It always helps me. I can give you a physical first and then we could talk privately, if you like."

Georg had noticed things she did not like; Von Wallenstein was one. His tall stature and short cropped light blond hair, his pale skin, athletic physique, the scent of aftershave he was wearing and his habit of speaking slightly louder than necessary when in the company of others, were causing her to react with ducking motions and lowering or averting her eyes.

Sister Anne responded better to Georg's attentiveness, which did not include attempts at making her speak. With tiny gestures of head and hands he began communicating with her. When they were ready to leave, Georg leaned over to her and with a soft voice he said:

"I will see you at your station. Tonight at 19:00 hours I can see you at my examination cubicle if you feel up to it."

To the visitors he said:
"Consider everything we have to be at your service."

Georg's hospital team went over to the other train. They dressed wounds and medicated patients, cleaned and sterilized the entire facility and replenished supplies to last until they would reach Berlin. Sister Anne pointed to her wristwatch and indicated that she would see him at 19:00 hours.

Georg had prepared his cubicle. He examined her gently. Once the physical was complete and a blood sample was sent to the lab, she finally broke her silence.

"Thank you." She had noticed that he found the vein in her arm with barely a prick and taped a little sterile tissue over the spot after holding it with his pointing finger for a few moments.

"Will you see me at my compartment, where we can talk?" Georg asked.

"Yes" she replied with a faint smile. When she was dressed, Georg lead her to the next car. He took her hand when she stepped across from one car to the next after opening the doors for her. He noticed the scent she was wearing but was unsure what it was. He liked it. He inhaled her scent in a deep breath. She looked at him in surprise. He gave her a reassuring smile. She was not used to be treated with such courtesy and attention.

"Jasmine," she said in response to Georgs deep inhale. Then she said: "Respect. I like it. You are treating me with respect." When they were settled, Georg said in a quiet soothing tone:

"Welcome to our home away from home. There is no rush. No one will enter until this compartment door is open. I will take you back to your train when we are done."

"Thank you." She said with a faint smile. She studied his features for a long moment: Dark brown eyes, black, short cropped curly hair, laughing lines at the outside of his eyes. Curious and friendly at once. And very young. Georg looked at her also: She was tall and athletic. She sat upright across from him and placed her hands in her lap after crossing her right leg over her left knee lacing fingers showing white knuckles. Her ash blonde hair was gathered in a tight bun with one strand dropping over each of her cheeks. Her eyes were blue and shifting side to side which he took as a sign of stress. Nice, I like that look. He thought. He began the conversation with a question:

"You do not like Dr. von Wallenstein."

"He looks like my father." She said, glancing out of the window into the afterglow of the young evening.

"What makes you not like him?"

"He frightens me."

"Would you like to tell me more? Does your father know what you are doing?"

"No"

"Oh?"

"He is one of them."

"Them?"

"An Olympic trainer. Track and field. Master race. You know what I mean."

"What about You?"

"I became a nurse. I had to train in secret. Mother knew."

"Do you feel guilty?"

"Yes and no. I love him, but he frightens me."

"Were you involved in sports? You seem toned and very athletic."

"Gymnastics. I am a tumbler I also do rings and uneven bars."

"Medals?"

"Oh yes. Gold and silver local and regional."

"How did you find time to train for nursing?"

"My best friend's mother trains nurses. She understood. She helpt. We combined homework and nurse practitioner training. She issued my certificate when we were done. My father never found out. I secretly enlisted and left right after graduating High School. I had to get away."

"Can you tell me why?"

"He loved me too much. He crossed the line and made me stay silent. Said he would tell. I had no one to help me with my guilt and shame. I have never mentioned this to anyone."

"You are brave. You are a survivor."

I guess I am, but now I feel like I am failing. First my mother then my father. Now my country by detesting what they stand for and what they do. My mother is obedient."

"Did she know?"

"No and yes. Everything must be in order in her world. She looks away. Eyes closed. She helped me get away. I think that was her way to redeem her feeling of guilt about the unspoken truth.

I detest war. Father sees all glory. He cannot not see the truth either. Now this doctor. He looks like he could be my father's twin. That shook me up. I am so confused. I am sorry." She began to sob. She put her hands over her face.

"It's alright. Have your feelings. Let them flow." Georg said, taking her hands into his. Georg felt compassion and sympathy. Through her tears she looked deep into Georg's eyes.

"You are so different from other doctors I have met." Georg let her wipe away tears with the back of his hands while she held on to them. She moved his hands to her neck where they made a cradle for her head. With a deep exhale she slowly drew him closer and closed her eyes while searching for his lips. Like a drowning victim she clung to him and like a rescuer, he committed to this moment, trying to replace her pain, to soften her confusion and finally to find a way to release her distress. Together, they found a way into complete ecstasy and satisfaction. Her tears never stopped flowing. They caressed and held each other for a long time until finally she spoke in a whisper:

"This is what I needed. I know we are on trains moving in opposite direction. This war is far from over. We must be strong. I will never forget you." She stood up and held him in another long embrace. He kissed her on her forehead and finally on the inside of her palms.

"You are right. This is how I feel also. This moment took my breath away. I do not count my breaths. I count the ones that were taken away from me and I thank you." He looked into her eyes. She looked back into his and they held this glance for a long time.

"Can you promise me something? He finally interrupted the silence. "Will you see someone about your distress? You will need help to unfreeze yourself from all that you have seen. I know you can, and I hope you will. You are a healer. Just this one promise? I want to be sure you will recover. Just do not try to do it without help. Promise?"

"Yes. I promise." Georg went to his bag and found a small tiger eye stone. He placed it into her hand as a keepsake. Then he escorted her to her train.

CHAPTER THREE
THE DOCTORS

Von Wallenstein swung his legs over the side of his bunk, which was one foot too short for this very tall man. The two doctors were seated opposite each other, after folding up their sleeping bunks. This was the quiet hour when Georg and von Wallenstein could talk in private. Almost everyone else on the train was still asleep.

The train was making a steady sound of steel wheels on steel rails with the unmistakable tat-tat at each seem in the rail. A screeching sound in curves interrupted by the puffing of the locomotive whenever the wind blew the sound and smoke into their compartment window. Lights inside and outside of the train were dimmed to make it less visible to gunners aboard enemy aircraft. The first light of a perfect autumn day revealed the splendor and color of foliage through layers of mist along the riverbed. Both men were transfixed by the beauty of nature.

Continuing a conversation, they had started the previous evening about Georg's origins, von Wallenstein said:

"Tell me more about your family. You said they are in public life. What is it they do? How did they get through the inflation after the first war? What are they doing now?"

"My father is a minister of the Protestant Church. My mother runs the parish house. I saw them struggle with life. The town's farmers were unable to feed the people. My mother is considered a saint in her community. Open doors, open gardens, open heart. She runs a sanctuary in the name of Christ. My father was getting depressed. Privately he had doubts about God's plan. During the early days of his ministry he began looking at philosophy and theosophy outside of his church. This put him in conflict with the strict doctrines they hold. Father says that this war is going on inside of all humans. War is a sure way to end all peace, he says." Georg paused while he was watching a village appear in the distance with a steepled church.

"We are descendants of a long line of ministers." He glanced into the distance. "Mother's lineage goes all the way back to the times of Martin Luther." Georg turned his palms up. "My father refuses to ask God for favors. Wisdom and strength for his congregation is his prayer. To live a responsible life in God's light. He does not want to delegate the heavy lifting to God. Father is fluent in Latin and ancient Greek. He studies and translates original scriptures. He still searches old bible texts to find answers. He fills notebook after notebook with translations and thoughts. He says that the bible was re-written almost as many times as history. His research revealed that every writer added their own spin to serve their own purpose. I could not help but to learn classic Greek from early childhood on. It was literally poured into my bottle with the milk." Georg sat silent for a moment, watching the sun come up. Von Wallenstein looked at his young college.

"Did your father have a problem with you studying medicine instead of becoming a minister?"

"My father knew I was interested in Anthropology and Archeology. He saw it as a logical consequence of his own studies."

"I meant becoming a physician."

"He saw my distress over the Nazis winning the election." Georg checked the door to be sure they were alone. "I was in opposition to National Socialism. I belonged to a boy scout organization, the Jungenschaft, that was interested in collecting oral history and documenting customs, songs and stories. We concentrated our research in Northern and Eastern Europe. We were concerned about people losing their identity, once they lost their stories. We travelled in this region of Europe. Now they are being overrun again. Many are even being relocated by force again. We traveled and lived with them to hear their stories. We were not surprised, when the Nazis shut down our boy scout troop. To them boy scouts are trainees for war."

"Why would they do that?"

"Knowledge makes the Nazis uncomfortable. They do not like anyone asking questions. We were concerned that National Socialism would be a threat to the cultural diversity of Europe.

"What happened? How did the power change from God given Nobility to fascist regimes?"

"I don't know. Maybe it was the shift of buying power from inherited privilege and wealth to industrial production and trade."

"Did the treaty of Versailles reorganize empires?"

"I think so. The treaty was designed as punishment for Germany. We are not even supposed to run hospital trains under the red cross. Everything was done in plain sight according to the demands of the winners. Everyone was glad the war was over. No one looked at the treaty. It caused a worldwide depression. The Weimar Republic did not have a chance to succeed. People lost all their money. National and local bankers claimed they had no idea how to save their depositor's assets. Money was not buying anything." Georg went silent.

"I know", said von Wallenstein. "My family was well to do until the big crash. We lost everything. How did life after the war affect you?"

"We were children. We wanted to ride the carousel. 22000 mark for 5 minutes. Every grownup was saying different things. People were hoping for the same outcome but considered different paths to get there. We knew the difference between what people were hoping for and what they were getting. No one noticed that people were being armed against one another while their children were starving."

"How could you tell? When did you notice?"

"Once I was twelve, I joined the boy scouts. We studied the folklore of people and found tales of heroism and the glory of battle. In re-telling their stories, people made wars sound like acts of God. Almost like a religious belief. Not just Catholics or Protestants. Christians, Hindus, Muslims and Jews also were holding their loyalty to their rulers higher than their faith to their God or to knowledge from their own experience. Always ready to lay down their lives for a cause other than their own. I think experience is altered by fear. If people fared badly, they felt guilty. They thought they were being punished for failing their rulers and their maker. When they fared well, they felt undeserving. How about you?" Georg asked.

"I was studying medicine in Prague. We were somewhat isolated in our ivory tower. We were high achievers. We let others worry about politics. How did the Nazis handle it? I thought they did everything according to law."

"They did. They declared martial law and replaced the justice system. With their loyalists they gave themselves authority to target minorities and dissenters. Most importantly, they wiped out the independent press. Now they have turned on former allies by breaking the non-aggression pact with Russia. Everyone is either joining the axis or has to go to war with Hitler."

"I can see why you do not like them. I myself was fed the party line.

Then came my military service. It was all about getting up in rank." Von Wallenstein replied. "I started questioning the Nazi regime when the news began coming from only one source. Schools became training institutions for technicians, engineers and chemists for the war industry. Mathematics was suddenly about ballistics. Physics was about wireless communication. How did this influence your decision?"

"It was simple. I could not serve in their army. My father understood that I could not be a soldier. I gave up my dream of archeology and decided to study medicine instead."

"I am on your side. I am coming from a long line of physicians. We save lives. That puts our entire profession in conflict with regimes that engage in violent conflict." Von Wallenstein looked out the window. In the breaking dawn, he could see women loading a wagon with straw. He turned back to Georg. "What did you do for basic training?"

"Cavalry. I am good on horseback. I used to do competitive trick riding." This memory made him smile. "There was a stable with Lipizzaner horses in our town. My family has teams of draft horses. I loved helping on the farm and in the vineyards. Horses are in my blood." His eyes gazed over the morning landscape. "We had several cavalry deployments in France. I never stopped studying during my service. I studied at night and mailed my papers to my professor at the University of Tübingen." Later at breakfast they continued their conversation:

"We are going to the front in Russia. Moscow and Leningrad." Von Wallenstein said.

"We are being side railed a lot. Sometimes for days. I need you to be our liaison to the local people. Whenever we have a chance to provide medical services, I want you to take it. Patients in need of medical services are everywhere." He said with finality in his voice.

CHAPTER FOUR
A DREAM

Von Wallenstein was almost a head taller than Georg. His pronounced nose and forehead were adding authority to his blue eyes and direct manner. People listened when he spoke. He commanded attention and received obedience without having to pull rank. Everyone appreciated and liked his leadership. His surgery skills were legendary. As roommates in the sleeper compartment the two doctors were a good match.

The tapeti-tap of the rolling wheels had lulled Georg into a deep sleep. *He was at home. Peter the mailman came to the door. Georg had known Peter all his life. Peter had shared vegetables from his garden with the minister's family. Georg's mother had returned the favor by bringing Peter's wife sugar from her rations during canning season. Peter and his family were members of Georg's church. Peter's children had gone to Sunday School with Georg. Georg opened the door. "Heil Hitler!" said Peter with a crisp clicking of his heels and the straight arm salute with his right arm. "Good morning Peter", Georg said at the same time. The next morning, as Georg opened the door, Peter said: "Good morning", as Georg said: "Heil Hitler" with a crisp Nazi salute. The third day both were wishing each other a good morning and offered a smile of relief over the irony of this situation. "This was crazy" Georg said."*

"I know," said Peter. He was smiling.

The screeching of the brakes ended Georg's dream. He was still smiling at the mailman.

"What's so funny?" asked von Wallenstein, who had seen Georg smile. "Nothing. Just a dream about Peter, our mailman at home."

"Is he one of them?"

"In my dream I thought he was. Only the next day we switched sides and on the third day we got it right. Both on the same side. That made me smile." Georg said. Von Wallenstein looked worried.

"Why do you think we are stopping?" He asked. "Did Hans or the other engineers in the locomotive say anything to you last time you went to see them?"

"No. Nothing." Georg thought for a moment. "I am still trying to figure out how they get their information. It is as if they can listen in on the wires. I must be careful. I Cannot ask direct questions. I do not want to spook them. No one trusts anyone anymore. I glean what little information I can get from what they volunteer when we are talking."

"They follow orders. Just like the rest of us."

"I suppose you are right. I have a hunch though, that they get more information than just orders. I have heard them say that they are no longer working under the authority of the army. The Bundesbahn is a public organization that is familiar with scheduling trains and moving freight through blocks of signals from depot to depot. They are in charge now."

"Are you going forward to see them this morning? Something feels different today "Von Wallenstein said.

"Yes. I bring them coffee and check in on them. I am treating a burn wound on Paul, our boiler man. He got scorched a few days ago when the red-hot fire box door closed on him in a curve."

"Keep your ear on the tracks for me. Perhaps you hear something."

Georg was never sure if the knot in his stomach was worse when he felt the train move towards the front while through the window he could see people continue life as though there were no war or when the train stopped and all possible hazards were about to erupt. By visiting the locomotive during siderail layovers and talking as a doctor to the drive team, he was developing trust with the locomotive crew. It had taken the doctor-patient relationship to build this personal connection. Georg now collected his medical bag, burn dressings and coffee. Careful not to trip on loose gravel in the predawn light, he slowly moved forward towards the locomotive. The steam and smoke were sinking to the ground together with the cold early morning mist. When Georg prepared to climb on board, he noticed that the four engineers looked ashen. He noticed a fifth person: A soldier carrying a messenger pouch aboard the locomotive. The four were pointing at him with their eyes. Georg could hear the hissing of the relief valve on the steam chamber of the locomotive. The steam was lit by the dim light from the glowing coal through the open fire box door. Georg was able to see the faces, lit by the fire.

"Heil Hitler" saluted Georg before he handed up the coffee. "I see you have company. Should I come back? I can bring more coffee." The soldier said:

"Thanks, but I have to move on." Turning to the train crew he said sternly: "Remember what I told you." He pulled his ear guards down, put on his helmet and fastened the chin strap. His winter boots hit the gravel with a crunch while the four gave a silent salute. The soldier disappeared into the steam of the engine and the chilly pre-dawn haze.

"What was he talking about, remember what?" Georg asked. "Top secret business." Hans said, once Georg was on board.

"You say one word you hear from us to the passengers on this train and we could all get fried." To make his point stronger Hans stepped close to Georg: "As far as the people in back are concerned, we are going on another detour. Track repairs."

CHAPTER FIVE
GOING SOUTH

Hans spoke the next words into Georg's ear:

"We are being sent south. Not Leningrad, not Moscow."

"What are you saying? Where are we going?"

"Kovel. Then Kiev, right down the middle of the Ukraine. That is all I know. That route has the same gauge tracks as this train. We will be instructed from depot to depot." Hans explained." There are major changes going on. They say nothing. Every time they say nothing, hell breaks loose. We have to use our own channels to get information. This will take some time. Railroaders have ways. "With much emphasis he repeated: "For your own sake Doctor Hofmeister, you know nothing!"

"Doctor patient privilege" Georg reassured him. This news was serious.

After some small talk over sips of coffee Hans asked: "How is Paul's burn wound doing?"

"I will know as soon as I change the dressing," Georg said, grabbed the tape that fastened the bandage to the injured forearm between thumb and pointing finger and with one swift movement ripped it off before Paul had time to react.

"You are good," said Paul, the fire expert. "Removing tape is always torture and you did this with your left hand, I didn't have time to feel it." Georg examined the wound, dressed and bandaged it.

"It looks good Paul, you heal well. One more day and you will be good as new." He said this loud enough for Hans to hear. To Paul he continued: "I would like to have you come over to my examination room to give you a full checkup. I want to listen to your heart and lungs and check your blood pressure." Georg was concerned about the hazards of operating a coal furnace. "Day after tomorrow you come see me at the office and if you are well, I'll let you go back to work." They all laughed. Stepping close to Hans, Georg said quietly:

"Suppose I was a boy scout and you were to tell me how to get to Ukraine from here. Just a travel plan with options of destinations a tourist would like to hear."

"Don't push it. I'll come to your examination room myself for a check-up tomorrow. You can check my ears and see what I've been hearing. I think it was a very big noise."

"See me at my office whenever you can. I'll have the nurse check your pulse. He has very good bedside manners." Another short chuckle and Georg was gone.

As he left the train, it was getting light. Georg could see a small stone building with smoke rising from the chimney. He noticed two armored vehicles in front of the building and by the tracks he saw two red signals. "I have a hunch something big is up". He said to von Wallenstein when he entered their compartment. He sat his doctor's bag down and prepared himself for a long wait.

"Any news besides hunches?" Von Wallenstein looked inquiringly at Georg, who looked worried.

"Nothing yet. A detour maybe. The engineers had a visitor with a messenger pouch. He left before I boarded the locomotive. I heard him say: "Remember what I told you." It sounded like a threat. Then he disappeared into the fog. When I left, I could see the depot with both signals on red. We are at a fork in the tracks. There were two armored trucks by the depot building. We will exchange locomotives here."

"What do our train drivers think?"

"Nothing. They are waiting for the soldiers to leave. Then they can contact their own system. Everything is top secret. Military leaves it to railroaders to manage rail traffic. Now it is up to them to find out what is really going on. I think we are in good hands with our drive team."

"You are their doctor. Take good care of them" Von Wallenstein said. Georg was in the habit of waking up at around four thirty in the morning. He usually walked forward to the locomotive with fresh coffee at around five. He had scheduled an examination for Hans, the head of the train crew for six o'clock this morning. There was no activity in the examination cubicle at that time. People on the train were having breakfast in the mess car at that hour.

Georg knew that his life was going to turn into twenty-four-hour non-stop mayhem soon. Everyone was going to be assigned six-hour shifts. Six on, six off, twenty-four hours a day. Georg wanted to find out where that might be. This morning, ice crystals had formed on both sides of the cabin window and the metal steps were slippery. Georg wore gloves and his ear flaps lowered. His white winter parka had a large red cross on the back an another one on the front. He lowered himself carefully onto the gravel bed and inspected the depot buildings in the dim light of this cloudy pre-dawn morning. The armored vehicles were gone. White smoke rose straight up from the brick chimney. The only sound he could hear were his footsteps and the occasional hissing of the pressure relief valve of the locomotive. Georg checked to see if a fresh locomotive was standing by for the hospital train. This was his favorite time of the day. The world came into focus.

"Heil Hitler and Good morning boys." He looked around. He did not see Hans or Paul.

"Paul is in his bunk. He had night shift." Said Manfred, the second engineer. "Hans is at the depot. He was busy all night. As soon as the army trucks left, he went into the rail roaders network. No one can talk to him then. Hans is a third generation Engineer and fifth generation railroader. It is all in the family he says. Right now, he is very focused. We know better than to ask questions when he gets like that. Last night's messenger visit got him going. Hans wants to keep us safe. We are his family. "Manfred checked the water supply and the pressure gages. "We will get a new locomotive. They have potable water for the hospital here." He began preparations for switching out locomotives. "It is difficult enough to run trains. Running trains through war zones can make you crazy."

"It is a mystery to me how you do it," said Georg. "How do you learn to run trains? When do you decide to become a train operator?"

"Most of us are born into railroad families." Said Manfred. "We are a tribe that was born when rails were first built all over Europe a hundred years ago. A million kilometers of rails were laid between eighteen thirty and eighteen seventy. It took a few years to figure out how to send trains down the line. The problem is that both sides need to know who has the green light to go. It takes telephones and signals. We also have to deal with different rail widths. East Prussia, Poland and Ukraine have European gauge. Same track width as Germany. Russia's rails are wider by about four inches. They have been invaded before. They decided to make it difficult for invaders. When Hitler broke the non-aggression pact with Stalin, all their trade agreements were cancelled. Some vital supply lines are still German track width. Hitler attacked his former trade partner. Russia has used their own long trains to evacuate civilians. They return with troops and tanks. They are a defensive force. As aggressors, we have to bring everything with us that we need to run a war. Panzer war is a logistics war. The army needs constant resupply for their Panzers. At times they forget that food and winter gear for troops are as important as diesel fuel, grease and ammunition. I say they did not think this through. This is not truck traffic. This is rail service. Tank warfare is a rail service war. Railroaders make tank war possible. France and Poland were easy. Russia not so much."

"Is there any coffee?" Paul stretched and climbed out of his bunk.

"Your coffee is cold. I'll stick it in the fire box. I was just telling Dr. Hofmeister"

"I know. I could hear you. You talk too much. Your opinions will get you killed one of these days."

"You always say that. Just because you don't have opinions does not mean that I could not have some." Manfred sounded defensive. Georg was getting to know his drive team.

"Where is Hans?" Paul wanted to know. "Hans is at the depot," said Paul.

"Right," replied Manfred. "He will come back and he will know more than you and I together."

"That makes him the boss," replied Paul.

At this moment, Hans appeared through a puff of steam.

"Burrr," he said." This is going to be a cold winter. "The frost is two weeks early." He saw Georg. "Hello doctor Hofmeister, I did not see you behind Freddy the armoire. I think I will need that ear examination today. The cold is doing a job on me. Do you have an opening at six? I will have breakfast first if that works for you." Hans said.

"Come see me first and have your breakfast later. I get better readings if you have an empty stomach. We can eat breakfast together at the dining car after the examination."

With a nod to the others Georg climbed to the ground and made his way back to his car, where he expected von Wallenstein to be waiting for news.

"So?" Von Wallenstein was sitting upright on his bunk.

"Nothing yet." Said Georg. "I have made an appointment for an ear examination for Hans this morning."

When Hans arrived five minutes early Georg said:

"I have to get my station ready and my paperwork prepared. Hard to get office help in these parts." Both gave a short chuckle. "Please sit at the edge of the examination table facing away from me and remove your jacket and shirt. I want to listen to your lungs." With swift movements he went to several places on Hans's back, tapped here and there, had him cough and breathe deeply, checked his heart and noticed a murmur. He noted this on his pad and went on to check reflexes in eyes, tapped the knee caps, checked range of motion in arms and torso, looked into the ears and nose, took out his elastic and tied off Hans's arm above the elbow and with his stethoscope under the elastic he listened to the pulse as he loosened the elastic tie. He noted the information on his pad.

"We need to give you more potassium. Otherwise your heart is beating strong. There is a murmur. What's her name?" They both laughed at the thought.

"You can whisper into my stethoscope. Your words are safe with me. What can you hear?" Hans spoke very softly into the stethoscope:

"The war plan has changed. Everything we have is being thrown to the south. Instead of resupplying the forces in the North-East, everything has been ordered to go South. We will be spending many days on side-rails now, waiting for transport trains to pass. They are supplying the attack on Stalingrad with everything they have. I don't believe that Stalingrad is the final target. Stalingrad has Russia's largest Panzer factory. We used to be partners with them. We used to supply them with steel and parts. They traded iron ore. That is why our rails in this sector still fit. Stalingrad is the panzer capital of Russia. We are not interested in that city. Hitler is interested in wiping out tank manufacturing. That is going to be a furious fight. We are really going after the oil further south. There is oil near

Baku. Where there is oil, Hitler must go." Hans paused. "I think the rise of the Nazi Regime has something to do with that. I think Hitler promised someone oil." Georg looked at Hans for a few moments:

"You seem upset." He said. Hans now spoke a little too loud for the stethoscope:

"Hitler has sacrificed half a million soldiers in the siege on Moscow. He has already lost more than three hundred thousand during the battle of Leningrad. I think he is over his head with this war." Another long pause followed. Under his breath Hans repeated: "Half a million soldiers stranded near Moscow without winter uniforms, tents, fuel or ammunition. They are doomed. Even their Panzers and trucks froze. The troops froze. This is what Napoleon found out a long time ago. Keeping it a secret at home is not going to make it go away. Talking about this to anyone will get you killed. I hate war. Now I am beginning to hate this incompetence." This conversation left Georg in as much distress as Hans was. He confirmed to himself and to Hans:

"You and I will have to be quiet about this. Losing our lives will not save anyone. We must save all the lives presented to us. That is our mission. We are together on the same train."

The following day the train was given green light to move to the next supply depot, after the locomotive was switched out and water tanks and heating supplies for the hospital cars were replenished. Hans had received orders to move the train to Kiev. He told Georg that information and orders were going to come in daily dispatches from one depot to the next. "This is a new kind of war" Hans had explained to Georg. "Fast moving tanks with armor piercing cannon and some with anti-aircraft batteries are now used. Our equipment is superior to that of the Russians. Thousands of foot soldiers are still running behind and in the muck and dust of these tanks. The old horse and buggy regime of warfare is still in use. It does not work. Especially not on the Russian front. It is too cumbersome. This is not part of World War One. This war is a fluid dynamic operation. Everything is a moving target and battles are no longer staged and buried in trenches. The only thing that gets buried now are everyone's casualties. Supplies cannot be moved as fast as battle fronts advance. Strategic understanding of these changes in warfare make the difference between victory and defeat. Our generals fall short on all fronts. They made a mistake sidelining General

Rommel. He had a proposal on how to end the war. But then ending the war was apparently never the idea. Smart maneuvering might win a day. Delays in transport will render even a military genius defenseless and exposed. Go too far too fast for resupplies to follow and you are doomed." Hans straightened up his jacket and got ready to leave. Georg sent him off with these words:

"I have never been enthusiastic about war. I think war is not the answer to resolving conflict. I think war cannot lead to peace. Maybe it never has." Hans looked around the hospital room inside his converted freight car. Then he replied:

"I understand rail service. We have changed the economy everywhere rails were laid. We have raised the standard of living for everyone by moving raw materials to factories and goods to markets. I am sorry Dr. Hofmeister. I am rambling. I have too much time on my hands, sitting on the side rail observing, waiting, thinking. My locomotive is moving the world. Unfortunately I am not. Thank you for looking after my drive team." Hans left.

The hospital train was advancing one block at a time, more or less 80 to 100 kilometers apart. Often they now sat for days at a time, waiting for the next green light. Whenever there was time for Georg to offer medical aid to people who lived near the rails, he was glad. He delivered babies and invented remedies from herbs and berries. Sometimes he even found himself treating sick farm animals or assisting farmers with difficult births of livestock. These services were offered freely. In return the hospital train often received gifts of food.

During one of their early morning conversations, Georg was feeling sad. Von Wallenstein noticed.

"What is the matter Hofmeister?" He asked.

"My fiancé is graduating this coming year. We were hoping to get married. If I can bring a little Hofmeister on board, she will not be drafted into making ammunitions. She opposes the Nazis' war on the world. She wanted to study medicine. She is on our side. I am horrified to see her make bullets to kill people." After thinking about Georg's words for a while, Von Wallenstein replied:

"We will be sending trains with wounded home and come back with resupplies and medical support staff. Let me think about what we can do to get you married." A few days later he picked up on this conversation: "You can escort a medical train back home and get married. I will issue orders accordingly. On the way back to the front you will be in charge of assembling medical supplies and filling in positions for our team. I will inform headquarters that you were given a promotion to First Lieutenant. This will give you authority to commandeer supplies for the front. That is an order." Georg stood to attention and saluted.

"Yes, Doctor von Wallenstein. Thank you."

CHAPTER SIX
DON AND VOLGA

After what seemed to have been a very long journey with more than twenty layovers, the hospital train finally arrived at its destination two-hours driving distance west of the battlefield of Stalingrad. This was the new location for this assignment. On quiet days, Georg was sent out to care for local farmers of this region. It looked pristine with its rivers, canals, and windrows of poplars, birches and willows. Some sections looked untouched as they had during the days of the Don Cossacks who have lived here and defended this region on horseback for centuries. There were some devastated corridors: After a battle group of hundreds of tanks moved through, the land looked as if a tornado had cut a straight path from one end to the other. Georg was puzzled by the discovery, that many farmers reacted to war the way one would react to a natural disaster. Tank and air warfare were something no one had ever seen before. Now they regarded them as hell. People looked at this new warfare as an act of God, soon to be over once all sins had been purged and forgiven. The greatest sorrow resulted from the conscription of eligible men to military service, leaving the disabled, elders, women and children behind. The loss of loved ones and unexplainable changes in behavior of returnees were breaking everyone's heart. No one knew what had happened to them.

Civilians and clergy were persons Georg was ordered to meet, to render medical services and to invite people to the hospital for conditions that required hospital care. Medical emergency services were widely appreciated and accepted. Georg had met people in this region ten years earlier as a boy scout, researching oral history and collecting songs and sagas.

The battle of Stalingrad was now raging and a massive stream of injured had begun flowing to the hospital day and night. Shoulder to shoulder, the surgeons stood with their teams and operated day and night until the stream of victims slowed. Georg and his teammates had lost track of time. They worked until their legs could no longer support them and their eyes were falling shut. They would sleep a few hours and then adrenaline would rush in and they were wide awake again. Back into the light green scrubs, a quick bite to eat, coffee, some chocolate, some water and back to the operating table. This way more than an entire month had gone by unnoticed.

"Good morning Hofmeister. Heal Hitler," said von Wallenstein, pointing his salute to the ground.

"Hello Doctor, how are you feeling today?" Georg replied:

"I am exhausted. This was some month. How many hours did you stand at the operating table every day? Twelve, eighteen, did you count? I lost track of time." Von Wallenstein tried to focus. After taking extra time to sleep, both doctors came back to life. Von Wallenstein asked:

"Have we run out of serum yet? You and your team have done outstanding work. The change in weather has slowed the fighting. We are almost caught up. I will need you to do some scouting again for civilian patients and possibly find blood donors before we run out of serum." Both tried to stretch and relax their shoulders. The weather had brought rain. Then snow. "As I was saying Hofmeister, why don't you scout things out for a few days. I will let you know when we need you again."

"Yes Doctor, Heal Hitler. I will take my leave now." After collecting his medical bag, Georg checked the contents and put it into his backpack. He stepped off the train and onto freshly fallen snow. The red cross on his white winter parka was now visible from a long distance away. White gloves, white parka and white pants were his winter uniform.

It is Christmas soon. This must be particularly hard on people, Georg thought.

The early morning light revealed a wide flat river landscape now covered with freshly fallen snow that made everything look pristine. Prominent standing out was a double row of birch trees, their branches covered with sticky fluffy snow. The color of tree trunks in white and gray matched heavy clouds, still lingering after the snow had stopped falling. From a farmhouse at the end of this lane, Georg saw smoke rising. This type of farmhouse looked familiar to Georg. Its roof covered both living quarters and stables. He had visited this region, had grown to admire these powerful, independent Cossack riders in their long white linen blouses, their wide loose sleeves gathered in cuffs at the wrist, worn with tasseled, richly embroidered sashes on festive occasions. Georg had been fascinated and fantasized about the romance of life as a mounted Cossack, wearing such a sash sent by the loving bride as a keepsake into battle, returning into her loving arms and the embrace of her three-generation family.

It was completely quiet. The snow muffled his footsteps as he approached the house. A woman in her mid-forties stepped out of the front door. In the distance she noticed movement. She could see a large red cross moving towards her. Then she saw a figure dressed in white and noticed that the cross was covering chest and front of a person. A pair of black eyes was approaching her house from the tree lined alley. Without thinking, the woman ran towards the figure, not sure if it was real or a sign from heaven in response to her prayers.

Georg was startled by the vehemence of her approach. She ran to him and fell to her knees grasping his hands and putting them to her lips and cheeks. After a long moment she got up and with a flood of words spoken through tears and sobs she led him to the house. Inside Georg had to adjust his eyes. After a while he could see the head of a young woman in a bed near the wood stove. The covers were drawn up to her chin, her black hair was gathered in the back of her head.

Georg gestured for more light after showing the woman his stethoscope while taking off his hat and jacket. He prepared to examine the patient. He gestured with his hands rubbing together that he needed water and soap to wash up while the woman indicated that the patient was with baby. She led him into the kitchen.

There was crockery, pots and pans for a large household and a cook stove large enough to cook for a big family. Georg inhaled the smell of this house, the wood fire, the scent of cooking and baking, the scent of farm activities, dairy and horses. The air in this house was a sweet reminder of Georg's home in Germany. He asked the woman to prepare a glass of water for drinking. Then he asked for a bowl with warm water, soap and several towels. She placed several candles on the table next to the bed while talking to the patient in rapid and exited words.

Stethoscope in hand, Georg pulled a chair next to the bed so he could be at eye level with the patient. He directed his questions to the older woman who was standing by, eager to help. He gestured that he needed the patient to sit up and that he was going to listen to her heart and measure her pulse. The patient was a young pregnant woman towards the end of her third trimester. She had a weak pulse and very pale skin. There was a bedpan next to the bed that contained a small amount of vomit. Georg pointed to the glass of water with the question if she had been drinking water. The older woman looked very worried. She pointed out that the patient could only drink very small sips of water, because she could not keep anything down. Not water, not food. Listening to her lungs, he observed shortness of breath. He asked her to cough and noted signs of chest pain. He found weak resistance to pressure on her hands, arms, torso and legs.

"She needs water, salt, thiamine and vitamin B12," Georg whispered to himself. "She needs food. She appears anemic. She is in distress. I need to find something she might be able to keep down." He thought of a porridge made of stinging nettles and oatmeal. He tried to explain to the older woman that he needed some supplies. First, he asked her to give the patient small sips of water with salt stirred into it, every five minutes. He now realized that he had not introduced himself. He pointed to himself.

"I am Georg." Pointing to the older woman he asked: "Name?"

"Katya" the woman answered. Pointing to the patient she said "Olga".

Making milking movements with her hands and pointing to the stables, she said: "Tanya". She repeated with her hand over her head "Katya. Then pointing to her nose, hand flat, palm down she repeated "Olga" then pointing to her shoulder, she said "Tanya". Turning to Olga and forming the round baby belly, she said "Don". Making a gesture of a bird flying away, she said "Cossack, war." With tears welling up, she took a framed picture of a couple in wedding attire and showed it to Georg. He understood that the father of the unborn child had gone to war. Georg was now trying to tell her with some urgency that he was looking for something outside, that he needed her help. After bedding Olga comfortably and feeling her cheeks and hands, he gave her a sip of water after stirring a spoon of salt into the glass.

Katya took a large woolen stole and wrapped herself in it. To Olga Georg pointed to his eyes and to the outside and gestured a circle, indicating that they would be right back. Outside he found what he was looking for. Masses of stinging nettles were growing near a cattle-run. Georg shook off the snow, ripped off an arm full of the nettle leaves and told Katia to do the same. They returned to the kitchen. Georg instructed Katia to prepare nettles for a spinach-like dish. He asked her to cook it for a long time. In a second pot he asked her to cook oatmeal. It was more a dance than a conversation. They were both laughing at his performance when Tanya entered with a jug of milk and a dozen eggs she had gathered in her apron. She almost dropped the eggs when she saw the handsome young man who saved the moment by swiftly taking the milk jug from her other hand. Blushing, she was just barely able to save the eggs. Katia explained with a flurry of words that contained Georg, Doctor, Olga and Christos with three crosses drawn over her heart. Tanya was having trouble keeping her eyes off the unexpected visitor. She was instantly taken by this stranger who had managed to slip into the very heart of her family's life before she even had time to finish milking a few cows and to gather twelve eggs. He had managed to take the milk from her hand before she dropped her eggs onto the kitchen floor.

Now Georg gave the next set of instructions for the care of the patient. He took a sheet of paper and a pencil from his Pack and drew two clocks. Above one he drew a glass of water and salt. He drew arrows pointing to each five minutes, indicating small sips of water to be taken. Above the other clock he drew a pot with porridge. Here he drew two soup spoons at every half hour and indicated that he wanted Olga to try to eat two spoons of porridge every half hour. He checked the stove and showed the women that he wanted the cooked oats and the nettles to be combined and passed through a meat grinder he had seen on a shelf to make them smooth.

He explained that he needed a horse and sled to go to get more medicine for Olga. He had drawn a train with rails and a cross on the side of the wagons, matching the cross on his parka. Eager to help, Tanja nodded that she could do that. He showed urgency by putting on his parka, hat and gloves and told Katya to explain to Olga that they would be back soon. Following Tanya to the stable, Georg felt excited to see horses. The warm air and the scent of horse manure transported him to better times. They made him feel safe like the smell inside the farmhouse had done earlier. Georg had not handled a horse since his deployment to France with the cavalry. It now occurred to him how much he had missed these gentle, smart creatures.

Georg and Tanya entered the tack room. With a deep breath, he inhaled the scent of the stables and the leather gear. He could see that this was the farm of Cossacks by the order and placement of their driving harnesses. He looked around and asked Tanya to show him which bit set and bridle to take. She smiled at him amused by his apparent get up and go with all thing's horses. She was curious what he would do and what else he would ask for. He took the holster and turned to the stable to find which horse she wanted to take. There were four white horses. Approaching the animals from the front, Georg let one horse tell him to put on the holster he was holding.

"Good nose. Never fails." He murmured. He had the approval of the girl. He had picked the right horse. He handed her the reigns, went back to the tack room and grabbed a towing harness from the front, gathering up the leather reigns so he could simply slip the whole set over the horse's head. She was even more impressed about the way he talked to the horse as he placed the harness over his head and neck. Now came the short walk to the shed, where he turned the horse and backed him into the tow bars of the sled. She stood smiling as he connected most of the lines in the right places, asking her when he was not completely sure and then begged her to inspect his work.

She gave Georg a two handed thumbs up. He took both her hands and with a bow he gallantly kissed first one then the other. She blushed. He noticed how cold her hands were and took them between both of his palms and rubbed them, before pulling the sled out into the open. The sled was simple but well-designed with a loading platform in back and a driver's bench covered with a sheepskin cushion and knee cover to keep a driver protected from rain or snow. They mounted the sled. Georg handed her the reigns and gestured "Go" pointing down the double row of trees he had walked when he approached the farm a couple of hours ago.

Dr. von Wallenstein was stretching his legs outside the train when he saw a horse drawn sled approach at a fast trot. He could hear a female voice slow the horse. The horse came to a stop right in front of the Doctor, when he saw that Georg was the passenger. He wanted to know more about sled and company but Georg had an expression of urgency that could not be misunderstood. The young woman did not move from her seat. Von Wallenstein asked:

"Is there anything I can help you with?"

"We have a medical emergency at her farm. Her sister is about to go into labor. She is dehydrated and has chest pain. She may be anemic" He told von Wallenstein. "I would like to give her thiamine and vitamin B 12. We are feeding her salt and nettle-oatmeal porridge."

"Take a blood kit, bring us a sample. We will do blood work when you get back." Supplies in hand, Georg returned and thanked the doctor. "This is Tanya, she is the younger sister. Tanya, this is Doctor von Wallenstein." Tanya nodded and smiled. Georg mounted the sled. "Pleasure is all mine", said Von Wallenstein with a short bow. Tanya nodded, smiled at the doctor and said "Ya" to the horse as she picked up the rains. They went back in the same tracks they had just made. Von Wallenstein could hear the ringing of the little bells on the harness fade as the sled moved away. When they arrived at the farm, Georg asked Tanya to wait by the front door. He went inside. Katya awaited him by the door. She could sense his urgency. Georg kept his coat and hat on. He was going to leave again. He took a blood sample from Olga and repeated the instructions he had given before about water and food. Now he fed Olga the new medicines and told Katya that the next dose was to be given in the morning. Then he left.

"Go, go, go.," Georg urged. Tanya clicked her tongue, turned the sled on the spot and took off at a canter. Without thinking, Tanya reached under the sheepskin blanket and took Georg's hand. He felt her hand and noticed that she was shivering from the cold and from excitement and fear. He pulled the blanket up higher, put her hand into his left hand and drew her close under his right arm. She tilted her head slightly towards him. He too began to shiver. It was not just from the cold. When they arrived at the train, von Wallenstein was surprised about this quick turn-around. He sensed that time was of the essence. He had the blood work done immediately. Looking at the result, he urged Georg to hurry back to the patient.

"Your patient's platelets are crashing. She might bleed internally. You may not be able to save the mother. You can save the child. Go!" Georg had no words to explain this to Tanya. He simply held her tight the way one holds someone who needs consolation for pain so deep that words are no longer helpful. Tanya sensed this. She took the whip out of the holder and snapped it over the horse's head asking for the fastest gallop. She began to sob quietly into Georg's shoulder. She knew.

When they arrived at Olga's bed, Katya was still there. She had not left Olga's side. She had observed Olga's breath becoming shallow. She had found a feather to hold in front of Olga's nose to detect if she was breathing. She had anxiously listened for the sound of the bells to return. Katya had lost her husband, her brother, the father of this unborn child. This past winter, both her parents had died. This was too much for her to bear. She was praying for strength and grace. She was searching her heart. Katya could not understand why. She kept asking:

"Why!" Katya had never felt this lonely before. She had always been the rock in this family. At Church after confession she had lit twelve candles. In her living room she had set up a little altar beneath the Icon of the Savior and the cross. She kept five candles burning here. "Please God, let us keep some life." She had repeated this prayer over and over. Then she heard the bells. Georg knocked but did not wait for Katya to open the door. He sensed the state of distress Katya was in. He saw Olga pale and barely responsive. He immediately turned back to the sled and asked Tanya to go and fetch the Priest.

"Batiushka" he called. Get the Priest!

"Olga" he said very softly to Tanya, his face close to tears. The grief of the women began to break his heart. He had tried words he remembered from his visit to Russia and some he had heard before in Ukraine. He could see that she understood. Tanya nodded, mounted the sled and took off as fast as she had come. Tears were streaming down her face. Georg entered the house, took off his coat, repeating the words:

"Tanya Batiushka, call the priest." Crossing himself while pointing to the family altar with the burning candles he said: "Sacrament." Then pointed to Olga. Katya could sense that this was the time she had been preparing herself for. Her face was as ashen as that of her child Olga. She crossed herself three times. Then an expression of resolve returned to her face. Katya was ready to fight.

After checking Olga's pulse and listening to her heart and lungs, Georg looked into her pleading eyes and touched her cheeks with both hands. He went into the kitchen and scrubbed his hands and arms. He checked the simmering samovar for hot water, took out his surgical kit and placed knives and surgery tools into a pot with hot water, then moved them onto the fire to bring the water to a boil for sterilization. He found salt which he used for sterilizing a board, on which he placed his operating tools once they were sterile. He took iodine and sterile cotton out of his medical bag, laid out medications for pain and a flask of ether and placed them on a surface he had covered with a fresh towel. He placed a stack of fresh towels next to that. Katya watched his movements. She knew the doctor was preparing to deliver the baby.

She heard the bells of the sled. The door burst open and a gust of icy wind blew into the room. Georg could see the tall figure of a priest in a long black coat from the corner of his eyes and behind him two figures dressed in black wearing black head scarfs. Behind them appeared the familiar face of Tanya, her eyes red from crying. Georg felt very tired. He had been at the operating table at the hospital train for weeks around the clock. Fighting for lives. Saving lives, losing lives. There, he was working mechanically without getting emotionally attached to any of his patients. Here it was different. Here it was personal. The energy in this room was elevated by love and heartbreak. Georg stepped back and bowed to the priest saying in ancient Greek:

"Yes, father we are ready for you. Last rites and a welcome to life if God will." He felt deeply grateful and with a tiny bow and with his eyes he thanked Tanya for bringing the priest and the mourners. They all knew what to do, they were part of Cossack culture: Men riding into battle, women left behind to deliver babies, care for the sick and injured and to bury the dead. Georg had goosebumps when he heard the deep bass voice of the priest begin to hum and the four women join voices in a chorus he had heard years before, when he attended church services in this region. It was the song Rest O Lord the Soul of Your Servant.

Tears were quietly running down his cheeks as the ritual was performed in the harmony of this moment, when the border between life and death was being crossed. There was the knowledge that a higher power was at work and that the Holy Spirit was present and ready to take back a loved one's life. The Lord's Prayer followed, and the last rites were administered. Georg was monitoring Olga's heart. At the moment of the priest's benediction and blessings Olga grasped Georg's hand and exhaled for the last time. Her heart stopped.

Georg nodded to the priest. Katya began singing Ave Maria, followed by the deep base of the priest and the harmony of the women changing the mood in the room to praise for the Holy Mother. Georg moved everyone back to continue their prayers at the family altar, where candles were lighting the family icons.

Olga's mother and Tanya were now standing by to assist Georg with the surgical delivery of the baby. He worked swiftly and time stood still until Georg handed Tanya a newborn baby boy. Georg's heart beat in his temples as he opened the babies' airway. From Taya's arms he took the baby, laid him on the table on top of the towels. He gave the baby life breaths and performed compressions on the chest to move the circulation of blood from this fragile distressed infant's tiny heart to his lungs. When the baby's first cry could be heard Georg realized that everyone in the room had been holding their breath also. Now sounds of joy and grief filled the room. Air was inhaled and everyone sprang to life. Far beyond Georg's expectations, the mourners were experienced midwives and were now taking over from Georg. With Katya's help, Georg began preparing Olga's body for the wake.

For the first time Katya and Georg were now able to let their emotions flow freely. Both had been clinging to life, the one that was taken and the one that was given and saved. Tears were washing away the past and softened the soil for the future. A new Cossack was born. Georg had become a part of this family. He was letting himself grieve and celebrate with them. Georg went on checking the infant. Without knowing how and why, he remembered and began singing a lullaby he had learned when he visited this region before: Bayushki bayu. The lullaby about a baby boy who can sleep safely because his father is a rider. Soon he too will grow strong and brave, mount his horse and ride off into far lands.

"Just think of your mother always;" the song pleads. Other voices joined Georg. In a ceremonial gesture, the priest now handed the newborn into Tanya's arms and committed him to her care. Tears of joy and tears of grief were streaming like the two rivers Volga and Don.

"Name him Don, like his father and the river." Georg suggested. "You are his father too", whispered Katya. "You gave him life."

"I am only the servant of the Lord. It was his will and his will only." The next song Georg heard was "Save O Lord Our people". Once again, the priest had begun with his very deep bass and the women joined in with harmonies clear as bells.

Georg took Tanya by the hand and led her outside to take care of the horse. The white stallion was still standing in front of the house steaming and in a lather. He needed to be rubbed down, watered and fed. Georg knew that a different horse had to take the sled for the return of the priest after the rituals. Tanya nodded yes and fell sobbing into Georg's arms. They stood, holding on to each other for a long time. The horse dug into the snow with his hoof several times and gave a whinny which was answered by the other horses inside the stable. That startled Tanya and Georg back into reality and reminded them of the chores at hand. Georg pointed to the cows and made a milking and feeding gesture, telling Tanya that he could help. They worked together with small gestures and the occasional deep look into each other's eyes. Tender touches brought tears back. Trying to kiss tears away led to increasing feelings of passion which neither of them was able or willing to slow or to suppress.

Once milking and feeding were done they harnessed a fresh horse, went back to the front of the house and stepped inside to check on the preparations for the wake and to feed the baby. Tanya explained to Georg that she was going to fetch a woman, who was nursing and could feed her newborn son with breastmilk, together with her own baby. She also explained that the wake required more mourners who would come and that food was going to be brought to be served here.

"Three nights and three days" she told him. "Then funeral." Georg understood. He pointed in the direction of the hospital train and said that he needed to return there, but that he was coming back to check on the baby, Katya and Tanya. With gratitude and a pounding heart, Tanya looked deep into Georg's eyes. Then she took his face into both of her hands and her eyes made a gesture that only he could see.

"I love you," they said. They were ready to return the priest to his church. The women were staying to help Katya await other mourners who would come, using their own sleds. Sleds began arriving, loaded with food. Georg knew this was the custom of this community. Every task was performed with skill, dignity and devotion. The singing of sacred music in many voices moved Georg deeply.

After having just arrived at the site of the most horrible battle in history, Georg was consoled and felt supported by the devotion of these people in his own shock and grief over witnessing this unprecedented loss of lives. The miracle of this newborn child humbled him. It left his emotions raw and reaching for life. Georg had never been aware of his own feelings with such intensity.

His eyes were tearing up and burning from fatigue. Now that food was mentioned, he realized that he had not eaten a real meal in many days. He ate. Tanya fed him. The soothing closeness to a human being took him away like water takes a log of wood down river during a flood. He gave himself into the loving hands of Tanya with all his passion and Tanya did not let him go. She was a strong woman and her ability to receive and return his feelings was boundless.

Georg accompanied Tanja on the ride to return the Priest. On the way to the train they stopped on a rise near an old linden tree. They could see the entire area. The village, the farm, the tracks and the train. The silvery landscape looked like a romantic painting in black and white. The sky was still heavy with clouds. The freshly fallen snow cover reflected every last ray of light, giving contrast to silhouettes of features in this river landscape with its willows, birches and poplars. The view of the steppe beyond with its endless expanses took their breath away. A sense of peace spread like a blanket over the end of this eventful day.

Georg melted into his rising attraction to the woman in his arms. He gave himself to her and to this moment. For the first time in hours he could breathe. He had an unstoppable desire to breathe into her. And to drink her as if she were a challis offered to him. Together they felt the presence of a higher power. They did not care about the world outside of the shelter of their soft sheepskin blanket and the fur covered bench seat with the padded high back. Tonight, there was no war in their world. Magic moments that made them happy until they were completely breathless and exhausted.

It was dark when they asked the horse to pull their sled to the train. Georg had a thought and told Tanya to wait for a moment. He went on board to report to Dr. von Wallenstein about the rescue of the baby, the loss of the mother and the fragile state of the infant.

"What are you doing here. The baby needs you." Von Wallenstein said in a mock warning tone.

"Yes Doctor, I did not want to stay without an order or before reporting to you."

"Go back to the farm. Finish the job. Stay the night. It is quiet here. Good night Hofmeister."

The scent of Georg's lover was lingering in his clothes. This had not escaped von Wallenstein's attention.

"Children. Much too young for this deadly business." He murmured to himself.

With the soft jingle of the bells on the sled and the muffled footfall of the horse, Tanya and Georg left to return to the farm, to the baby, to the grandmother and to each other.

CHAPTER SEVEN
TANYA

Georg's heart added several beats when he left the hospital train to join Tanja. He was overjoyed to let her know that he was coming back with her to the farm for the night.

"I am also Don's doctor, not just his father," he said smiling, holding both of Tanya's hands and kissing her upturned palms gallantly first one, then the other.

"Take me to the patient please." He begged.

"Yes doctor, as fast as I can." Tanya replied through a burst of happy laughter that came deep from the bottom of her throat. Not too far along, the horse could be left to find its own way home. Georg told Tanja:

"I have been ordered to stay the night with the new mother and the baby, if she thought this to be necessary."

"It is, it is. "Tanya hurried to say. "Do you see yourself leaving the baby and his new mother in the dark of the night? Do you? Really doctor. Do you?" Tanya whispered into his ear along with countless tender kisses. "I do not think it is medically responsible for me to leave," Georg whispered. "I must stay. You need me. You have a baby. The baby needs me. The baby needs you and I need you."

"You need food. They cook much food, the whole village coming by morning, viewing poor Olga. Many friends and girlfriends, drug and druja she said. You are not nimjetzky you are drug. My drug. I teach you, she said. I am your druja. You gave baby life. You gave village new Cossack. You are father of Don. I am now mother of Don. You are Family. You are Cossack." Georg was not completely sure what she had whispered to him. He knew it came from deep in her heart and that part he did understand. Hearing her voice made his heart sing. Feeling her touch made him breathless, brought him close to fainting. Georg and Tanya arrived at the farmhouse where more sleds were now assembled. They took care of the horses and did the chores. Georg was familiar with farm work. He found what he needed to water and feed the animals. They milked the cows. Tanya watched him in amusement and was comforted by how natural this seemed. He tried to put the harness away, which was not easy with two people trying to sort out which hand was doing what and both had never done this during a continuous tight embrace. Some entanglements made them laugh so hard, they were crying and now their raw emotions were going back and forth from joy to grief. The horse's ears were pointing straight up and went back and forth, following the two lovers. Georg told Katya that he had orders to stay the night, to look after the baby and the new mother. Tanya stood there, looking as if she had just rolled in the hay. The blush on Tanya's cheeks did not escape her mother. The exhausted new grandmother sat down in relief and with a very faint smile and an even fainter movement with her head she said:

"What are we going to do with you youngsters? I give up".

Georg finally ate with a giant appetite. The only reason he did not hurt himself with too much food was sitting next to him touching his knee and feeding him as if he were a little injured bird. The eyes did as much eating as the mouth. Many eyes in the room were following their every move and they could not have been more pleased. Here was the miracle of a new life and the timing of the young doctor's arrival at the farm. There was also his way of naturally blending in with their culture and religion and they could not help but treat him like a long-lost son. The two lovers were in a new and different world. Georg examined the baby boy and spoke to the wet-nurse, who's baby boy he also examined. He found both babies to be in excellent health.

Georg was too exhausted to stay up while Katya continued receiving new mourners and well-wishers. Tanya took charge of sleeping arrangements and made the nest as warm and cozy as two lovers deserve and as can only be achieved when there is happiness and perfect harmony. She brought a large jug of warm water and filled the bowl on the washstand with the mirror. Standing behind Georg, Tanya looked at his image, carefully removing his shirt. She began to give Georg a gentle rub down, the way Cossack women bathe their riders after a long absence, doing battle on horseback.

She had to laugh when he did not remove his stethoscope. They both were exploring each other, and both were more than pleased with what they discovered. Finally, the stethoscope fell, but not until after the doctor had examined her heartbeat and breath which sent them into unstoppable laughter and the instrument began to be at risk of being destroyed by getting in the way of their passionate embraces. They stepped over their clothes, which had fallen in random order to the floor as they explored more of each other and garments seemed to be getting in the way of hands and lips. They found each other and had no thought of letting go until a deep sleep got the better of them. There are no dreams that could make a pair of hearts race faster or longer than this moment of pure bliss.

They woke up at first light and slipped into their clothes. They checked on the mourners. Georg examined the babies. He found Katya to let her know that everyone was well and that they were off to do chores. The two realized that they were missing four hours of sleep. Working well together they did the feeding, grooming, milking, collecting eggs and mucking out. They decided to be careful this time with eggs and milk.

After finishing with the horses, they replenished hay and added some more oats and wheat chaff into the trough, the lovers stood for a long moment, leaning on the bottom of the split stable door to watch the sunrise. Freshly fallen snow reflected the first light in shades of ultraviolet and blue, picking up the sun's rays for a brilliant show of light reflected by snow crystals. The rumbling of thunder in the distance broke the spell of this moment and they knew, that it was not thunder they heard. It was war. The kiss they shared now was given in the recognition that each moment together was a precious gift that had to be received with gratitude as a first and honored as a last. They loaded firewood onto a wheelbarrow, balanced the basket with eggs on top, put scoops full of oats and chaff into a small wooden trough to give to the mourner's horses. They filled buckets with water and let the horses drink. Feeling giddy and happy, they returned to the front door without breaking a single egg. Before they entered the living room they could hear the chorus of voices singing hymns of devotion and gratitude.

They delivered the eggs and asked if there was need of flower to bake more bread or pastries. The women showed them a pile of food they had brought along for the wake and assured them that all they needed were some hungry mouths to eat some of this food.

"We will bring some hay for the horses", said Tanya and off they went back to the stables where Georg took a fork and loaded it expertly. A large amount of hay ended up balanced over his head until he dropped it in the snow in front of the horses, which Tanya had arranged in a semi-circle. Georg could hear the bells of the harnesses, moved by the chewing of hay and he saw the wide smile on Tanya's face. It made him forget the war for another moment. When the priest returned the following day, Georg assembled the women. Tanya helped him give a short speech during which he explained that the doctors on the hospital train were treating any wounded soldier and any sick person no matter which army or nationality they belonged to.

"Our profession obliges us to save lives and to treat the sick. This is not a horseback and rifle battle anymore. This is panzer war fought with large cannons mounted on top of vehicles." Georg explained. "We hear that there are many thousands of tanks facing each other. Too many soldiers die. Injuries are horrific. We lose lives because we do not have enough blood. I am begging you to consider giving blood. Every soldier is some mother's child. Every drop of blood donated to us will save a precious life. We have one rail car for blood collection. For everyone's safety we ask you to send blood donors at night. You will be fed a meal. Transports of injured have been left unharmed. Help us save them." The women heard him, and the priest gave his support. He understood the gravity of the situation and gave his blessings to saving lives. There was a murmur of approval when Tanya and Georg left the room. Tanya took Georg by the hand and lead him to the room where they had spent the previous night.

"You look tired. Forget world," she said moving her hands through his short, curly black hair." You look like Cossack; you have Cossack son. You are Cossack. Come here. You need rest. You need care. I take care now."

"You feel wonderful. I will faint and wake up in our dream. There you are. There we are." He felt her soft skin; her black curly hair was pouring over his head. He forgot the world. Poetry of Nature took over and composed a symphony of feelings, emotions and sensations they would never forget. Georg was aware of the heartbreak that was going to be the fate of every person alive during this time. Lovers were not exempt. Only Tanya and Georg. Only for this moment. These two were exempt. After a long time they fell into a blissful deep sleep. They could hear the familiar muted sounds of the farmhouse with stables at one end and the living quarters at the other end with the wake and the singing of the mourners all mixed with the sweet scent of life. Georg was searching for ways to explain the future. He was relieved when he discovered the deep understanding Tanya was bringing to this situation.

"We lost a lot of lives in my family and in my community." She told Georg. "I know there will be more before it gets better. When you came it was sign for us. I will now hold our mother in my arms and raise our son." Tanya said this with her eyes gazing into the future. She had wisdom and compassion far beyond her age. She was able to calm Georg in his anticipation of unfathomable grief by pointing him to his task of saving lives and reminding him of the baby she called his son. "This is what you were sent here for. We may not be able to save everyone we love. We may live with a broken heart, if we live. We ask for guidance to do what is right. We have loyalty. I have received absolution for my sins. The priest is my guardian and my spiritual advisor. I am mother of a Cossack now. You are father. That will never go away. Look at Don my love." Georg looked at the child. Feeling Tanya leaning back into him with her cheek against his, he was holding her with his arms, his hands gently caressing her.

Tanya represented life in the face of death, and he could feel the power of everlasting life in the love he felt for her and in the gratitude he felt for the creator. With their love for this child and their love for each other, death did not have a chance. At breakfast they sat together as a family. Katya said a blessing. Then she said:

"The world is burning and we are sitting here together. God has mercy."

"War is driving everyone mad. As Doctors, we are in conflict with all governments at war. I spoke to my commanding officer. He thinks they have all lost their minds. We hear it from patients on both sides. Civilian casualties inside Stalingrad are tragic. No civilians have been permitted to flee. They were ordered to dig in and learn to shoot. Women and children are being trained to be snipers. That makes all civilians a military target. This is new. Stalin refuses surrender. He will sacrifice every last life then surrender a town that bears his name but has lost its soul. It is all about ego. Hitler did the same thing. I think Dr. von Wallenstein is right." Georg thought for a while, then he said: "We must remember our mission. Saving lives. The men in the locomotive tell me that a medical train is on its way here. It is a red cross transport full of wounded. They pick up patients and take them back to Germany. It is a very long train. They have added freight cars. This is the last stop. Twice the wounded, half the doctors and nurses. I was ordered to go with them."

"You know people along the way", he said, "you have been able to find food, salt and water. You will keep patients alive. Having you on board will help their nurses and medics. In Germany you will load fresh medical supplies and personnel to bring them back to us."

Georg had been successful with his blood drive. Once word got out that the doctors on the hospital train were treating the local population and also wounded Russian soldiers without taking prisoners, people came from near and far to donate blood and to get treatment. He was sent back to the farm several times to see the baby and the women. He was present at the funeral. He was welcomed as a member of this Cossack family. Georg was sad about having to leave and escort the medivac train. He was excited about seeing Rose and a chance to marry her. As young as they were Rose was his anchor and his compass. He could not reconcile the fractured parts of his life. It made him very sad.

"Shhhh," said Tanya. Kissing away his tears. "Remember God gave us moments, not years. Years he gave to Don. We have love. Pure beautiful God given love while the world is on fire and dying is all around us. Cossack women protect babies and families. Our love never dies. Cossacks were here before Tsars. We will be here long after Lenin and Hitler. Cossacks belong to the Earth. We will always be Cossacks."

It was time to baptize the child. They named the boy Don Georg after his father and the one who had saved his life. The women started humming the song Ave Maria and raised their voices when the priest joined in with his resounding bass while blessing the holy water in the basin. He proceeded to perform the baptism with dignity and beauty. The infant was submerged three times in the water and placed into the hands of Tanya who stood ready to receive Don Georg with a large towel. A few days later the medevac train arrived. The transport was organized, and patients were transferred. At the farm Georg was much less calm than the women.

"I fear for you and for your community. I have voices in my heart that will not be calmed." Georg whispered.

"Talk to our priest. He is wise. He helps us survive. I will take you to him. He will bless you and take your confession. You can speak ancient Greek with him." Tanya said, caressing Georg's forehead with her fingertips. "I will give you my brother's wedding shirt. It will show Russians, that you are one of us. It will remind you to come back to me and your son. It will give you something to wear at your wedding after you have made it safely home to your Family. It is a garment of celebration. Wear it on you always. It will give you the same strength you have given us. I am with you always. That is the way of Cossacks." This gift and Tanya's generosity made Georg break down in a new stream of tears.

"I should not be so weak. I do not deserve your love." Georg sobbed. "Shhh," Tanya held him in her arms and hummed bayushki bayou to soothe him as if he were her other baby.

Georg's meeting with the priest left him reassured. It helped him to put in perspective the enormity of the fate of the world. The priest validated actions Georg had taken in response. It calmed him when the priest heard his confession and gave him blessings and absolution.

Georg snuggled up to his lover for the last time before she returned him to say goodbye to Katya and Don Georg. Tanya dropped him off at the train, turned her horse and galloped off, leaving a cloud of snow whipped up by the hooves and the runners of her sleigh. The sound of bells faded into the distance and Georg took a deep breath.

"I am ready," he said to Dr. von Wallenstein.

CHAPTER EIGHT
MEDEVAC

The return of the medevac train to Germany went as well as anyone could hope. Georg paid special attention to patients who lay quiet without complaint. Hans and the others on the locomotive introduced Georg to the drivers of the medivac train as they maneuvered their own locomotive in front of the train to assist pulling this long train. Hans had a snowplow mounted to his locomotive which was key to making the trip safely north and west to Germany. Georg was busy with the overloaded train full of wounded who were screaming every time the train braked or accelerated and when bumpers between cars were magnifying the shock into the nerve endings of their wounds.

Georg was as much a chaplain as a doctor and it was his task to declare the end of life of those who did not survive their wounds. He was strict about sanitation. The locomotive crews kept his train in good supply of heating fuel and fresh potable water. Now and then Georg was able to visit peasants he had met on the way out and was given generous gifts of food and chickens for soup, well received by the kitchen staff who hated serving watered down tasteless tea instead of food.

Georg discovered that the Cossack shirt he wore wrapped around his waist was a source of strength for him as was his gratitude and love for Tanya and his little Cossack son Don Georg. Once in Germany Georg delivered his report and the pouch with Doctor von Wallenstein's orders. In a brief ceremony Georg was promoted to the rank of first lieutenant with new stripes and authority.

The wedding of Rose and Georg was prepared and celebrated in a whirlwind of activities. Georg insisted on wearing his Cossack shirt. The bakers of the wedding cake mistook salt for sugar, which was taken as a good omen. Together with his loving community and many adorable children a great feast was held.

The Bliss of the moment lit the black cloud of war long enough to let the light of love sweep Georg and Rose away. The newlywed couple had just long enough to remember the vows they had made to each other including that they were never going to leave the country. They had vowed to stay and fight to build a new world after the Nazis were defeated.

"The war is coming apart." He told his bride who had just graduated from high school. "Our children will be the messengers from the spirit world. They will bring new answers to our prayers and lead us into the future."

When Georg left to return to his headquarters, Rose was with child.

Georg oversaw the loading of the medical supply train which was running as a regular freight train.

"We are running with supply trains. No hold ups or side railing at depos. That gives us better protection. We look just like any freight train," said Hans. Paul gave his opinion:

"Germany has no business to be anywhere but in Germany and the generals know it. Hitler fires Generals left and right and has taken over command himself. He does not tolerate disagreement or intelligent conversation based on facts or experience. Medical trains are now a strategic target. Have you ever heard of such a thing? We have to keep it secret where we are. War is more about the response of the public at home than winning battles."

When they approached Stalingrad, Hans noticed that messages became hard to understand. Troop transports and supply trains were running both ways. No talk about the next return of wounded. No details about rail conditions. Then total silence. Something had gone wrong. When their train pulled into the depot, they saw it: The hospital train was gone. It had disappeared. Not a trace. Not a word. It had simply vanished.

"What are you going to do now?" Asked Hans, who had prepared a letter for Georg to keep and to present to railroaders and depot crews as he handed him his pouch.

"I don't know. I have no marching orders beyond this assignment. Unless I find my commanding officer, I am a deserter. You too have no marching orders. Good thing that you are not military. Someone will find something for you to do. Let the word out that you have medical supplies and they will take them. Both sides will. Transport is moving both ways. I pray we meet again. It was a privilege to know you and your team. I must disappear now. My uniform is a death sentence. I am now on my own."

Georg grabbed Hans in a tight bear hug and said, "God keep you safe." Hans said into Georg's ear:

"Remember all the friends you have made along the way. Check in with my railroad people. Mention my name. Show my letter. Some railroaders may not know my name, but everyone knows the medical trains. Some might be able to communicate. Promise. We need you alive. Godspeed!"

Georg took his pack and extra medical supplies for the farm and with a deep hollow in his stomach and an aching heart he set off towards the home of his Godson. He could not wait to see Tanya and the baby. It was getting dark. The air was cold. Georg was fighting for breath when he arrived at the stables. The horses recognized him first. There was a whinny and the horses were stomping hooves. Tanya's heart did a leap. It made her feel dizzy. She ran towards the figure in the dark. She knew it was Georg. Both have no memory of the next hours of a reunion that was defying every description of urgency and passion, tenderness and intimacy. The two young lovers discovered that every living cell has a heart that beats in a rhythm ordained by a greater universe. At the core of this bliss was their undying sense of loyalty. When they woke up Georg did the chores with Tanya. After greeting Katya, they went to see the baby and the wet nurse.

Georg examined the children. He was amazed how much his godson had grown.

"Was I gone that long? He looks a year older." To the boy: "Can you say papa Georg?"

"The Germans have been defeated at Stalingrad." Katya told Georg. "They have surrendered. Their weapons are in the hands of our Russian generals. Thousands of prisoners are now marching east into an uncertain fate. There is no more food. Not even for the Russian army. Stalingrad is starving. There are still German snipers in the region. They may not know about the surrender of Stalingrad." Katya fell silent.

Tanya, her right hand behind Georg's neck and her left on his hip feeling for her brother's wedding shirt, said fiercely:

"I will not let you stay here. You will not survive here. They will catch you. No one has food. Most prisoners will starve to death or freeze to death. We have lost too many lives in our family and community. I ask you to return to your country and I demand that you survive. That is the only way you can honor the lives we have lost and the life you have saved for my family. You have saved many lives in our community. Now you have one more life to save: Yours.

You will save many children and many more lives. You will be a teacher and a doctor. We will pray for you." She spoke these words from the very bottom of her heart. Powerful and strong words no one would ever forget. This war had made grownups out of children. Tanya was one of them. Through his tears Georg said:

"I don't know how I can answer this. I have carried your brother's shirt. I have worn it when it counted. You just gave me a new order in the most loving way. I will obey you and try to earn your trust and fight for my life as if it were Don Georg's or yours." Georg whispered. "I will need civilian clothes and a tent sheet. I will need Cossack riding boots. Your brother's shirt will be my shield and a key into people's lives."

Katya and Tanya were helping Georg with purpose and forcefulness. They arranged a meeting for Georg with father Gregory so he could ask for blessings and advice. Katya and Tanya spoke to their elders about arranging safe houses for him. The priest gave him a letter to present to other priests asking them for their protection and help. When preparations were complete, Katya looked at Georg in his Russian clothes, his Cossack boots and pack. She checked his provisions one more time and with an inviting gesture asked Georg to board her daughter's carriage. Katya kissed both of Georg's hands and placed his right hand for a few moments on her heart. Georg took Katya into a tight embrace as if to plant the memory of her scent and her family deep in his heart. He held her for many long moments, then kissed her forehead above her eyes. Then he let her go. She turned quickly and went into the house.

Seated in front of the carriage with Tanya, Georg gave the house one last look. He searched and found Tanya's hand. He wanted to hold something besides her brother's wedding shirt which he still wore like a sash around his waist. Tanya was used to goodbyes with uncertain future of departing family members. It was part of Cossack life. Georg was in a state of grief, excitement, anticipation and fear.

PART TWO

WORLDS AT WAR

CHAPTER NINE
CROSSING BORDERS

Today everything felt different. Tanya did not know why.

"Georg, my heart, I know we have said everything there is to say and I know you heard what I have said. I know how you feel about me. I know how you feel about your godson Don Georg and about my family. Now I need you to survive. The region of Kalach-no-don is now under the control of the Russian army. That has changed things over night. Pockets of Hitler's army are still here. They are most dangerous to you. It is Spring melt. Rivers are running high and no vehicles can move without grinding themselves into the mud. This is your best chance to evade capture. Russian soldiers may be nicer than Germans. But they are just as deadly. You have to trust me on this: Both will end your life when they catch you. The Germans will shoot you on sight and Stalin's troops will capture you and starve you to death. Stalingrad is completely out of food and water." Trying to look strong Tanya added: "They will be coming after our farms very soon, looking to steal our seed potatoes to eat them instead of letting us sow." She glanced to the horizon. "There will be famine. Like ten years ago. They will eat all the seed."

"Yes, but why can't I stay and help you?" Georg sounded desperate. "Shhhh." She squeezed his hand.

"We have talked and talked and now we are all talked out." She put her hand caressingly over his face and feeling his kisses moved it down to grasp his hand. She held it so tight, that her knuckles were white, and his hand hurt but he did not pull away. They began to move towards the river

Don. The horse walked with purposeful steps and the bells on his harness rang softly in a steady rhythm. Tanya and Georg held onto each other's hands as though they would never let them go. Tanya had timed Georg's departure so that he could cross the river at night, using a small fishing skiff a church member had hidden for her under willow bushes next to a small boat landing. Georg looked like a fisherman. No one anticipated the Russian army to interfere with a fisherman. They would take the fish but not the boat or the hooks. They would take the potatoes but not the cart or the horse.

Tanya found the skiff. The owner had stocked it with a bucket full of freshly caught fish. On this last trip together the two had not spoken much. They exchanged long glances at each other as if to etch the other's image into their memory. With stern expression on their faces they had looked down the road over the horse's ears. At the landing they moved the skiff to the water's edge, stowed his pack and checked what fishing gear there was and were about to finish sliding the craft into the water when the horse made a snorting sound that broke the silence by the river. Only the lapping of the slow current against the hull could be heard. Georg sensed the hair on the back of his neck stand up. The horse took a step sideways. Georg heard the snapping of a twig in a thicket of willows not more than fifty feet away. He felt a rush of adrenaline. His heart began racing. It sent him into hyper vigilance. Everything appeared to Georg to be happening in slow motion:

The helmet of a German soldier appeared in the thicket. The figure of a tall man in combat uniform rose to full standing height. The butt of a sniper rifle was rising to the soldier's shoulder. The head tilted and the sniper's eye aligned with the scope on top of the weapon. Georg could see the grin in the shooter's face as he levelled the gun to take his shot. It made the blood in Georg freeze. He saw the alignment. It was aiming at Tanya and not at him. Georg pulled his weapon with his left hand, aimed and fired. His bullet hit the sniper between the eyes as he covered Tanya's heart with his right hand. Both shots had gone off at exactly the same moment making it sound like a single rifle shot.

Georg felt a hot stinging sensation between his ring finger and little finger. He saw the sniper drop to his knees and slowly with a thud fall forward on his face. Georg felt Tanya sinking to her knees sliding down his thigh with her shoulder. With her last breath and her eyes breaking Tanya said:

"I love you my Cossack husband." She slipped to the ground exposing the exit wound. Georg turned away and vomited. He went into a state he had never experienced before. His willpower was drained. He exhaled a deep breath and dropped to his knees. "Focus damn it focus." He told himself. He wanted to close the wound on Tanya's chest with the shirt he was wearing around his waist. Then he realized that he had lost Tanya. A gut-wrenching scream escaped his throat muffled by the Cossack shirt he had automatically pressed against his face. Inconsolable sobbing turned him inside out. He now heard Tanya's words spoken earlier:

"I demand that you live." He heard his own answer: "I will survive my heart. I will save lives. I will earn your love." Through his sobs he now whispered: "I must send you home now." Automatically he felt for her pulse. He noticed blood running from his hand. He could feel nothing. His breaking heart was shredding him to pieces. He took bandages from his pack with his left hand and using knees and teeth to do the holding he prepared the gauze by cutting the end down the middle and making a knot to make ties for fastening the bandage. With tongue depressors he made a spline after sterilizing the wound with alcohol from a small flask. He bandaged his right hand. Georg did not feel the sting of the alcohol on his wound. He felt sick. He vomited again. He was lost, drifting in his overwhelming grief. He could not breathe. He made himself focus on poor Tanya. Kneeling beside her he held her for a long time.

"We should not have come here. Now you must go home." Georg whispered. He placed Tanya's body in the back of her wagon arms crossed over her chest. He placed the sack of potatoes under her knees to keep her from rolling. Softly though flooding tears Georg hummed Bajuschki Baju as if to lull her to sleep. He turned the wagon and patted the horse on its forehead and neck one last time He looked around again, then gathered the weapons of the German soldier and placed them on the driver's seat.

"Nothing personal" he said to the soldier's body. "You have three victims. I am the one who has to live." Pointing to Tanya he said in his choked-up voice: "This is Tanya. She is the bravest woman any coward like you has ever shot. She will live on as a saint in the memory of her community. She has loyalty and heart. All you have is blind obedience to a mad man. You had a choice; she was no threat to you. You are the third victim. May the Lord forgive you. May the Lord receive and keep Tanya's soul. Her Godson will hold her memory in his heart and never forget her as long as he can ride as a Cossack and speak of his brave godmother Tanya." Through his tears and with a broken soft voice Georg spoke the Lord's prayer. Then he took out the whip and with a snapping sound sent the horse east on its way home.

As in a fog he stepped into the little skiff, collected the oars and soundlessly rowed away into the still water of the mighty Don towards the west. It was now completely dark. The water, the sky, Georg's soul all had lost their light. At this moment Georg wished he would never be able to see again. He felt completely lost. Streams of tears kept washing over him like waves of a stormy ocean. The water's surface was eerily flat. It seemed like blood. It reflected nothing.

"Slip over the side and sink into the water." Georg whispered. "End the killing. End the suffering. Do it now." He inhaled deeply. There came a second thought: "Dedicate life to the living now. Solve the problems of the world." The first voice answered." My heart is broken. It is useless. I have killed a human being. I have broken the compact with my life. How can I live with that?"

Georg was standing up and was about to cross the final border when suddenly Tanya's voice spoke through his heart. "I need you to live." Tanya's voice made him cling to life. Georg could hear his own voice whisper the vows he had made to Tanya:

"I will live. I will save lives. I will teach children. I will honor you and learn to earn your love." He sat back down on the bench seat of the boat and heard himself add these words:

"I will never forget the Godmother of my Godchild. Tanya you live on in my heart. I will be your eyes and ears. I will be your heart. You will feel everything I feel through me. I will be your life. This is my assignment. These are my new orders."

With these words he reached for the gun and the extra bullets and slipped them over the side of the skiff. Blindly, Georg rowed on until he could feel a slight breeze which told him that he was nearing the other shore. He could hear the lapping sound of the water. The skiff touched the ground with a soft grinding sound and came to a halt. Georg got up and with his left hand pulled the skiff to high ground. He tied it to the exposed root of a fallen tree. With automatic movements he rolled himself into his tent sheet higher up on the riverbank behind a tree trunk and placed his pack under his head. In his heart he searched for gratitude. With every exhale he said:

"Thank you" and with every inhale he said: "Tanja." The following hours of restless sleep were interrupted again and again by dreams about loved ones in Germany, his parents, Rose, her parents, Katya, Tanya, Gregory with his deep voice, all standing together, pointing him to go north and west, asking him to live. He saw Hans handing him the pouch with the railroad letter. He saw the dark eyes of baby Don. Pain in his hand woke him and reminded him of his situation. Georg could smell the scent of river air and damp soil. He felt the chill of early morning. Empty and numb, he unrolled himself from his cocoon. He thought he was going blind. Everything looked soft. No sharp contours. Every feature seemed wrapped in white cotton. He tried to focus. The image did not change. Finally he noticed that it was the mist rising over the pre-dusk river. He decided to take with him from the boat a small bundle of fishing gear, a lure, some hooks, a line and a lead sinker. He also took the container with fish. He shouldered his pack with some difficulty. Using the Cossack shirt, he made a sling for his right hand by tying together the sleeves at the wrists and hanging the loop over his neck. He wrapped the body of the shirt around his forearm and hand. The bear was waking up. Adrenaline was bleeding off and pain was rising. Being able to relax his arm and shoulder made it more bearable. Feeling the wet soft ground under his boots, Georg began walking. He was carrying the fish with his left hand. He followed a wagon trail until he could spot dim lights from the inside of a farmhouse in the distance. A dog came running towards him. He softly spoke to the dog to calm him and to keep him from attacking. "I am your friend. There now that's a good dog. Yes, I have fish but that is for everybody." A woman stepped out and called the dog while raising a shotgun, saying: "Raise your hands." Georg held the fish out to her, saying:

"I can't. I am Georg. This is for you." He looked like a Cossack fisherman. She saw the sling holding his right arm.

"Did you say your name is Georg? Did you come across the river?"

"Yes."

"We have been waiting for you. Gregory the priest from the other side sent word to expect you. What happened to your arm?"

"I was shot.""Who shot you?"

"A German sniper. He killed Tanya. He shot through my hand into her heart. He did not survive. I feel sick. I need water. I did not sleep much. You can cook this fish. It is fresh."

Georg was spent. He was weeping. He tried to apologize. The woman took control.

"Come inside. Take your pack off. Let me have a look at your wound. Then we talk. I am Valeska. I know you are Georg." Georg looked around. The dim light revealed a house very similar to Katya's. The smells were familiar. It was clear to Georg that he was at another Cossack's house. Men at war, women in charge, used to caring for the injured. What surprised him was the familiarity she treated him with. Tanya had said.

"You are Cossack now." She had meant it and it was the truth. He could not stop his tears every time he thought of her.

"Pain?" Valeska asked when she saw his tears. She was in her mid-thirties; she was in the company of a young girl who was playing with her dollhouse.

"This is Sonya. She is six years old. She is mother's helper. Aren't you Sonya darling?"

"Yes mama ", the girl said, "who is our visitor?"

"This is Georg, the doctor your aunt was talking about. The one who saves lives."

"Have you saved a life today?" Sonya asked.

"I tried", said Georg, "it does not always work. I always try." To Valeska he said:

"My pain is not terrible. I was thinking of poor Tanya. I could not save her. That is what made me weep. I am sorry."

"It is war. You are doctor. You are fighting on both sides. Here you are one of us. Let me look at your hand." Carefully and with sure hands she removed the bandages. She examined the hand. She touched his fingertips.

"Can you feel this?"

"Yes. It hurts, but yes."

"You know how lucky you are? The bullet missed your bones. It went through your spread-out hand. It will heal with bandage."

"How do you know so much about wounds?"

"I am nurse. Most of the women in this area are nurse or midwife. We are Cossacks. Our men ride. Women keep house and animals. We take care of wounded warriors." Valeska was in charge now.

"Do you have disinfectant?" Georg tried to reach for his pack.

"Let me. You are my patient now" She said as she put his outstretched left hand back to his side. "You rest. I take care of wound. Your hand needs time to heal. We will cook fish. You eat, you sleep, you heal."

"Thank you Valeska I have no words to thank you."

"You already have. We have heard about you. This is small world. Let me help you take off your boots." She said and turned around to grab the heel of one boot, pulled it off, then the other. She could see how Georg was wiggling his toes to help, it made her laugh.

"My men would use foot to push my behind", she laughed "they are at war. We pray for them." She sounded sad. When she was done with his new bandage, she said:

"There, done. Now we cook. Then we eat. Then we rest. Are you hungry? Of course, you are. Everyone is. We have chicken tonight. Chicken heal everything." Valeska went about her work around the kitchen.

Resolute, no nonsense, Georg thought to himself. While she cooked potatoes and chicken, she dropped some eggs into the borscht she had going on the stove for breakfast. Then he told her his story of life on Katya's farm. He was in tears again.

"I am sorry. I am very tired. Tired for more reasons than I can tell. I do not want to impose. I am a doctor. Not a good patient."

"Shhhhh, you were shot. You are not first one of our men to get shot." She assured him. "I will care for you. You will sleep and get well. I put herbs into your tea that will make you heal and sleep and get well. We need doctor with two hands. You were lucky Your hand was open wide when bullet went through. It feels like bones did not get shattered. You will be good soon. Let me show you to your room. Follow me." He followed her as she lit the way with a candle. It was still dark inside. It had started to rain. There was a chill in the damp Spring air.

"I clean you up. You rest. Then you eat." Georg wanted to thank her. Valeska interrupted him. "No, do not thank me. This is what we do. This is what I do. You are my honored guest. I will help you. The Priest told us to

59

do so. We do what we are told by priest. You saved life at my cousin's house. That makes our house your house. You saved lives in our community. That makes you one of us." Valeska sat him down by the washstand and gave him a washcloth bath, expertly manipulating his wounded arm and hand.

She is a good nurse, Georg thought. To Valeska he said:

"We could have used you on the hospital train a few months ago."

"I know. I was there. I gave blood. You saved a lot of lives. You were in charge of blood drive. Your speech is famous. People say God sent you. That is good enough for me. Now you put your head on this pillow and I will give you another pillow for your hand." With this she was gone. Georg made one toss and one turn and was asleep. He did not wake up until the moment he heard the sound of a bell. He dreamed. There were bells placed for celebration on the festively decorated harness of four Belgian draft horses at his aunt's house when they made the team ready to pull a harvest wagon for the blessings of the fields through the vineyards. Georg was eight years old. His job had been to polish the bells. Then he saw Tanya's sled when the bells on the arched harness rang as he backed the horse into the sled the first time. He saw Tanya's smile of approval when he succeeded. He saw the carriage move away with Tanya's body and heard the sound of the bells fading in the distance. His heart tore apart in unfathomable pain. This caused a flood of tears. His grief was as black as the night and as deep as the river. The bell rang again.

"Ah. Dinner," he thought, and his hunger pains had no objection to trying some of Valeska's chicken and potato. He was thirsty. His hand felt a little better. He was breathing into the pain. He put on the sling Valeska had made for him and went downstairs.

"How long have I slept?"

"All day long" Valeska laughed. "Can I get you anything?"

"Water please. Something smells good. The smell of your food and the house make me feel at home. We have horses and cows, chickens and pigs, just like you. My father is a minister. We live next to the church. Our family grows food and grapes for wine. Apples and berries for juice. We live in a small town next to France in the west of Germany. My family is more French than German. My father also teaches piano and violin. My mother feeds the hungry, the homeless and her own large family. She even takes homeless in when they cannot find shelter. You remind me of her."

"You sit here. Here is some water. I put in mint." Valeska liked to be compared to his mother but she was too young to feel complimented to be like the mother of a grown man like Georg.

"Here is your dinner. Let me cut your meat. I bring you what you need. No, do not move your right hand. It needs to heal. After dinner we change the bandage for the night." She smiled. She liked the power of a nurse. She was very good at it.

"You are good with your left hand. Do you shoot with your left?"

"I shoot pistols with both left and right. I aim a rifle with my right eye and pull the trigger with my right index finger. I prefer saving lives over taking them. I prefer riding horses over eating them." This thought made them both smile.

"The truth is, I like to use both hands to operate with. I like to ride horses. I was a trick rider when I was a boy. I was trained in the Cavalry. It reminded me of the Cossacks I visited when I was sixteen years old. We collected stories, sagas and songs. That is why my commanding officer sent me out to contact people. I feel lucky to be in your care now."

"Yes, my friend, now you eat. You need strength. Then you rest. I will have to tie your right hand to your chest, so you leave it be." Georg's eyes showed his appreciation. He enjoyed the food. He began to like the sensation of being the patient and not the doctor. Looking at his water brought back memories of the night before. Memories came in waves, as did his tears. To Valeska they looked like tears of gratitude. There was no way she could imagine the grief he was feeling. It was not his hand that hurt. He felt his tears run down his cheeks and get slowed by his week-old beard. He felt like not shaving again until he got home. He was concerned about the use of his hand. Nothing could be done about tendons and nerves now. Not for months. He told himself to let it go. He reminded himself of Tanya's words.

I need you to live. He was startled by Valeska's voice.

"We have apple butter and bread for dessert. I hope you like it. We cook it for a long time behind the fire. That makes it thick and sweet." Her words brought him back to the present.

"Your food is delicious. Why would I not try dessert? I don't know how to thank you."

"I told you. You already have."

The wound was expertly cleaned, disinfected and dressed. His arm bandaged across his chest as Valeska had told him, so he could not move it or put pressure on his wound. This made him relax his muscles as did the care he was receiving. It also helped to relax his mind. Georg slept for a very long time. Days and nights became a blur. He was as profoundly tired as only one could be who was shouldering the burden of life and death for more time than he could remember. His hand was healing well. Valeska was a strict taskmaster.

"We are holding our Spring feast," Said Valeska. "We will celebrate the victory of Stalingrad also. Paulus the German General has surrendered. We will also help you escape." Georg took a deep breath to answer. "No, no. Don't say anything." Valeska said. "You are one of us. That is what we do. I washed and pressed your Cossack shirt. I polished your boots. You will look good. You are our honored guest. Don't even think of dancing. We will dance for you. We will dance for the ones we have lost in this war." Georg's mind drifted off. He thought:

I am not ready to celebrate. My nightmare puts me into the boat in the middle of the black Don river. The flash of rifle and gun, the bang of the pistol next to my ear, the complete silence on the water. At peace with the thought of slipping over the side of the boat. Disappearing forever. My fear of dying is gone. Fear of living is ever present. They say you live only once. I think you die only once, but you live every day and right now that scares me. He felt slightly nauseous. Valeska's voice startled him.

"You can sit in front with me" he heard her say. "We do not travel during day. We wait until dark. This war has made the world crazy. We are like you. We have to hide everything from everyone. We have been plundered, our food stolen, our animals driven off. Ten years ago, famine killed everyone who was not prepared. We had to dig cellars deeper. Hide everything better. Be better armed. Be better connected. Cossacks are always treated as the enemy. The Tsars, the Reds, the Whites, the Nazis. We are hoping to find peace one day. Our priests are living in hiding. We have never lost our faith. We love our children. Look at Sonya. Is she not adorable? Soon she can wear grown up dresses. We love our children. Sonya already knows to dance. And she knows to make borscht. Don't you, my heart?"

The feast was set up in a hay barn. The plank floor was swept clean and soap flakes were spread to keep the dust down. Tables were set at one side of the room. A makeshift kitchen was set up with a cast iron stove to heat and finish food. Chairs were also set along the sides for the dancers to rest and to watch. Everyone was dancing with everyone. The food was a medley of the most popular dishes of the region.

"We all bring food" Valeska said. "We all drink too much."

"I remember most of your food. That is Borscht. We had it when I came. Are these Potato Pancakes? That over there is Salo, pork on rye bread very good for your health. This is my favorite dish: Varemitzi Banish, grits with mushrooms. How am I doing?" Asked Georg. "What was the delicious drink again that you make with herbs and honey? I think it is made with vodka?"

"That is our favorite. Medovukha. We go without most everything all the time. When we celebrate everyone brings favorite dish to eat and Medovukha. Then we celebrate."

Fiddles, guitars, bass, drums, cymbals and harmonica appeared. People began singing. Georg was moved by songs grounded by the priest's very deep bass. They matched his emotions. He loved to see joy in this community that had suffered so much for far too long.

"Still in shock and grief," Georg spoke about this with the priest.

Gregory said:

"We eat food after blessing it, life is a gift. We bless our life and pray to find the strength to endure what we cannot change and the courage to change what we cannot endure. Today we celebrate. Valeska, give our guest a glass of Medovukha. I will have one too. Cheers to life and health!" Gregor said, emptied his glass in one shot and held out for a refill. "We both do things for community." Said Gregor. Georg tried to hear him over the music. "We both help babies come into world. You help with body; I help with soul and spirit. Cheers!" Both drank their Medovukha bottoms up, after clinking glasses. Georg:

"You hear confessions and give blessings. I treat fever and infection. I work for body; you work for spirit. Cheers." Glasses were kept full as if by magic. The conversation deepened and so did Gregor's voice. Attention given them by the beautifully dressed girls felt better the more of the magic drink they had sipped. The dresses were richly embroidered in colors from orange to pale blue with wide cut skirts and puffy white sleeves trimmed with ribbons. Breasts were pushed up by laced bodices. Georg had seen these dresses when he was here before. The image of these beautifully dressed girls had stayed with him ever since. There was one girl who paid special attention to Georg tonight. Georg had known a teenage girl who had encouraged him back then. These two looked very much alike and Georg was reminded of his teenage infatuation. Back then he was still trying to figure out how to remove these pretty garments. Now as the number of drinks went up so did his desire to dance with her. He no longer paid attention to the short boots that were good for riding a horse or wading through the mud outside. Her skirt was floor length, making her look tall. He liked the way her hair was pinned up, braided like a wreath. She was looking at Georg with friendly curiosity and attention. There was a spark in her eyes. He was looking back. The one he instantly liked was soon the only one he could see. She made him forget how heart sick he was. He could not help but to look deep into her eyes, thinking he had found the girl from when he was sixteen. He said another toast to the past. Before he knew it, they danced. The good mood of the moment rose to new heights. Each sip of the honey and herb drink made it easier for him to forget his hand in the sling. They danced. She held him close. And they danced. And danced. There was much need for affection and tonight hesitation to show it melted away like the last snow in spring. Georg began giving in to his growing desire. He was swept away by the moment and into the arms of this beautiful dance partner. She had no hesitation to move with him from joy to pleasure and she expressed as much need to give as hunger to receive. He sensed the need coming towards him. It came with permission to respond. Responses rose in him and he decided to let one thing lead to the next. He had to admit to himself that he was on the brink of either giving in to this moment or falling into a deep depression. He was happy and unhappy at once. He gave in to the moment. He gave in to happiness and to her. He told himself:

"Celebrate Tanya's life. Each one of these girls is Tanya. Especially her. She knows how to make me please her and she makes me feel good". He looked at his favorite. She took his tears for tears of joy and gave into the mood like a mother who holds and consoles her child. By the end of the feast, as by magic everything was getting sorted out. Georg was well fed and more drunk than he could remember. The world was swaying around him as he found himself returned to his bed in the arms of what felt like an angel.

Georg had lost track of time. Daylight was rising like an eyebrow. Another deep long sleep followed. He woke up alone in his bed. The scent of something beautiful lingered. Otherwise he would have believed that he had woken from a delicious dream. He had no memory of this night, except that he had felt no pain.

Georg's hand healed and soon he was able to use it, even though his little and ring fingers were beginning to curl in. He was getting ready to move on. He felt gratitude for everything Valeska and little Sonia had done for him. He remembered dancing. To little Sonia he said:

"Did you see me dance? Your mother healed my hand, so I could dance."

"I know. I saw you. I was watching you. Both. You also danced."

"How did I look?"

"You looked like a happy Cossack."

Children they know everything and miss nothing. Georg thought.

"I have to continue my journey." Georg said to Valeska. "My hand is much better thanks to my excellent nurse. The struggle to survive will be good for me. Only time can make me feel better. I will miss you. I will miss Sonia. I will miss my Cossack family. Before I leave, I would like to see Gregor one more time. Do you think you can arrange this for me?"

"I am sure I can. I will send word." Gregor came and Georg had a chance to speak with him. It made Georg feel better. Gregor explained to him:

"We have been hunted by the communists for years now. Everything religious is done under the veil of secrecy. Cossacks are torn between being Russian and being independent of any regime. We just want to be left alone. Everyone wants our men to fight their wars. Then they want to take our food. We still remember a great famine, because they had taken land away from their rightful owners. The government wanted to do everything. We believe that government cannot grow lettuce or potatoes. They eat seed and punish people when nothing grows. Some people here were hoping Hitler would liberate our country. That makes things even more difficult. Instead of food, it sows death and destruction. In the end we try to hold on to our own ways."

The priest had handed Georg a small parcel. "Katya sent this. It is from

Tanya. We are all sorry for our loss. Her heart was as pure as gold and God will receive and keep her as we will honor her memory. She wanted you to live. This is a small keepsake for you to take with you." Gregor thought for a minute, then he continued: "The Spring feast left us with our spirits lifted despite the knowledge that hard times are coming and Cossacks will be targeted again. We are already squeezed into the margins between the rivers. They have taken our best land. Many Cossacks have fled and migrated in search of a safer home. They have settled on difficult terrain that no one else wants. You can find Cossacks everywhere. In Mesopotamia, Iran, Albania, Turkey, Romania, Slovakia and some in Hungary and Austria even. Some have chosen to run with touring circus companies. Cossacks need to preserve Cossack culture. Therein lies our strength. Our loyalty is legendary. We can disagree on issues, but nothing ever touches our loyalty."

"I feel a deep sense of gratitude and friendship to my Cossack family and you, their shepherd. We are lucky to have you as a guide." Georg said. "I am going towards Kiev. I will follow the route I have travelled before on the train, as far west as Poland. I think I can slip by patrols with the help of people I have met in medical need. Looking like a Cossack fisherman I am hoping to avoid capture from all sides. Valeska said I look more Russian than German. My medical skills will continue to be helpful and a life saver for others as well as myself."

Georg was sent off with Gregor's blessings and supplies packed by Valeska the way Cossacks go to war. He took his surgical knives, his stethoscope, the medical supplies and his fishing gear. His bedroll included a woolen blanket and the gray tent sheet to roll himself in during the night. Valeska and little Sonya stood by the door and waved until Georg's dark silhouette mixed with the mist and the morning light and he began to fade and finally disappeared into the light. Georg was in deep thought about events that had placed him into this beautiful landscape, connected him to these remarkable people who were stripped from their social and communal power to hold on only to a faint memory. He remembered one of his conversations with Gregor:

"Your loyalty is one of your greatest assets. Your fierce independence is present and has survived undiminished in the face of two wars in less than one generation." Georg had said. "And you have prevailed hundreds of years under the Czars. You have told me that wars have nothing to do with your people. You are forced to participate time and again and you do it to maintain the respect you have earned through time. War has left your people weary of authority. I understand that some have begun thinking that dying is a better way out, than having arguments with those who point a rifle to your chest or a cannon at your house of worship. The threat to your spirituality has been the glue that binds Cossacks to their identity and to one another, no matter where they are forced to move to or on which side they are forced to fight."

"You understand." Said Gregor." This is why you are one of us." Georg added:

"I have always felt kinship with your people. Your example gives me strength to struggle instead of giving up. I have to commit myself to surviving day after day."

"You have a talent for meeting people." Gregory replied. "They trust you. And you are a healer. I give you my blessings and I will pray for your safe return home."

One night in his bedroll Georg lay sleepless. He took inventory. Something he would have done by written letter to Rose, if he could.

"I have met the people who are going about doing their work as though there were no wars. I met people walking the same trail with me. I knocked on doors and asked for shelter. I have fished, foraged for food, lived like a bear from berries and herbs and made fire to cook when the fog was thick enough to conceal the smoke. I have traveled in and out of the valleys of many rivers, using the early morning mist to avoid detection when I stumbled too close to military staging areas. I have crossed passes on goat trails. I am travelling west to reach the silk road. It still has an ancient population who live by memories of better times and who know how to serve the needs of travelers without asking questions. These Silk Road People were never in line with governments. They are crossing borders. Like railroaders, they deem governments to be incidental to their lives. They are like doctors. They serve everyone. That is what they have in common with me. They all care for humans." He finally drifted off to sleep.

This morning was different from other daybreaks. Georg was startled by the bleating of an animal in distress. It sounded like a cow in pain.

He realized that he was sleeping in his tarp roll near a barn with cows. Now he could hear exited voices. Georg approached and made a throat clearing sound to announce his presence to the farmers, an old man in his high sixties and several younger women in their fifties. He held out his stethoscope. With a combination of gestures and whatever words came to mind, he told them that he would be willing to help them. Startled at first, the old man and three women saw no better choice than to accept the unexpected offer as a good omen. Georg looked at the animal. He saw a cow with difficulty giving birth unassisted. He directed the farmers to bring fresh straw. He asked for hot water and soap. Making hand washing motions. Lots of soap. He looked around for rope and some sticks. He asked for a large towel. Showing them a face drying motion and outlining a large rectangle. He asked permission to examine the cow. The animal looked exhausted. She was laying on her side. She appeared to have been in labor for a long time. The calf Georg found, probing from the outside, was large and he suspected a breech position. Georg began by soaping his arms and hands. He reached in and realized that he was right about the breech position of the calf. Now he had to turn the calf. For this he needed to get the cow to stand up. He asked for the towel, took it to the water trough, dipped it and told everyone to step back. Standing by the cow's side, he patted her on the head between a pair of enormous horns. To everyone's surprise, he swung the wet towel high over his head and slapped the cow across her back with a loud bang. Startled, the cow jumped up. After applying lots of soap and warm water, he reached in and turned the calf to a normal position with head and front feet posed to come out first. He checked that the navel cord was not wrapped around the calves' neck. He asked for more fresh straw bedding, which made the cow lay down again. There were no more contractions. Georg reached in again and attached a piece of rope to each of the calf's front feet by slipping a loop over the claws. He tied each rope to a piece of wood the thickness of a broom handle. He directed the women to pull as he indicated with his head. First one foot, then the other as he guided the calves' head through the birth canal. He had lubricated the area with lots of soap to prevent tearing. They managed to get one front foot and the head out and turning the shoulders sideways. This made the passage. Then they repeated the sideways movement with the calves' hip and guided by Georg's hand, they finished the delivery. Georg soaked the towel a second time and slapped the cow over the back, making her jump up again. He then cleared the calves' airway. Five minutes later the cow was licking her calf. Two lives had been saved and four hearts won.

The farmers asked Georg into their small cottage. They brought out the best of what little food they had to celebrate their good fortune. Georg showed them the letter from the priest and after some consultation they led him to a rabbi, who was the person in the village who knew how to read and who helped everyone with letters. The rabbi told the farmers to show Georg to the Russian orthodox priest. The priest welcomed him and assured him of his support. He added a second letter. As in a relay, Georg was able to find refuge and connections to other churches and to people with medical needs. They in turn sent him to relatives who were living a few villages distant in his direction on roads that were not often patrolled. As he travelled, Georg was mindful of thickets for shelter. After resting during the day, washing his clothes and drying them by his fire, whenever it seemed safe to do so, Georg was often sent with fresh provisions to his next destination. One family introduced him to a farmer who was taking a trip with oxen to a small market town. His name was Sergej. Sergej offered to take Georg along. He too travelled at night hoping to slip by military patrols to avoid having his freight confiscated before he made it to market. Travelling on the back of a farm wagon gave him a chance to rest and to save his boots from getting worn. Sergey introduced Georg to other farmers who were moving hay. He now traveled on top of freshly dried hay, which was being floated across a lake to winter quarters on a barge. Georg looked like a farmer helping with the harvest. Another time he accompanied a shepherd over a mountain pass to reach the next river. He was headed toward the Danube, which he was hoping to follow all the way up to Ulm. Traversing Mountain ranges and river crossings were challenging at times because of alpine summer snows or thunderstorms. Freezing nights and sudden flash floods were making crossings hazardous in the mountains. The increasing Summer heat was not as much of a problem for Georg, who made his best distances after sunset and before sunrise. Georg found help from people in remote mountain dwellings. They showed him the safest trails, avoiding border crossings. Some raging rivers needed to be crossed over logs, when water was too wild or deep and bridges were not an option for him to use, because they were often guarded. People were helping him to find fallen trees to bridge streams. Georg found himself crossing rivers and lakes on small fishing boats. At times Georg was unsure which country he was in. Only his sense of direction and a basic knowledge of geography helped him to stay on course. He was trying to stay on the side of the watershed belonging to the water basin of the Donau. Many of the people he met did not know more than the immediate valley they called home. Often, he could not make out what language was spoken.

Georg was reminded of his travels as a boy scout ten years earlier, that the region between Hungary to the south, Ukraine to the east and Poland to the west, was inhabited by many people of diverse religious and cultural background and origin, people who had been forced to leave their homelands and were clinging to their identity as best as they could.

His genuine interest in their cultures made his connection to them possible even though he did not speak their language very well.

CHAPTER TEN
FREIGHT TRAIN HEADED WEST

Early one rainy morning Georg stumbled upon a rail depot. Just as he stepped out of the shadows all hell broke loose. Sirens sounded an air attack and anti-aircraft guns were firing everywhere. Georg saw a locomotive and boarded it, hoping no one had noticed his approach. He recognized the drivers.

"Is this locomotive for hire?" He called out over the hammering of the guns and the sound of explosions.

"Hello Georg", said a familiar voice, "Did you bring coffee?"

"How did you know it was me?"

"Your voice. No one has a voice like you. Smooth but grainy like freshly ground coffee."

The laughter about this joke was deeply felt by the train crew and Georg alike. Everyone was extremely nervous. Bear hugs were exchanged. Before Georg could say any more, the men on the locomotive pushed him into the coal tender, took his pack off his back, wrapped his tarp around him and shoved him into the side of the coal pile, his face away from the entrance, placed some kindling and wood logs on top of him and started shoveling coal into the firebox. A soldier climbed up into the locomotive: Georg heard him ask:

"See the saboteur?" The soldier asked.

"See what?" Hans replied.

"We saw a person with a backpack crossing the tracks. Before we could get a shot at him, he disappeared near the head of this train. Watch out. He might be armed, and your train could be the target."

"Tell me about it. We lost a locomotive to an ambush near Moscow on a supply run. We need our trains in one piece. We will blow the whistle if we see something. We are about to move west. How long for you to check the train?"

"Give us fifteen minutes. We will clear you to move when we are done. Heil Hitler!"

The soldier was gone. Hans told Georg to stay put until they had the all clear and the train was moving.

"Wow. what are the odds of seeing you again?" Georg breathed a sigh of relief. He had held his breath during the exchange with the soldier. He realized that holding his breath might have been a mistake, judging by the noise his exhale made. He noted that shallow breaths might work better in this situation. He had not only avoided detection; he had learned two things. One, his friends on the train had just risked their lives hiding him and two, they were about to move the train west. This area was swarming with German soldiers under attack and in a state of confusion. Fifteen minutes later the "clear" was given and the train moved out of the depot. Friendly Aircraft were now patrolling the tracks in periodic fly overs. Hans looked up at them and said:

"Too little, too late." Georg had escaped detection. Now the train crew took care of him. He knew he was in the company of friends. His heart rate was close to twice the normal speed. He was concerned about his recovery time.

"Thank you, Hans. You were fast as lightning hiding me. That was close. Capture would have meant certain death for me. I am still out of breath." It took time for Georg's adrenaline to bleed off. The pistons of the locomotive released steam and a loud deep choo sound escaped with every revolution of the big driving wheels. The fire box door was wide open, and coal was being shoveled into the white glow of the fire, sending sparks up through the chimney mixed with steam that trailed back over the length of the train. After a while Georg could feel the rhythm of this huge steam engine again and he could hear the familiar roar of steel wheels on iron tracks. The daybreak revealed a misty summer morning. The glow of the rising sun from the east was lighting the fog that still lay ahead of the train, making it appear like a solid white wall that broke off into swirls of white light as the locomotive sliced through it. The sound flattened out as the train picked up speed. The forward movement of the locomotive could not disguise the fact that these rails were no longer as flat as they had been before the war. There was now a definite sway in the moving space, the train operators occupied. The windows to the front on both sides of the engine were shrouded with curved hoods like eyebrows to prevent objects from hitting the glass. To the sides, the windows were part of the doors. They could be folded down for ventilation once the air temperature had risen and the engine room was getting hot.

"That was very close. Too close." Georg said to Hans, beginning to shake.

"You were lucky we happened to be there." Hans said as he pushed the lever forward that added more steam to the pistons. They had to raise their voices above the driving noise.

"Maybe it is your lucky star. There were another twenty trains sitting there, ready to be dispatched all over creation. You picked our train. Our locomotive. That was Karma. That we were driving this train was Kismet." Georg was still out of breath.

"Where are we going?" Instead of answering Hans said: "You must have missed our choo choo."

"Yes, I have. I did not know how rough your bedding is. I would have brought a white feather bed. Are you going west? How far can I ride? Where will you drop me off?"

"Questions, questions, questions. Let's have breakfast first. Then we look at my maps. We can do better planning on a full stomach. I always relax better when the train is moving. I hate to be a sitting duck." Hans said and checked one more time all his gauges and levers. They shut the fire door. The train was moving alongside a river with curves following a stream. The side to side movements made them feel like being on a ship in moderate seas. The men sat on low stools that were mounted to the floor, their legs braced wide. The sun was beginning to burn off the mist. The view forward was framed by the oval windows with their hoods and the light was now constantly changing with the changing direction of the tracks along the river. Georg was thinking how amazing it was, that local farmers were able to maintain their world in such good order, while the world was at war.

"Today we have eggs." Georg was pulled out of his musings. "The depot family gave them to us. They even sent a chicken we can cook tonight." Hans announced.

"Would you like to sleep some more in the coal hopper after breakfast? You looked cozy." Laughter all around. Comic relief felt good under the circumstances. Guillotine humor, they called it.

"You should see what Paul has come up with for cooking chicken. The ancient Romans would have been envious. After the war Paul will open a chicken roasting operation." He showed Georg Paul's stove pipe with one end cap riveted on and the other end removable.

"Paul is still working on the best thickness of metal. For now, this stovepipe is his prototype. He packs it with vegetables like carrots, beets, potatoes, parsnips whole onions and whatever the cat has dragged in together with the chicken and then prays that it will not blow up in his face. You will have a sample for dinner."

"Tell me about the Hospital train." Georg asked. "Any word about what happened to it?"

"We have no clue what happened. Remember I was in Germany with you. When we came back, communications were down even on the wires along the tracks. Normally we have communications on these wires. No trains can run without them. No matter who they are running for. They were all down. We think that command at the highest level had something to do with it. Or Stalin's army was switching their own equipment back in. My people will know before too long. I think the war is coming apart. Did you ever ask yourself why we can even run trains during a war? We are not like ships. We are sitting ducks."

"How do you come up with these questions?" Georg asked.

"I have a lot of time to think. I get information about where I have tracks to move on. I get information about my destination. I get signals red or green. The information that makes me think comes in through the cracks."

"What do you mean?"

"Think about it from the perspective of a bomber pilot who can destroy fifty tanks that are driving in line one behind the other. It has happened many times. He can do this undetected. He goes in from behind and takes out one after another. Think about a railroad. Just like tanks all in a row. All in the same row at the same location. One behind the other.

They can see our tracks from the air. They know where there are people and fuel, most do not even have anti-aircraft defenses. Now ask this pilot what he would do to stop the war. Do I have to spell it out? They could stop this war in twenty-four hours and render the entire rail system inoperable by destroying locomotives and depos. One night. One day. Not a single civilian should be sacrificed. They could announce the attack beforehand. They could even tell the train crews to evacuate all personnel. Or they could simply cut the tracks."

"You are right. I never thought about it that way. So, what is the agenda?"

"Some things have to play out. Think about this: Hitler promoted General Paulus to General Field Marshal. That is a fact. Everyone knows this. Facts have consequences. We now see the consequences."

"Maybe I can't see them. Maybe no one can. What do you see?"

"Similar to Stalin's no surrender order for the defenders of Stalingrad, Paulus was given a no surrender order for the siege on Stalingrad. They took away his resupplies, moving them north and south. They claimed victory. Claimed Stalingrad had fallen, which was a lie. There were eight thousand Russian tanks moving in on Paulus. He was encircled and had no defenses from the outside and no supplies to survive. The no surrender order was a suicide order. A General Field Marshal would have to take cyanide before disobeying a "no surrender" order. Stalingrad has cost almost eight hundred thousand German lives. In the city, Civilians had been trained to be snipers in house to house combat. That made all civilians combatants. Stalin moved thousands of tanks to attack the Germans under Paulus from three sides. Paulus stopped the carnage. He surrendered. Paulus must have suspected that his blunt remarks to the Fuehrer, disagreeing with assessments of battles in Southern Russia and the Ukraine had driven the Fuehrer to an even more extreme position. Unless there was a different agenda at work altogether."

"How do you figure?" Georg wanted to know.

"Hitler is confronted by his Generals time and again about decisions that prevented ending or winning this war. Or that would have forced renegotiation of the Treaty of Versailles. Hitler replaced his best Generals with people who do not disagree with him or ask questions. He takes blind obedience for loyalty. That is the Nazi. A dictator."

"Give me an example."

"Look at the fate of General field Marshal Rommel, the other Panzer warrior, who had proposed to end the war by forcing England to surrender, using artillery and air strikes on royal airfields and harbors to keep the royal air force on the ground and to disable the royal navy."

"That would have prevented attacks on London and other civilian targets. It could have saved untold numbers of lives. What did Hitler decide?"

"Hitler gave General Rommel a promotion like that given to General Paulus. He made both General Field Marshals." Georg guessed.

"Rommel was considered a military genius." Hans added. "He was popular with the German population after he took France as if it were an outing of Tanks taking a drive through all of France. Most French people had no idea they were at war. The French people did not realize the tanks were not theirs. As I said. Rommel suggested to end the war."

"What did Hitler do?" Asked Georg.

"After promoting Rommel to General field Marshal, Hitler put him in charge of the Afrika Korps, where he left him stranded without supplies and equipment, similar to General Field Marshal Paulus in Stalingrad."

"What happened to Rommel?"

"Rommel pulled off the stunt he became famous for, by driving the British attackers off the battlefield with cardboard contraptions that looked from a distance like tanks. It still left him defenseless and unable to do what he thought his mission was as a soldier. Being called the desert fox did not help him end the war. He was laid on ice by the Nazis. Hitler had hoped Rommel would never return from Africa. In my opinion, Africa was supposed to be a suicide mission."

"Are you saying that Hitler sacrificed some of his best generals and millions of his own troops to disguise the fact that he had a different agenda from that of winning the war? Is he working for someone else? The Nazi not working for the people who elected him?"

"This is exactly what I am saying. I have only circumstantial evidence. They control the news."

"How do you know all this?" Hans reduced the speed of the train.

"I watch the money." He said. The train moved through a small tunnel. Hans almost shouted:

"Remember the state of the economy of the Weimar Republic before the Nazi Regime was elected? The currency of the country had run out of value with hyperinflation. Everyone lost their savings and their income?"

"Yes, I do. People brought their pay home in wheelbarrows but were unable to feed their family the following week because the money had already lost all its value by Monday. Small businesses closed everywhere. People were unable to keep their shops open or find work. They were desperate. Bankers claimed they had no clue what to do." The locomotive moved into a tight curve the screeching of the wheels almost drowned out the conversation. Hans shouted:

"What do you think happened after the election was won?" The sun began to shine right into the little hooded window. They had to shade their eyes with their hands. Hans made an upward gesture with his right hand, then he said:

"The money became Reichsmark and was suddenly stable. Internationally recognized as a hard currency." Georg recalled:

"The Nazi told us that it was because of his brilliant finance minister who saved the currency and the economy, right?" The train had to be slowed down to make a couple of tight turns.

"Did the people who lost their money in the great depression get their money back? Did the government refund the gold that was lost?" Hans asked.

"I don't believe they did. No gold deposits were returned to their rightful owners. As far as I know, the middle class had been robbed and wiped out financially."

"The Nazi is sitting on the gold now. If you tell me they were able to restore the value of money overnight with the stroke of a pen, I will tell you that Santa Claus is now travelling by plane or submarine and tomorrow the sun will rise blue." Hans looked at the pressure gages.

"More coal" he shouted.

"What did you say?" Georg was unsure if Hans had asked him or Paul to load the furnace. The locomotive made a sudden move to the right. Hans put his hand on the brass lever and pulled it down. It slowed the train. Then he engaged the breaks slowly, one clicks at a time. To Georg he said:

"Time to feed the monster water and coal. I am afraid we will have to put you to bed in your favorite sleeping compartment again. These depots are infested with soldiers checking trains. They do not want any riders without tickets. Georg was hidden in the same disguise that had saved him before. The locomotive came to a stop under the waterspout. Paul climbed forward to open the round hatch of the water reservoir. From here he observed the situation. He was concerned about snipers. He wore his helmet and a bullet proof coat.

"The weapons are getting deadlier and the ammunition is more lethal." He had told Georg earlier. This depot was at the outskirts of a small town. The sun had burned off the mist and now without the travel wind blowing over the engine, Georg could feel that it was a very hot summer day. For him that was good news. It made the soldiers placid and now they were more interested in lunch than in raids on their train. Hans liked the opportunity see the depot crew and to get news without being watched or questioned. Today's timing helped with his important passenger in the coal bin.

Paul was just a child during the first war and details were still in his memory as if it had happened yesterday. Now he was glad to be working for Hans, because no one had more and better answers to anyone's questions. Riding the rails gave them a lot of time when they were watching their gauges, while talking about the strange world they were travelling through. Including the one big question no one could answer: Why are trains still running?

Georg exhaled a sigh of relief after a very tense moment when the coal tender was being re-filled and he could hear the sound of the steam-engine change from idle to the powerful choo, choo, choo of the main pistons after the release of the steam pressure from the breaks. He had escaped one more risky moment with just a black face. They ate lunch after they were well outside of this town and the train had settled into a comfortable speed. Hans asked Georg to report to him about his travels since they last saw each other. When Georg had finished, Hans picked up the morning conversation:

"We are railroad operators. We started running trains when all of Europe was owned by a clan of Nobility, related by marriage. They spent more money than their farms and forests could earn. Some became highway robbers. You can see their little fortresses in strategic places everywhere.

Some of them began borrowing money from merchants, industrialists and bankers, who saw new opportunities because trains opened resources for them and gave them access to raw materials and markets. Nobility with raw materials under their land became rich and the ones with forests and farms engaged in politics. With emerging industry came a need for more workers. Some were guarding resources; some were extracting them, and others were working in factories or as soldiers. That gave them the idea to start wars for profit. There is never a good reason for war. Especially not justice, peace or security. One nation becomes more secure at the expense of the security of their opponent. You want to know what I think as a railroader?" Hans did a wide sweeping gesture. "World wars are wars waged against all people, financed in collaboration with industrial interests to divide the pie. They supply all sides with weapons and loan them the money to pay for them. The workers eventually catch up by paying high taxes, while living in cheap industrial housing. People never benefit from war. They pay for war, believing in the quest for freedom and a better tomorrow. They believe in the glory of war. They send their children to war. We know. We have hauled millions of them in and out of wars. We have seen the wounded and the disabled. We know the cost of war. Railroaders watch it all happen." Over the noise of the locomotive Hans almost shouted: "They have no plan for peace. Everything needs to be destroyed first. Then they finance reconstruction of towns and countries everywhere and employ people to do it. They send them to work in their new factories. We transport the raw materials, the products and the people." Hans adjusted the steam to slow the train through a curve. His mind was trying to reel it all in: "The war industry needs money to buy raw materials to build weapons. They finance it. Railroaders transport the goods. No war has anything to do with people. Except that they guarantee the debt and do the work." He looked at farm fields again with people at work. "Justice is a trivial concern, merely a distraction from what is really going on."

"And that would be?" Asked Georg who was trying to hear over the screeching of the wheels.

"It is about resources. The three resource this war is about is first people, second natural gas and oil and third, real estate. Nobility owned all three when trains started running. Now the new world is being traded by new interest groups. If you don't believe me, watch the money. There will be a conference on international monetary policy to bring this all under one umbrella. Watch in 1944. I am not sure where it will take place. I think the place is called Bretton Woods." The train almost came to a halt. There was a switch and the signal turned. Georg was curious:

"Are you saying that new power structures are being built that have nothing to do with national interests? Did you call it a new world order?"

"Exactly. Resources are worthless unless someone digs them up: People. Factories are useless unless someone goes to work: People. Goods made in factories are worthless unless someone buys them: People. War is both a market and the people are the buyers whether they want it or not. Watch. They will create a world bank. They will create an international monetary fund. After they have destroyed enough of the planet's infrastructure, they will create a new rescue mission. And international development banks. No one can do anything without their permission. Hitler could do nothing with the money of the Weimar Republic. That was the big opening shot at the world. That is why they do not stop our trains."

Hans slowed the train and at a slower speed crossed a bridge. Georg looked out of the window, seeing a river to the right as Hans observed the same river on his left. Georg asked:

"I am a doctor. I save lives. Are we like the Finance industry? Providing people? Weapons that injure our patients are financed by people who invest money to make weapons for all sides. The raw materials come from the same mines. Will it end when they run out of people? Children and women are already being used as snipers. Am I serving this new world order?"

"Women are working fields and boats out there." Hans said, pointing at the afternoon landscape with women in fields, on rivers and lakes. That is all they want to do."

Georg looked at the peaceful world laid out before them. He said: "For the paymasters, people are the other natural resource. They will go anywhere and work everywhere. Just like soldiers, no national boundaries for workers." Hans replied:

"Soldiers put their lives on the line. They are told patriotic tales about freedom and women are told to have babies. The Nazi has gone so far to start breeding stations for his super race. They don't know when to stop." He thought about it some more: "First they ruin the economy to make people fear famine and unemployment. Here the population is still mostly concerned about the last famine, caused by mismanagement of seed and people on the most fertile soils of Europe. Look, that is what people do. See any men? Only old men and women. We railroad people can relate to these people, who are the real heroes of this war. That is why we still eat. They are not decorated the way we decorate people who have killed thousands of people in the name of freedom." Georg replied after some thought.

"Like railroaders, doctor's cross borders and survive regimes. We are needed by everyone. Like you, we serve people. Now we must find a way to connect politics and industry, healthcare and education to serve people. Now like you, we must learn to connect the dots. They claim to be fighting for people. Truth is, people are fighting for them. They claim to do it in service of justice. I say if one single person is holding a gun to another person's chest, there can be no justice, no security and no peace." Georg was now angry. Hans asked:

"They?" Georg made as sweeping a motion with his arms, just as Hans had done earlier:

"Politicians, industrialists, bankers, judges, universities, teachers and labor unions even. In every country. Right now they have everyone running around in arms. This war is completely out of control. There are armed people in uniform who have no idea who they are fighting for, no idea who they are fighting against. They fight one another. They have lost their compass and their identity. Instead of agreements, they make accusations. Then they shoot." Hans pointed at the old farmers.

"The real people out there are the victims. We need a master plan to stop victimizing each other. It will take every one of us and it will take for us to find common ground." Said Hans. "We need everyone to act the way railroaders and doctors do: Service, not destruction. Collaboration, not control. Ask the people in the field out there." Georg still did not give up: "Is there a master plan? It seems there is only one that does not serve the people." Hans thought about what he had observed earlier.

"You are right. The plan they are working on is to reorganize geo economic reality. They want international organizations to control resources and money at both sides of every border. They want People to become the other natural resource. They want to lose the borders. Fear of war will be used to get permission to finance defense expenditures. Their goal is to control everyone by armed force. That is why cities are being bombed. By all sides. People everywhere are simply hoping for peace, while tanks and bombs are creating only fear. They call everyone a terrorist who is not working for them. Once the borders are down, the war will be a worldwide war on terror. They will try to allocate resources for war as part of a fictitious economy under a fictitious threat, backed by fictitious laws." Georg did not understand. "Mark my words: This will all be reorganized before the war is over. The talk is about the creation of an international monetary fund. Nations are being united under the guise of the financial interest of reconstruction and redevelopment, after the war lets some people come up with new rules. Then the war will end." Hans seemed pleased with his conclusion. He continued:

"There is another side to that coin: A new enemy will have to be invented to keep fear alive and to make people pay and keep on paying. There are no winners in violent conflict. Those winners have already won the war." Hans raised his voice more. "Look at yourself. Did you not fall in love with Russian girls? Do you not try to save lives, no matter what the ethnic, religious or national origin of your patient is? Do you not get inspiration from the diversity of people and cultures on this planet? Do you not live by the oath of Hippocrates, doctors swear to save life? Did this not put you where you are right now? Are you not a refugee from a threat to your life from all sides of every border? Despite of all this? Are you not in opposition to all warring parties as a doctor?" More in confidence he added: "That is why you and I are having this conversation. That is why you can find refuge on my train as long as they don't catch you. We are the model of a new master plan" he said. "I told you that I think a lot about war. I am an engineer. I study how things work. As a railroader, I am crossing borders on land in kilometers and between governments in time. No one can run a country without railroads. Not anymore. The Nazi tried to run trains under military command. It did not work. They could not do it without railroaders. We are a peacetime organization. We are an instrument of peace. This modern war cannot be run without running trains. There is a problem though."

"What is the problem?"

"You cannot make war with instruments of peace. People, doctors, scientists, architects, composers, musicians, poets, artists, farmers, foresters, and teachers: All are instruments of peace. They will have to make the plan, instead of blindly obeying some dictators."

Georg saw the train of Hans's thoughts.

CHAPTER ELEVEN
MASTER PLAN

"If no one shows up to war, there is no war. Right now, Railroads are protected by everyone to continue this war."

"You have a point" observed Georg. "How about aircraft and ships?"

"Same thing there. Blow up airfields and harbors and there is no war at sea or from the air." Georg followed up on his idea about a plan: "What would be your master plan?" Hans gazed into the future: "Very simple. War is not winnable. No one can win wars. Trust me. I am in logistics. I connect the dots. Everyone is already at war with everyone else. The population will be pillaged, raped, kidnapped and abused. It's happening in Italy and in Greece right now. They do it to each other. Ships are still running and air forces are multiplying like rabbits in Springtime. War is a diversion, creating one humanitarian crisis after another. They are terrorizing civilians by bombing big cities like London, Dresden and Stalingrad. It makes the first war look like child's play. Meanwhile our trains are still running."

"Give me the plan. You have just taken away all my hope. What do you see in your crystal ball?" Georg was beginning to feel physically sick. Hans answered:

"This war will strangle itself. Afterwards, we need to create new mandates. Just like railroads that serve the economy only in peacetime cannot be run by the military, your Hippocratic Oath works best when it serves everyone in peacetime. We have made this planet uninhabitable and we are approaching the end of the human species, if we keep moving down this track. We need to create new rules for individuals, governments, corporations, universities and schools. Rules that serve and conserve, protect and heal, create security without gunpoint diplomacy, trade without robbery. We must learn to make agreements without threats. Just like railroads and Doctor of Medicine. He continued after a long pause:

We need to teach everyone about a livable planet. Economic activity needs to serve people and to protect life. All forms of life. We must put all human activity under the umbrella of sustainability. Freedom is not a privilege for a few, who are better armed. It is the precondition for life on this planet. Religious freedom does not work, if everyone has to obey by one faith only. That leads right back to war. Humans will not survive, if they are the only species left. The diversity of cultures matches Nature. It takes the entire palette to survive. We have good examples all around us. Physicians and Railroaders to start. See how art can transcend around the globe. See how people connect. All everyday people are in concert."

While Georg thought about these words, he leaned out of the window. He was wearing the flak helmet. It made a melodic sound in the wind, depending on how he tilted his head. It was a stream of hot, aromatic late summer air. He checked the chin strap to be sure not to lose the helmet. The landscape had flattened out and a vast plain had come into view. The tracks were running straight, while the river was wide and meandering through a great open plain. Georg could see railroad bridges now and then, built with long, slanting ramps to make room for river barges. Hans saw him look at the river and he explained:

"Rivers were the first avenues for transportation. Wait until you see the Danube. Upstream, barges are still being pulled by horses. Even though railways have made all of this obsolete, the river people and their horses are still there. Have been for a thousand years. It was and still is the silk route. You do well to make friends with the river keepers. You never know. They are even better connected than our railroad friends. They cross borders with the rivers."

Georg felt like taking a nap. This conversation had made him profoundly tired. He was still interested in Anthropology and Archeology. Art seemed to be the answer. He used to detect a glimpse of hope through the eyes of the anthropologist, looking into the future. He was now afraid that from the past nothing could be gleaned that would help save the future of the planet. The wrong ownership concept had been used over and over. It had left everything in ruins. The power of destruction became progressively greater, with new technology and the reach for global resource extraction and control. Georg now knew that he had a long road ahead. Not the one to finding the fastest way to enslave people or to destroying the planet, but the one of learning about the resiliency that comes from diversity of humans and nature. This would be a road to creating a true connection to a spiritual world, which to him was not separate, somewhere in outer space, but integrated inside the complete world of every living cell. Georg missed the daily correspondence with his love at home and he hated the fact, that he had to stay underground until he set foot in the office of his commanding officer at his home base. He hated this war. He also knew that hatred was not going to be helpful in getting him home. Nor was it going to be helpful in changing the world into a habitable planet. Right now, his world was neither safe nor habitable. Hatred was not a component of Georg's master plan.

"A deadly virus has infected the world and it is my job to find a remedy as a human being, as an educator and as a doctor." Georg said to Hans. "That will be my job." Georg wore a Flak Jacket and locomotive driver's hat when it was quiet and a flak helmet during stops at depots to refill water and coal. They had started to service their own locomotive to keep it running. Hans and his team had been moving their train towards Krakow during the night. The jokes about Georg's coal bin bed were getting old. He had survived because of the quick response by Hans and his team. He was grateful for their friendship, the shelter and everything he learned from them and shared with them.

Georg and Hans had spoken at length about his story of crossing the River Don and his decision to choose life over ending it and to travel unarmed, using his stethoscope as a means of protection, the way a priest uses the cross. The hospital train came up in their conversation often. Hans was as upset about its disappearance as Georg. They agreed that it was unlikely that the Russians had taken the train but suspected that the army had sent it south. Together they now looked at the maps Hans had collected. Hans explained:

"You could stay north and go via Prague, Nuremberg, Heilbronn to Stuttgart. It would be the shortest route. You told me you have studied medicine in Prague. This corridor is the most dangerous route for you to take. Troops and supplies are moving through it. They are being guarded. Prague is being attacked by the allies. Take the silk route from Vienna up the Danube. The risk for you to be detected is great everywhere. There is a rat in every cellar. If anyone has a chance to slip under the wire, it is you. Make that your personal master plan: Move like water, become the river." Said Hans as a final piece of advice.

"I will miss my railroad family. Your friendship and advice mean more to me than I can say."

"I wrote you a new letter for railroaders. I included words for the skippers of barges on the Donau while you were asleep. Here is your pouch." With these words, Hans handed Georg the messenger pouch containing the letter, maps and personal remarks for good luck. Hans slowed the train enough for Georg to drop his pack and to jump off.

Provisioned with water, bread, salami and cheese, Georg walked into a forested area near Krakow. At daybreak Georg could hear a bell from a chapel calling for services. He entered through the sacristy and startled the priest who was preparing the coal dish for burning incense. He made a throat clearing sound. Then he said in polish:

"Good morning father. May I have a moment of your time after the service?"

"You certainly may. Sit in the chapel and worship with us. Would you like me to hear your confession?"

"Yes father." Georg went to the back of the congregation. The service was accompanied by beautiful choir music which elevated the congregation from feeling the ravages of war to a state of bliss and internal peace. After the service, Georg took his place in line for the confession. Someone touched Georg's sleeve and said in a whisper:

"Are you Georg Hofmeister, the doctor?"

"Yes I am. How do you know me?"

"You sang with the choir. We recognized your voice."

"How did you know my voice?"

"You came to our house a year ago. My grandson had epileptic seizures. You helped us." Georg searched his memory "Is his name Boris?"

"Yes. You remember!"

"How is young Boris?"

"You taught us how to help him. We are experts now. Thanks to you. Would you come with us to see him? We will wait for you outside."

"Yes, I will see Boris. I see you after confession." Finally he had his turn at the confessional.

"Bless me father for I have sinned. It has been many weeks since my last confession. I am overwhelmed by events I was not able to control, understand or to stop. I do not even have good recollection of everything that has happened during the last eight weeks."

"My son," the priest said, "you are in the sanctuary of the Lord. Your words are safe with me. In the name of the Father, the Son and the Holy Spirit I will hear your confession."

To the priest Georg said his confession. He told him about Katya's family, the loss of Sonya and the child's birth, his love of Tanya and her command to go home and to get married, and Tanya's insistence for him to return home and live after his medical train had vanished and he was without marching orders, subject to execution by anyone without a trial.

Heavy on his conscience was his failure to save Olga earlier and later his failure to protect Tanya from the German sniper. He explained his automatic reaction to the rifle leveled at Taya and his pistol shot between the snipers' eyes. He explained his desire to end his own life but his choice to live, while crossing the Don, when part of him wanted to slip over the side of the skiff and drown himself to end the war that was now raging inside of him. Georg shed tears when he spoke about the feast and getting drunk while slipping back into a childhood infatuation with a girl from a Cossack family in Ukraine many years earlier. His shame about giving in to his loneliness and desire, the drunken seduction, being unable to stop himself from finding comfort in the arms of this young woman, spending the night with her without remembering anything, not even her name. All he was able to remember was the sweet smell that lingered on the pillow after she had disappeared before he woke up. He spoke about his decision to choose the hard road of survival over the easy way of giving himself up to Russian or German soldiers or to ending his own life. He spoke about his breach with the compact of his own life by taking the life of Tanya's murderer, his lack of repentance or feelings of guilt and his conflict of having been with women other than his newly wed wife Rose.

"You love Rose?"

"More than my own life. I need you to stay alive, Tanya had said."

"You love Tanya and the other woman who seemed to be your childhood friend. You love them all. This love you will now turn into the strength to survive your impossible journey. You will do this to honor all of them and your own love as a doctor for all people and the patients you feel responsible for. That is a very heavy burden for you to bear. As your priest I will include you in my prayers," the priest whispered. "Your penance is to live. This is God's master plan for you."

Georg was given prayers to appeal for the help of saint Johannes the saint of healing for inspiration and prayers asking his name sake saint St. Georg for strength and guidance on his journey, St. Christopher for blessings and protection and for good relationships with people ready to help travelers. Finally, to say Hail Marys' for his indiscretions and his giving in to lust and emotional needs.

"The holy mother understands. Your sins are forgiven." Georg walked taller. He felt as though a burden had been lifted from his shoulders. He thought that Boris' grandparents had gone home by now. They were still outside, patiently waiting for him. They noticed how he was looking around.

"We can take a footpath. It is hidden and very few people walk on it." Boris' grandmother said. Georg was surprised that he could understand the language. They even spoke some German. Then it came to him. He was in Poland.

"How is our patient doing?" He asked. "Oh, you should ask him yourself."

"I will. I would like to hear from you about what happened after I left him. If I remember correctly, Boris was having at least two epileptic seizures a day? Did anything change?"

"Oh yes. But not at first. We did exactly what you told us to do. Soon he began to look at his seizures differently after you spoke to him. He seemed to stop being afraid and ashamed about his illness. We do not know how you took this fear away from him. That fear was almost more difficult for him than the illness itself. He wanted to be like everyone else. After you left, he began to plan for his seizures. He began to prepare himself. When they happened, it was no longer a surprise or something he was desperately trying to fight. He seemed calmer and more grown up about it."

"Did you find him trout to eat and fish oil from sturgeon? I know fish oil was almost impossible to get. The trout you could catch from your own stream. The fish oil was more of a problem to come by. How did that go?"

"We took more trout from the stream then we needed. We took it to town and used it to barter with a person who is smoking trout. He liked our trout. We supplied him regularly. He said it would be difficult to get sturgeon oil, but that his smoked fish was popular with some important people and that they might be able to smuggle in some fish oil to him, especially since a small quantity would go a long way as you told us."

"You became a trout dealer? Was it all barter? Did you have the supply of trout you needed?"

"More than that. We built a trout pond. We became his main supplier of trout and were able to have him organize for us other things we needed." The husband said.

"How about Boris. How did he react to the food and the oil?" He began sleeping better after a while. The sleep made him stronger and he was less afraid." Said the woman. "After some weeks had passed, Boris told me that the seizures were happening less often."

They had walked along an overgrown trail alongside a stream that was almost entirely covered by the branches of willows that showed signs of regular cutting for basket work. Georg could see that the branches covering the stream were left to grow to shade the water.

"You have shaded the stream on purpose, it seems. Why?"

"Trout like to swim in cool water. This is where they place their eggs. Then they migrate into our trout pond. Wait until we show you. We did not know much about trout farming until you asked for trout. We began to learn. And now we are cultivating trout in our pond and in our stream." The husband said.

"You made us do it. For Boris" She added. When they rounded a bend in the trail, they could see a rise in the path and a rocky spillway from what promised to be a body of water. It was built with natural field stones added artfully to existing bigger rocks to create small whirlpools that looked inviting as a fish ladder for trout to jump up through the water to reach the pond. It was also a way to aerate the water to add oxygen to the stream. "This is beautiful, "said Georg admiringly. "If I were a fish, I would like to live here." When they had reached the level of the pond, a view opened that was like a romantic painting from a hundred years ago. The last time Georg had visited this homestead, he had not noticed the river. Georg now stopped to let this idyllic picture sink in, with the path surrounding the water's edge and a little bench, the variety of vegetation, an old chestnut tree and a small boat launch onto which a small skiff had been pulled out of the water. There was a pair of white swans at the opposite side of the pond and a chicken was running back and forth excitedly to attempt to call six ducklings back to shore, making a funny scene that made Georg laugh.

"That is how I feel half the time as a doctor when I do not speak the language of my patients. I too get excited when they cannot understand what I am saying." He said, laughing. "You did not tell her she was hatching ducklings, did you?"

"No. we did not want to confuse her. Well, now she is confused anyway." The woman said. They all were amused by the spectacle. The light was glistening on the water's surface when a trout jumped up to catch an insect, causing tiny circular ripples in intersecting lines to spread over the entire pond. The air was still, just a few white clouds in an otherwise blue sky. The swans raised their wings to display their plumage as if to show off to their visitor.

"Let me show you more of our pond and trout farm. The wife will make breakfast and Boris will be up by then. Teenagers" He said with an air of exasperation. "Sleep into the day and stay up into the night. I will have to send him off to learn blacksmith after he finishes school, before he turns into a no-good slouch. His mother has been too easy on him for far too long. Seizures this and seizures that. I should have had it that good. I was getting the belt with the buckle over my back."

"Does he still get seizures?"

"No, they became more and more seldom and about two months ago they stopped altogether."

"Hold off with the belt buckle for another two years and let him finish school. I think he is doing well from what you have told me. Better than I had hoped. He has a strong heart and a good mind."

It was Sunday and a celebratory breakfast had been served to Georg. The roasted grain coffee was served sweetened with honey and cream that had been skimmed off the milk for this event.

"Dr. Hofmeister, I thought I heard your voice!" Boris joined them. "How do you feel, Boris? You look good. How is your sleep?

You are still sending your grandparents to church. Are you asking them to thank God for your recovery? Can we talk after breakfast, just you and me? Maybe you show me the trout pond? I have some questions about trout that only you can answer." For the next hour, Georg and Boris wandered around the trout pond. Boris said:

"It worked. My episodes became less violent and soon were happening further apart. Then my grandparents began trade with a trout smoker in town. He was able to get the fish oil you have asked me to take. This led us to the idea to cultivate trout and to become a supplier of trout for the smoked trout market. After your visits, the first thing that happened was that I was feeling less fear and my grandparents were less excited. That made me feel less guilty for being a failure. I was able to relax. Something changed in everyone's attitude and my brain did too. We will forever be in your debt."

Georg told Boris that he was not at liberty to speak in detail about the reason he was no longer with the medical corps. Later over dinner, he did speak about his need to make it to Austria and that he was at risk of getting caught. This prompted some soul searching. Suddenly Boris' face lit up. He had an idea.

"Dr. Hofmeister could travel with the circus." He said jubilantly. "Circus Sarrasani is in town and the program said that they are on tour to visit Krakow and Vienna. I think they had the last show today. Monday they will pack up the tent and Tuesday or Wednesday they are back on the circus train. I am sure they can use a doctor. Grand Papa talk to the trout smoker. I am sure he has done business with the circus." Grandmother noticed the coal dust on Georg's clothes. She said:

"Give them to me. I will have everything fresh, clean and dry for you in the morning".

Boris' grandfather agreed to speak to the trout smoker the next day when he was going to make this week's delivery. The next day, they went into town to see about contact with the people of Circus Sarrasani. Once they reached the town square, it seemed safer for Georg to stay in the backroom of a small café, where they had an extra table the owner was using when there were no guests. Boris' grandfather introduced Georg as a distant relative from Germany. They handed Georg a newspaper. Today's news was, that a week ago a brave officer had arrested a performer of the

Circus Sarrasani equestrian team who had been fingered by a secret police agent as belonging to a communist resistance group in Leningrad which had recently been disbanded by the SS. Georg suspected that all of this was a lie.

Georg had barely finished his coffee when Boris' grandfather came in and asked him to leave the café through the back door. His host led him through small back alleys to the railroad station where they slipped into the locomotive of the Sarrasani Circus train. Georg spoke to the engineer. He handed him Hans' letter. After reading it, the engineer said:

"You are welcome to wait here." Grandfather said:

"I will ask the director to see you. They are packing the tents soon. The animals will be loaded last. I will come back with your pack in an hour." He left across the tracks to return to the town center through the main entrance of the station. Georg could see how guarded and paranoid everyone had become.

CHAPTER TWELVE
CIRCUS SARRASANI

"I am Georg" he said taking back the pouch Hans had given him. "Remember. The less anyone knows about you, the better" Hans had cautioned him.

The engineer had read the note and had nodded with a gesture of welcome and an invitation to sit while he was waiting for the director.

The director was a short, energetic man with a potbelly and a cold stub of a cigar in the corner of his mouth that looked like it had been there for days. He wore a black suit that matched the cigar in the wear and tear department. It barely covered his beer belly. A black round top hat completed the outfit.

"Hello, I am Georg", hand outstretched in greeting.

The director ignored his hand.

"I read about the arrest. I am sorry."

"Bastards", the director squeezed out between his teeth and the cigar, black eyes blazing with hatred. He looked Georg over like a cattle dealer, then he continued: "I am Janosh. The boys call me Ja. The girls call me Nosh. I am the boss here. Whatever I say is the law. You see, this is a zoo of a circus in every sense of the word. We travel. The fishmonger told me to talk to you. He said you are a doctor. Everyone is a doctor, I told him. He said you are a real doctor. What do you want?" Georg hesitated. *Tough guy*, he thought to himself. The director waited for a reply, then he said:

"All right let's go to my car. I see you want privacy. I hate doctors. They always come when someone gets hurt." He snorted. "Step into my office". He was out of breath. He took a deep breath and continued with a dry cough that did not want to end. Once inside, he started over: "Damned dry air". He had almost lost his cigar. "So you are Georg, the dragon slayer? You patch the dragons after you stab them?" He laughed about his joke and coughed some more.

"Ja", answered Georg with emphasis. The director liked that.

"I see you listen. Where are you going? The fishmonger said you are going places."

"I lost my hospital unit near Stalingrad. Long story. I am officially a deserter. I must return to my unit headquarters at Tübingen. Then I get new marching orders. I promised someone that I will get there alive."

"Selfless to the last drop. Like a good wine," the Director laughed, following the exhale with another coughing fit. Georg pulled out his stethoscope without thinking.

"Take off your jacket, I have to listen to something." Georg had changed his tone to that of authority. Without thinking, the director obeyed doctor's orders.

"I like your style. Now you will tell me what I can do and what I cannot do." Said Janosh.

"Ja. You need a new cigar. This one is getting old. We want you to get old. Not your cigar. Inhale for me. Again. Again. I know Sarrasani. I saw your circus in Tübingen. Now exhale all the air out. Slowly. Then slowly fill your lungs as full as you can. Good. I liked your show, especially the trapeze act with the Lipizzaner and the girl on top of her partner." Janosh exhaled, barely avoiding another fit of dry cough.

"The Nazis took him" he exclaimed. "Bastards, just to scare folks."

"I read it in the paper. They made an example of him. They reward snitches. They have nothing to hold him for more than a couple of weeks. Meanwhile, I can stand in for him, if you let me travel with you towards the Danube. You are going to Vienna?"

"Yes, but hang on just a second. This is a tall tale. What gives you the idea that you can do that? Stand in for him, really. Now I have heard everything." He laughed then had another coughing fit.

"We saw your act. With my trick riding partners, we almost killed ourselves learning how to do it. Ok, now give me a couple of small coughs. There. I will make you a tea to drink and a special steam to inhale. My host the fishmonger will get me the ingredients. I was in the same position in the act. We did it in a smaller circle. That was harder. I did it again two years ago in the cavalry for a recruiting demonstration." The director opened the door and yelled out:

"Get me Wilma. Get her now". Again, he coughed. "We will settle this right here and now." After he had put on his jacket again and Georg had stowed away his stethoscope, the door opened and a slender brunette with a big smile entered the room. She greeted the director by putting her hand on his arm above the elbow, then turned to look at Georg. With a big smile that revealed a perfect set of very white teeth, she said to Georg:

"Hello" and to the director, "who might our visitor be?"

"This is Georg, doctor of medicine and trick rider from Tübingen. He claims he can do Manu's act without killing you, himself or the horse. And if he does, he can patch everyone up. He is a surgeon he claims. Georg, this is Wilma, the girl everyone wants to love, and no one ever forgets." Wilma blushed. Janosh moved things along:

"Let's go outside and see if he can hold you without dropping you. We'll do a test with the horse later, once you tell me he can do it."

"Nosh, are you sure?"

"No. I don't believe a word he is saying. Outside. Both of you."

When Boris' father crossed the track, he noticed a girl standing on top of a man. They were moving around from side to side, backwards and forward, then he saw her jump to the ground, catch her fall with a forward roll and immediately climbed back onto the man using his bent knee and his upturned left hand as step supports. This time she put both hands on his shoulders, moved in one swift motion into a handstand, from which she tilted slightly to place her right hand on his head and pushed herself up for a one-handed stand balanced on top of his head. Slowly the man turned, and it became clear that it was none other than Georg in the middle of a dry run for a circus act. A small crowd of spectators surrounded them. The girl pushed herself up and after saying "Catch me", dropped into his outstretched arms, then elegantly slipped to the ground with a curtsy to the spectators.

"Not bad", she said with a smile to Georg who was rubbing his neck. "Good" she said to the director who was breathing hard. "Let's try it on a horse."

"What are you all looking at?" Yelled the director to the spectators who stood clapping. "Don't you all have something to do?"

"Ja" everyone said, turned away and went back to their chores.

"You can drop his pack in the next car" he told the fishmonger." I need to keep this man. He can feed the horses." Everyone laughed. They knew this was not a funny situation. Boris was right, Georg thought. Georg stepped close to grandfather.

"I need another favor." Georg said. "I need you to find me chamomile blossoms and mint leaves. Both fresh and dried and a jar of raw honey. We need it for the director, he said quietly. Turning to the director, he asked:

"Janosh, what time does your train leave the station tomorrow?"

"Eight o'clock in the evening".

"Can you bring these things here? And please give my very best regards to your wife and to Boris." Georg said.

At six o'clock the next day, Boris' grandfather returned with a large package of smoked trout and Georg's prescriptions. The test in the tent was also successful. At first they had Georg on a lanyard to see his stance and balance on the galloping horse. They decided that it would take only a few practice sessions, before they were able to bring the act back. What made it special were the beaming smiles of Wilma who liked Georg in every way with his handsome looks, his dark complexion, his finely curled short cropped black hair and his black mysterious eyes. Most of all, she liked his chivalresc demeanor towards her and the other ladies of Circus Sarrasani. She liked the fact that she was the one who got to work with the new boy under the big top. She could see that he was a natural with horses who had a calming influence on them even as he asserted his authority and the horses seemed to respect him. Secretly Wilma's body began to ask for a little play as well. She had a lively way of talking and often used eyes and hands to make a point and to touch her new partner in a trusting and exciting way. At the next town they were able to get the act ready for the public. To celebrate, they danced to the music of the circus band, who never missed an opportunity to play for Wilma. They felt inspired by the way she turned their sound into motion. She could become part of the musical act as a dancer, they told her all the time.

"You wish", she would reply with her big smile. Partner or no partner. Everyone loved Wilma. Everyone wanted to take her home. "This is my family" she told Georg. "My parents disappeared from our home in Prague while I was at school. I was thirteen then. I have a brother with Downs syndrome. The Year before, the Nazis forced us to hand him over to be put into a special home. When we tried to visit him, we were denied. My parents protested together with other parents who were missing their children. Protesters began disappearing. All they had in common was that they were parents who loved their children. My parents disappeared one day too."

"I am so very sorry. I studied medicine in Prague." Georg said, reaching out his hand, asking her to give him the grooming tools. "I wrote my doctoral thesis in support of life worth preserving in the face of a government that was claiming there was life unworthy of living. The Nazi is eliminating flawed humans. They talk about a master race. I am lucky they also do not like to read. To them my doctorate was just another paper. Had they read it, I would be dead now. Your parents must have become victims of this new doctrine. People disappearing is the most frightening experience for the population, especially when no one knows where they were taken or what happened to them." He ducked under the horse's neck to groom the other side of his white silky fur coat, Lipizzaner's are famous for. Georg and Wilma had ten more horses to go after this one. He rubbed the stallion's head and nose and blew a breath of air into his nostrils which made the stallion shake his head. Georg was introducing himself to the horse. Wilma's hand appeared from the other side to steady the horse's head and their fingers met, while their eyes investigated each other in a long, exploring glance which neither was about to break off. Then the stallion gave off a whinny and reared which broke off touching fingers and glancing eyes. Someone was approaching.

"Janosh" Georg exclaimed, running the brush from front to back, stepping out into the isle.

"Are you not done yet? What is taking you so long? These are horses, not patients, doctor. We need to speak to the musicians. I have some ideas I want your input on. Hurry up already. How many more do you have to do?"

"Ten." Georg answered, cleaning his brush. He had learned grooming from the best the cavalry could offer. Ja. was still chewing on his worn-out cigar between his teeth. Another coughing spell made Wilma give Georg a concerned look that reminded him to prepare the treatment to make Janosh's lungs feel better.

"We need to get him a new cigar. Do you have any money left? I know, we can always trade with tickets to the show."

"Yes, and yes. Don't worry, I have ways to get comps and change them into cash if need some. I offer to buy supplies in town sometimes, but I pay with tickets and liberate the cash."

"I have to watch you. You have ways."

"He gave her a quick peck on the cheek as he moved to the next horse. Doing one side of a horse each, made it quicker and gave them opportunities to exchange contacts in creative and secretive ways as they went from horse to horse. They both loved horses and the animation did not stop with the animals.

"The boss has music ideas for our act? Do you know what he has in mind?" Georg wanted to know.

"He probably wants a big bang from the big drum when I drop from your head into your outstretched arms." She laughed." Then he can call for the snare drum to chatter when you drop me."

"This is not funny." Georg scolded laughingly and gave her a little slap on the behind as he crossed to the next horse. She grabbed his head and planted a kiss on his mouth but pulled away quickly to get to the other side for more grooming. Georg reached under the neck, caught her hand, pulled it across, took the brush out of it and kissed the inside of her palm. Then he returned the brush and continued his work.

"I will not drop you, mein Schaetzchen." He said.

"You are part of my act now. It is Kismet, the palm reader Gertrude has told me," replied the girl.

For now, everyone in the circus was still nervous about their act. They were surprised about his skill. Like Janosh, no one had believed his story. "Karma" he answered the palm readers claim. "I have done my homework."

"The universe gave you the girl. That is Kismet. A gift. You are a lucky boy. What you do with her is Karma. And it better be good." The fortune teller had said to Georg.

The palm reader was an important part of the circus. People were nervous about getting from one day to the next. She read Tarot cards also. She was good at telling people what they wanted to hear. That made her also a good pair of ears on the ground of the enemy.

"Nazis are my best customers. They like to believe things. They are not interested in reality. They like to follow their Fuehrer." She had told Georg. "They are the most superstitious of them all." The fortune teller burned incense, had things smoking inside her colorful stand behind printed Indian cotton curtains and strings with beads and bells. Her scents were exotic. She commanded respect. Georg noticed that people were a little afraid of her. He was curious about things she knew about the healing properties of plants. That was something Georg liked to talk with her about. He was interested in the medicinal use of herbs and the wisdom she had in formulating recipes.

One by one Georg met the circus members. It was an assembly of interesting misfits that had found a home here with the security of acceptance, which was as thin as the canvas of their tent but better than the world outside of the big tent, where almost all of them were outcasts. Inside the tent they were a big family. The circus was visiting a series of towns every year in the same sequence, which made it possible for Janosh to hire local contractors to help with setting up, reducing the travelling crew to a skeleton team of experts in different areas of the complicated structure of the big top as well as lighting and sound systems. Animals were accompanied by their own trainers. Keepers were also trainers just like Georg and Wilma who were working with their horses, they were feeding and grooming them also. Helpers oversaw water, hay, bedding and manure. They were in charge also of loading and unloading the animals. Everyone was from a different corner of the known world and most were refugees under the protection of this canvas tent, tolerated by outsiders because they were amusing the world without having to be integrated into it. Georg felt that this assembly of United Nations deserved the Glorious parade that finished each show with flags and signs of respect for the countries that gave them permission to perform for them as well as flags of their countries of origin. The refuge the circus gave its members was answered with fierce loyalty for each other.

"We appeal to the child in each member of our audience and the children are our allies. Occasionally someone gets picked out of our lineup of characters. There are secret police and snitches in our audience. They sit right next to innocent children, who love no one more than our clown Foo Foo." Wilma told Georg one evening when they sat in front of a small fire. "Foo Foo acts like a toddler but makes only fun of himself." Georg saw a tear running down her cheek. He moved in behind her and holding her in his arms he tried to make her feel safe. Their cheeks touched. He nibbled on her ear. Both knew this was only for a small moment in time. The circus train was side railed for a couple of days in a small railroad station with a depot for railroad supplies and a small freight yard. Georg was curious about the delay and the letter Hans had written for him to show to station masters was helpful when he went to find out. He went over to the small brick building with a red clay tile roof from which traffic was directed. After introducing himself and presenting the letter, the stationmaster poured Georg a cup of coffee and brought out a couple of pieces of cake. After studying Hans's letter, the depot master said:

"We can speak freely. You are one of us." Pointing at the cake he said:

"Mother baked this for me. She always makes more than I can eat. We have been following your progress. We love Sarassani. You came down from Warsaw. It was quiet up there. Everything is changing. Warsaw is the main corridor where the offensive into Russia was staged." He looked out over his rail yard with its empty tracks except for the circus train. "I know things are going crazy. Now we have fronts everywhere and Stalingrad was supposed to be the game changer for Hitler. Now we are fighting on all fronts. One up in Moscow and one at the black sea. One in Italy one in Africa. This has created trouble and emboldened opposition and resistance to the Nazis in Austria and Hungary against the rear guard of the Wehrmacht in this region. The army keeps calling for reinforcements. No one is listening. People have begun to defect and soldiers from former colonies have no idea whom they are fighting and who is giving them orders. That makes everyone extremely jumpy. The area around Budapest and the lower Danube has seen more sabotage lately. The Nazis are expecting resistance to return to Poland as well."

"Have you talked to the engineers on the circus train? Are we at risk here?"

"Yes, you are. I am afraid we are having trouble right now. That is why you are side railed here at our sleepy freight yard. The army is building camouflaged machine gun stations where they bury one gunner or two in strategic positions, guarding small backcountry roads, bridges and depots. They find this very effective, even at the chance they shoot someone from their own axis. At night they will shoot at anything that moves. We told the train crew to tell the director to call for a curfew and to let no one wander off after dark. Not even to take a shit. There are eyes out there. Anyone out of doors might get shot just to be sure they are not resistance fighters or saboteurs." Georg wanted to visualize the threat.

"Any particular pattern? Are there hunting stands?"

"That would be too obvious. These boys are up against the most dangerous and experienced resistance fighters. Some come from the fighting after the Ottoman Empire was broken up at the end of the First World War. They eat dirt and drink blood. The Nazis are spooked."

Georg had begun to look out of the windows to get the lay of the land. He saw a harvested field that made for a clearing from which someone could cover the entire area of the freight yard, the depot and the building they were in. The field was surrounded by small pieces of forest. There were field ways leading to small farms. Georg grew uneasy. He asked himself what he would do. Both in offense and in defense. He saw piles of manure on the field still steaming, ready to be spread by hand. In offensive mode he would use the forest as cover for an assault. It was not a place to attack, because the forest gave shelter to both the defender and the attacker. And there was no target inside these forests that would be interesting for the resistance. As a defender on the other hand, a single machine gunner could hide under one of these smoking dung heaps, perfectly hidden. There they could wait for a suspect or suspects to approach the depot to perform acts of sabotage. They would shoot them from the back. You could not even see from under which pile of dung the shots had come. Once you saw it, your clock had run out and it was too late.

"I understand." Georg said to the station master. "I will have a talk with Janosh, the director. Pray for us. We are just a circus. Nothing to be scared of. Thank you for coffee and cake. My highest regards to Mother. Maybe I will see you again. May God keep you and your family safe."

Georg returned to the train. He was deeply concerned for the safety of his companions and his hosts, who had kept him safe and hidden in plain sight. Just the thought of Wilma being a target made him almost lose his mind. He felt the rush of adrenaline that people experience during fights. He was transported back to the river landing at the Don and the sniper. Before he saw the director, he located his surgical kit and found his scalpel.

"Janosh, I have to talk to you. I have just come from the station master.

I have some information."

"Why would he talk to you? Why would he not talk directly to me? If he has something to say, I would be the one to talk to."

"I agree. You are absolutely right. He said he already spoke to you."

"What makes you so special suddenly? You are nobody. Just a cowboy with a medical degree. You are not much of anything, really".

"Again. You are absolutely right. Except I know his family, I cannot tell you how, but I do. That makes it so that he cares for all of us. These people love your circus. They want you to be safe."

"Why! Why you. Why not me. I am the boss."

"Because you are my family too."

"Ok. Talk to me. If you were not my doctor, I would send you to eat horse apples. Make it quick."

His lungs are better, he can run a lot of steam, Georg thought. *Minty steam, chamomile steam inhaled with a towel over his head. To get him to do that took a whole box of new cigars. To make him drink the tea with honey took the intervention of the fortune teller and sweet Wilma to prepare and serve it to him twice a day. But yes, he sounds better.*

Georg shut the windows and the door to his office. Then he spoke: "I have some new information to do with why we are waylaid here."

"I know. It's repairs to the tracks. They said so. Our engineer said so."

"There is more." Georg spoke in a low, confidential tone.

"The Nazis have machine gunners stationed in this area and especially at rail yards as a rear guard, to protect the movement of troops and supplies to the Black Sea. The resistance is increasing sabotage behind enemy lines. Our lines are all over the place. So are loyalties. People are falling off the Nazi bandwagon and are thinking it is safer on the other side. That has made these soldiers extremely nervous. They are jumpier now than ever before."

"What does that have to do with us?"

"We are being watched. This rail yard is a target. They think we may be used as a shield by the resistance. Maybe a diversion or another obstruction to the rails. This is not a major strand of rails, but it could be a detour.

Like I said, German gunners are jumpy. And they could be anywhere. You cannot see them."

"Are you trying to scare me with something I cannot see? Are you a palm reader now too, or a priest?"

"No. This is serious. I agree with the stationmaster. He wants you to call a curfew from sundown to sunup. They say it is not even safe to step out at night to take a leak in the dark. Someone may get shot. The Machine guns are not the old type most of us have seen. They are fast and furious now and one burst may not even obliterate the target but could penetrate the rail car walls and randomly injure people. Believe me. I was in Stalingrad on a large hospital train. I have seen it all. You want the curfew and you want the lights blacked out at night."

"What gives you the idea that you can control the United Nations of Sarrasani Circus?" The director snorted angrily.

"I feel obligated to try. Everyone is the master of their own fate. You and I are giving everyone a choice. If something happens, I have no idea what I can do to help. You do not get hardened to the tragedy of war. You lose control and you gain a new kind of control and power. You become hypervigilant. Or you die." Georg said with intensity in his voice.

"I have no idea what you are talking about"

"It does not matter. Will you please just tell everyone that we are under curfew? I know the stationmaster has told you so."

"That will take getting everyone together."

"Yes, I know. Only you can do it. Will you do it for them? Do it for me."

"I owe you nothing."

"You owe your circus everything." Georg grew passionate:

"As much of a pain in the ass as you are, they all love you and respect you weather you like it or not. Sarrasani is not a piece of paper. It is the people who love you. I beg you."

"Ok. You are the doctor. I'll do it."

Georg opened the window and the door and excused himself. It was still daylight and the horses were already done. He told Wilma that he needed to check something on the train, that there was something with the brakes that his engineer friend showed him needed to be checked occasionally. This layover was the break he was looking for, he told her. Georg proceeded to climb under the train and from an observer's point of view it seemed like he was looking at the break mechanisms. He even used a mallet to make banging noises. Every time he rolled over to move to the next set of wheels, he looked at one of the dung heaps for telltale signs of an elongated dark spot facing the tracks, that could be the slot for the muzzle of a machine gun. He went systematically from right to left as he moved from one end of the train to the other. Where the cars are hitched together, he was able to get up and check the connections of the pressure hoses that fed the brake action to the entire train. This gave him time to look from another angle. He had just about given up on the idea of locating a hidden gunner's position, when he caught a glimpse of light that might have been a reflection. The dung was fresh and still steaming, especially in the morning and in the evening. But there was no moisture on the dung that could reflect light and more importantly, there was no source of light coming from the train to be reflected. He now focused on the spot where the light had come from. Sure enough, there was the glow from a cigarette being smoked in a cavity under one of the dung heaps. He remembered the words of his drill sergeant during basic training:

"Never light a smoke when you're dug in. It gives you away to the enemy.

More of you have died a useless death because you did not believe me."

"This one did not believe him," he thought. Once again, he made himself busy with the connections of the hoses and the mechanisms. What he was really doing was to memorize the exact location of the gunner and some landmarks in the woods, including the silhouette of treetops and branches against the sky to act as points of orientation at night. He had decided to take out this gunner if he were to take a shot at someone and before he could take another shot. His approach would be from the back, so it was critical for him to know exactly which the correct starting point was. He had one more trip to do during first light, to check the view of the train from the shelter of the trees and to locate the heap with the gunner as seen from the back side facing away from the train. He checked the viewing angle of the gunner.

There must be a hidden entry on the back side of his dugout. Georg thought.

The following morning before sunrise at his usual time of waking up, Georg slipped into the overalls he was given by the circus. Silently he made his way to the end of the sleeper cars. He left the train and headed in the opposite direction to avoid being detected by his horses. Describing a large rectangle, he walked first south, then west, then east until he reached the forest he had seen on the other side of the train. With patience and stealth, he worked his way through the woods to the far side of the field, mapping in his mind the best approach in the shelter of low hanging pine branches at the edge of the field. At one point, he came across tire tracks in an overgrown logging path, which led him as close to the nearest sheltered point to the gunner's dung heap. Signs of disturbed grass and the smell of feces and urine reassured him that he was exactly where he needed to be. From here he observed the location of the gunner's shelter and the silhouette of the train and the terrain beyond. Now he could find the right heap of manure even in his sleep. Turning back, he also scouted out the closest sheltered approach and confirmed the viewing angle of the gunner in case he had to rush him. While he did this, he noticed the entry to the gun shelter and saw that it was visible to trained eyes. Instinctively, he tapped the narrow pocket at the side of his pant leg, designed for foldable carpenter's rulers, in which he kept his scalpel. Undetected, he made it back to the train in time for feeding and grooming. After breakfast, Janosh assembled the entire team on the other side of the train. He gave his speech as promised and everyone nodded in agreement except for some, who did not like to be told what they could and could not do during their free time. To them, this was a principle issue. No rules outside the show. Georg and Wilma had become very close friends but were hesitant to go beyond friendly banter with little kisses, innuendo and some chuckles. Touch and hugs, kisses and intimacies were maintained in the realm of loving siblings. One day when they were out in town, someone from the orchestra came right out and asked Wilma if she wanted to sleep with him. "Why", she had said, "a lot of guys want to sleep with me. If I would sleep with anyone, it would be Georg. So, no. But thank you."

The threat of a machine gun pointed at the circus train raised Georg's hair permanently. He could not share the information he had. Not even with the Director of the circus. He kept the details of his discoveries to himself. He was paying close attention to any movements of people on and off the train after sunset. One person who was especially dear to him and Wilma was the clown Foo Foo. His antics with his big shoes, his red nose and his corresponding semi-circle of bright red hair were legend. His ability to act like a six-month-old baby while doing impossible stunts of pulling himself back from certain doom with the magic hand of an imaginary mother that every child could see, made Foo Foo a household word for charmingly crazy wherever he had performed his act. Everybody loved Foo Foo. But no one was going to tell Foo Foo what to do. He was independence incarnate. He was a country to himself. That cost Georg sleep. This night was especially quiet, a clear sky with a sickle moon, surrounded by planets was clearly visible in front of a brilliant milky way. Georg was alerted when he heard the muted whinny of his horses. This would have been enough to make him go to their wagon to see what spooked them. He had been sleeping in his overalls, covered by a light blanket. He went to the window, his eyes well-adjusted to the dark and the dim light of the stars. He could see a figure walking alongside the train, then heading towards the dung heaps where he stooped down to squat to relieve himself behind a manure pile in the second row, about fifty meters from the side of the train. Silently, Georg slipped off the train. In a fast sprint he flew alongside the train. He entered the sheltered part of the forest until he had reached the safe zone, where he could not be seen by the sniper. He began to cross the open field, cutting a path between the steaming dung heaps, when he heard two short bursts of machine gun fire. Out of the corner of his eye he could see the figure he had noticed earlier picked up by the first burst of bullets and knocked clear over the pile of dung. The second burst ripped him apart in mid-air like a moving ceramic target at a carnival.

In one swift motion, Georg flung off the cover to the entrance of the shooter's dug out. Before the shooter was able to react, Georg's scalpel delivered a deadly cut to his kidney. As the shooter sank to the ground, he exhaled the remaining air from his lungs and without another sound he fell over. At the same moment Georg tapped around to make sure there was no one else in this tiny space. He left and replaced the cover. He knew that no one would see the dead gunner until the manure was spread and the dugout was exposed. He also knew that his time with Circus Sarrasani was over. When he returned to the train, he went to the horses, hoping that in the confusion someone would see him in a place where he was be expected to be, whenever there was a disturbance that could excite the animals. He had done this alone and he wanted to keep it that way. All this happened so fast that only a few animal trainers were up, and Georg was patting and speaking soothingly to his horses, calming himself and the spirited stallions, when Wilma arrived. He turned to her and took her into a long, deep embrace that said all he was able to say at this moment. When Wilma took a breath to speak, he said:

"Shhhhh, not now." As in their act on top of a galloping horse, she trusted him with her life. They remained in this embrace for a long time until his tears had stopped running and the chill from his wet shirt was getting his attention. He felt it. She knew. They both knew. There was a deadly silence. No more gunfire. Janosh was the first to arrive at the severely mangled body in front of that dung heap. In all his lifetime he had never seen a body torn apart like this. He dropped his cigar and sent for a stretcher. Even though he knew there was nothing Georg could do, he sent for him, suggesting he might be with the horses. Cautiously the train crew arrived at the scene with some lanterns. They assured everyone that there was nothing to see other than the sound of two bursts of gunfire and the shredded body of poor Foo Foo.

"This could have been the end of Circus Sarrasani." The head engineer said to Janosh. Georg and Wilma arrived at the scene together. Georg was white as a sheet and had to step aside to throw up before he could take a second look at Foo Foo. He reached forward and closed Foo Foo's eyes. Then he traced three crosses, one on the forehead one on the chin and one over the place where the heart had once been. Everyone was silent for a moment. Georg spoke through his tears:

"Foo Foo, you have made the world laugh and you have made us cry. Your memory will make us laugh forever. Losing you will forever make us cry. The world of our children and of the child in every grown up who knew their Foo Foo will never be the same. You had the largest, saddest most loving heart and you gave yourself to all the world. We are all Foo Foo now."

Georg pointed to the gunner's dug out and said: "Someone has already dug a grave for you." He directed his next words to Janosh. "The gunner has lost his life. We can do a memorial for Foo Foo later when we are in Austria or beyond. This is a war scene. Do not let the sun rise on this. We need to bury everything right now." Georg lead the procession with the stretcher to the dug-out, where Foo Foo was to be interred together with his assassin. Both were victims of a war that no one wanted or understood. When the sun rose, no trace was left of the tragedy that had happened during the night, except in all the hearts of his distinguished circus family, there was a huge void.

At the end of the following day the circus train was given green light and it moved slowly away into an uncertain future. Georg and Wilma spent one more night together on the moving train. He told her and she understood, that he could not stay with her or with the circus any longer. Now in the melting of grief and love, their passion found unrestricted relief with questions asked and answers given that surprised both lovers. This was a night everyone should experience at least once in a lifetime. Deep in the center of his lover's being, Georg noticed a change in Wilma and he was sure that he had given her a child and that she was going to make him a proud father. The heartbreak and hope of war in two hearts aching for a future had added the beginning of a new heart on a train with a circus rolling through the night.

Circus Sarrasani pulled into Vienna. For a last time and with tears streaming down their faces, Georg and Wilma fed the horses and groomed them together. Then Georg stepped out of his overalls, put on his peasant jacket, put on his Cossack shirt which he had not worn in a long time. With his pack in his hand, he waved one more time, then disappeared into the night.

The night sky was overcast with low hanging clouds. Georg's heart had no light left at this moment. He had not begun to process what had just happened. He was not obeying orders like a soldier. He was not in the business of taking lives. He felt that he had no choice about the machine gunner. His chosen vocation was saving lives and failing that, losing lives. Taking a life to save lives was different. It was personal self-defense with premeditation. He could not even begin to forgive himself. The shock settled in slowly and the darkness of the night was matched by the darkness of his thoughts. He had no idea how to justify what had just happened.

"I need you to live!" sounded in his mind again and again.

CHAPTER THIRTEEN
REACHING FOR THE RIVER DONAU

Georg touched the stethoscope which he had put back around his neck. He felt the embroidery on his shirt collar. Georg looked like a peasant without any particular markers of national identity. As was his habit as a doctor and scout, he kept himself meticulously groomed and clean shaven. Wilma had cropped his hair skillfully very short a few days ago.

"You look handsome," she said when she had finished.

"Then let me shave your legs in payment" he had laughed. "You show them off in your act and I need you to look at least as beautiful from what they can see, as you are on the inside. Not handsome, but beautiful." Half an hour later he felt his work and said: "There. Smooth as silk and not a nick." He remembered how impressed he was with the appointment of her dressing room. Elaborate makeup station, mirrors, the lights and all that is required to create a show that is the complete opposite of the world as it had presented itself to him for too many years now. Georg felt his head, touched his hair and was transported back to a world behind a thin canvas tent that was possibly saving more lives than tanks, guns, cannon, or airplanes ever could. More than medicine, even: A world that had no borders.

Georg was pulled out of his musings when he heard the footfall of a team of horses and the grinding of wagon wheels ahead, moving in the same direction as he was. The driver was holding on to the holster of the horse on the right of the team. He was limping and clearly in pain. Georg was glad about the unexpected distraction. We announced himself to avoid startling the driver or the horses. The first to notice him was a black Hungarian sheepdog standing on top of the load. Georg began talking to him as he repeated the call to the driver. "Good morning". These words had become a concealed way to determine if someone was a Nazi or not. The reply would determine how the conversation would continue. It was still quite dark, and Georg was under the impression that the horses were guiding the driver rather than the other way around. Georg looked into a pain distorted face.

"What's good about it?" Said the driver of the wagon.

"That depends on how you want to look at it." Said Georg. The smell of the horses made him intensely sad at this moment. "Everyone has bad moments to deal with. Often we have to learn things first."

"Learn what?"

"To understand the problem. To ask a good question."

"How would you know?"" I ask questions all the time."

"What would you ask me?"

"Why are you in pain. Are you wounded?"

"No. They mustered me out."

"Did someone look at your leg?"

"No. all they said was: 'Next'."

"When was that?"

"Three years ago. I have hated these bastards ever since."

"Why?"

"They made me the laughingstock of my village.
'Have your teeth pulled and sit with grandpa', they said."

"Would you want someone to look at your leg?"

"There are no more doctors here, not since the war started."

"I am a doctor."

"And you think you can help me?"

"That depends on two things."

"And that would be?"

"First, you'd help me ask some good questions and second, you'd do as I say."

"How do I help you ask questions?"

"You think about your answer before you speak."

"Then what?"

"Then you speak the truth"

"How do I know I can trust you?"

"I see you are in pain. You can trust me on that. You know that is true."

"Good. Then what is the second thing?"

"You take some time off and let someone do your work and take care of your animals for you. You have to learn how it feels to feel no pain."

"There is no one."

"Yes, there is. I am Georg, I am here."

"You said you were a doctor. What do you know about horses?"

"Everything."

"Give me an example."

"Say you could not walk all the way home. Say you climbed back on your wagon. Say it was pitch black, as it is right now."

"Then what?"

"Then your horses would take you home."

"How do you know my horses?"

"I don't"

"Then how would I know?"

"We make a bet. If I am right, you let me help you."

"Strange bet. It sounds like a sure win for me."

"Exactly. But you have to do as I say."

"I don't even know what you look like."

"I knew the Wagon was pulled by a team of two horses in the dark. did I not?"

"Yes, you did. How did you know?"

"I smelled them long before I heard their footfall. Up close I saw you and that you are in pain, long before you said so. More than three years of pain. What is your name?"

"Johann."

"All right then Johann, are you in?"

"What do I have to lose. I have one good leg that is no good without the other one."

"That's my man. You can worry about what I look like once you win your bet."

"When does it start?"

"Right now. Do you have a few potato sacks?"

"How do you know I might have potato sacks?"

"Men like you have potato sacks, in case they come across potatoes."

"All right, I do. What do you want me to do with them?"

"We use them to make you comfortable. Get on your seat." Johann stopped the horses and climbed up. "Put your leg up. We use the sacks to cushion your back, your seat and your leg. We need your leg to be up above your heart." Johann completed the arrangement of the sacks. He made himself comfortable. Georg checked and made a few improvements to Johann's posture. He took the seat next to Johann. Then he took the whip and flicked it in the air, which made the horses pull on.

"Home", he whispered. A long silence followed. After five minutes Georg could hear Johann's breathing get deeper and slower. He was fast asleep. Johann woke up from the clatter of iron rims of his wagon wheels on cobblestones. The horses made a turn to the right and Georg could hear the studded horseshoes do a tap dance as they stepped over to pull the wagon straight onto the main street. A few houses further down, the horses stopped. Johann rubbed his eyes. There was a large gate in a tall stone wall of a pretty village, and it was getting light.

"Where are we?" Johann asked before his brain began to function again.

"Home I guess, that is where I told the horses to go. Now did I win? Look." He pointed at the dog who had left his place next to Georg where he had been cozy as soon as Johann began to snore, jumped off the wagon and now stood with his tail wagging wildly by the small entrance door, barking enthusiastically.

"That answers my question. We are home unless you have a girlfriend on the side, who gives your dog special treats." Georg laughed.

"I have not slept this good in a long time." Said Johann. "How did you do this? How did you find my house?"

"I had help. The horses know and your dog would have told me, if the horses had forgotten where we were going. But they went home, just like I asked them to. Your dog is very friendly and a good companion. We must teach him to let you put your leg on his back inside when the treatment starts. Did you feel any pain during the last four hours?"

"No pain. I forgot all about it."

"Then the treatment has already started. Will you let me continue?"

"Yes, Doctor Georg".

"That's my man. And who might this be?" Georg pointed to the woman who had stepped out of the small door into the wild greeting of her dog.

"This is my wife Hilde. Hilde, meet Georg, he is my doctor."

"Ja ja ja ja, did you have one drink too many again? You can tell me your story over breakfast." To Georg she said: "Thanks for bringing him home. Are you hungry?"

"I could eat a horse. I was not the one who brought him home. Your horses did. Your dog reassured me that they knew the way. He is a shepherd. He would have herded them home if they had gotten lost."

It occurred to Georg at this moment that he had not spent another second to dwell on that which he could not change. He was grateful for his good fortune to have this diversion. He could not deny that deep inside he was broken hearted and deeply injured in a place no one could see. There had been no light inside of his heart. Now there was a glimmer. The wagon was pulled into the courtyard. Skillfully Georg backed the wagon into a space under a roof, guiding the horses to steer the front wheels. When Johann tried to help, Georg simply raised his right hand.

"Go inside. I will be right in. Let me take care of the horses first." Johann shrugged his shoulders and followed his wife into the kitchen. The dog was not sure if he should stay with his new friend or go inside. He stayed with Georg, knowing he could get more attention from his new friend than from his owners. Johann said to Hilde:

"Germans. Know everything better and are so damned serious. I prefer Hungarians. They are never right but at least they are never serious." Hilde looked up. She had not heard a joke from her husband in a long time.

"Then why did you bring him?"

"It's a long story. I had no choice"

"Did you meet him at a pub? Did he drink you under the table?"

"No and no. Why don't you ask him? He'll be right in."

"You two better come up with something better than a mystery or a poem. How come you let him take care of the horses?"

"He seems to know more about horses then the two of us together."

"We'll see about that, "she said and cracked one egg with each hand simultaneously into a large skillet with sizzling butter and finely chopped onions. She added bacon and wiped her hands on her floor length blue and white apron. Georg appeared in the door and when Johann tried to get up to greet him, he raised his hand again and pointed at the chair.

"Sit and stay." To Hilde he said: "It's Hilde, right? Is he always this jumpy?"

"Not lately. I am surprised. He hates Germans. He thinks they are always right. Something is very wrong with his leg. Maybe his horse stepped on it when he went on a bender a few years ago. Maybe he is being punished for some sin he committed while he was drunk. He goes on quarterly binges."

"Why are you telling him all this? You don't even know him!"

"Why do you let him handle your horses? No one ever gets to touch your horses. They are the apple of your eye."

"The horses told me to let him drive and our dog agreed."

"You better eat something. You are getting lightheaded." She said and put a heaping serving of food on each of the two large plates she had set out for the men, and a little portion on a small plate for herself.

"Georg is a doctor," Johann dropped this remark as if it was nothing. "Doctor Georg."

"He is what?" She replied incredulously.

Beautiful, high minded and a sharp tongue, Georg thought.

"It smells like I am in heaven," Georg heard himself say while he looked around the room, studying carefully all the antiques that looked like they had been here for hundreds of years: Ceramic sculptures, pewter plates and pitchers of different sizes, family pictures in gilded frames and pictures of saints in a glass cabinet with rounded framed symmetrical doors and a crucifix in a small altar setting with a chestnut colored lion paw legged prayer bench, upholstered in a beige, green and gilded brocade. She pointed at one of the chairs. Thanking her, Georg sat down. The dog placed himself in front of and on top of Georg's feet under the table.

"He likes you." She smiled." How did you and Johann meet?"

"We spent the night together. I walked the same road and caught up with them. I saw a figure limping in pain leading the horses, rather than riding the wagon. It was Johann." Georg smiled at her. I will bring her around, he thought. She liked Georg better, once she had learned that he was not a drinking partner.

"Enjoy your meal." She said.

"I feel fortunate to have met you and Johann."

"Did you travel all night?"

"Yes, I have, most of the night with Johann. Johann slept most of the time, once we made him comfortable with his sore leg up. We are both still very tired. Like I said, there was no pub. We can talk more when we are rested." Breakfast was devoured and Johann excused himself to try to get more sleep. Georg turned to Hilde.

"Do you have apple cider vinegar?" Hilde gave him a long look.

"A doctor." she said. "Now I have heard everything. Yes, I have vinegar."

"Do you have ginger?"

"Yes, I do."

"Can I have a glass of water and vinegar? "He added: "Do you have baking soda and honey?"

"Yes, doctor Georg". She laughed and he could tell, she was still not buying the doctor story. While she handed him the items he had requested, Georg pulled out his stethoscope and placed it before her on the table. He now spoke in the serious tone of a professional:

"We have to prepare a drink for Johann. He is suffering from Gout.

That is serious. He could lose his leg." Hilde stopped laughing. "I need you to pay close attention, Hilde." Georg said.

"With your permission I will be your guest for a few days. But only if you agree to help your husband. I can only do so much. Like a minister in church, I will show you the way, but you must go it. I am not a repair man. I am a physician. I am willing to teach you. This is war. I am a doctor. I am between assignments. I am willing to do your husband's chores for a few days to keep him off his feet. He will get better and you will learn how to manage, so the Gout does not come back. I will depend on you to follow up after I leave. He needs you to continue treatment, support and to heal him. He cannot do this by himself. This will take several weeks. He told me he was pain free just from putting up his leg on the wagon. But this is only one thing. Watch me. Remember. Say yes. I promise you; he will be a changed man."

"Yes, doctor Georg." In almost a whisper she continued: "I am sorry, this has gone on for a long time. No one knew what was wrong with Johann. I admit I thought he had a drinking problem. He probably does now. I saw him drowning his pain. He does not treat me well when he is drunk. He gets angry. He threatens me. Worst of all he makes me feel like I am not even in the room. I can do nothing right then. I am afraid of my drunken Johann. I was thinking of leaving him. But I have no family and nowhere to go. And I do love him. When you first came, I thought you were making fun of me like everyone else." She picked up her apron and wiped away some tears. "I am really sorry. I started to believe that everything is always my fault. That I am the bitch. I am so sorry." Tears were welling up again.

"I understand. We can talk more later. Know this: Gout can make a wonderful, sweet man into a raging monster. But it is reversible. I will be here for a few days until we know he is getting better. And you will be getting better too. Now watch." Said Georg.

He took a knife and chopped a piece of ginger root into very fine pieces. He put a small spoonful into the glass, together with a teaspoon of baking soda. He measured three spoons of vinegar into the glass. It started foaming. After adding a big spoon of honey, he carefully filled the glass with water and stirred it for several minutes.

He looked at Hilde. The sunlight flooded the room. Her long apron did not disguise her strong, muscular figure, enhanced by the long neck of a dancer, framing a beautiful face with a classic nose and dark brown eyes, featured by a frame of braided hair that she wore like a crown. She reminded him of his love at home. Her dark blonde hair showed off her curious eyes that looked like they were made for laughing. Georg could see the crow's feet that formed when she smiled her warm and friendly smile. He also saw some lines across her forehead that spoke of sorrow and pain of the kind she should not have experienced at her young age. Georg looked straight into her eyes and said:

"If we want to help Johann, we need to reduce uric acid in his body. That is what causes gout. It will require his help and yours. There can be no alcohol, no pork, no red meat. Serve him a little chicken breast. Use the rest of the chicken in soup. He can benefit from eating sauerkraut, pickled red beet salad, sweet potatoes boiled and served with a little cottage cheese. Give him vegetable soup and Salad. This will cleanse his system. Once his pain is gone and he stops drinking, he will be a happier man and you will be the happy woman you were meant to be." Georg looked at her eyes and continued," I know he thinks the world of you. I saw the way he looks at you, I heard the way he talks about you." He checked his memory and focused once again. "Can you get lemons? They probably bring them up the Donau from Turkey or Lebanon. You might have to use some of your connections. Do you know a spice dealer? Can you get kurkuma powder and cinnamon? I better write this down." He pointed to the bedroom." Let me show you how his leg needs to be supported. Let's give him his drink now. One glass now, one at noon and one at six in the evening." Georg could sense the relief she felt when she began to believe that there was hope. Her face lit up not just from the sunlight outside, but from the inside. Her shoulders moved up and back a little, her posture straightened, showing her tall slim stature completing the picture of a very beautiful young woman. Georg knew that life with a man in pain had not been easy for her. When she brought Johann his drink, she was smiling at him. Georg could see how this smile surprised her husband.

"This is what doctor Georg wants you to drink three times a day. It will help to heal your leg," Hilde said to Johann who swung his legs over the side of their four-poster bed to take the glass she offered him. Georg came in behind Hilde to show her how he wanted his leg to be supported.

"Thank you," Johann said to Hilde. This surprised her. She had not heard a kind word from him in a long time.

"Thank doctor Georg." She said softly. Johann drank the potion and scrunched his face around his nose. He drank the whole glass. They tucked him in with his leg raised.

"Let me show you the guest room. You too must be tired after travelling all night."

"I could sleep standing up. Thank you for the wonderful breakfast. It was delicious and better food than anything I have eaten in a long time. This war is causing a big food emergency." Georg moved his pack into the guest room. It was tastefully furnished with a light natural pine armoire with four pictures of saints painted in fields on the doors. There was a little writing desk and a pine chest of drawers with a big ivory colored ceramic bowl. In it was a large matching ceramic water pitcher, two chairs besides the windows and a trunk at the foot of the bed. There were nightstands at each side of the headboard. All in matching blond wood like birch or hickory. This told him that the area near Vienna had been spared from the ravages of war up to this point. The two small windows had white lace curtains with heavy brocade blackout drapes. He pulled them shut. Turning back to his hostess, he said:

"Please check on the horses in case I have missed something. I did not clean their hooves. They deserve a treat.

Georg turned in as soon as she was gone and fell into a deep sound sleep. He had a strange dream. *Colors were radiating from the center of his vision. He now saw the image of Foo Foo the clown rising in the color of blood at the moment when the machine gun fire hit him in mid-air and tore him apart. This was a very painful image for Georg. He was able to return the image back to the center and select other strands of color and follow them to the outside or dismiss images that emerged by moving them with his mind back to the center, where they disappeared. He was curious to see if he could see the future. He selected a rose-colored strand of radiant light. It opened an image of the Alps as it merged with hues of green, light blue and white. He saw the crest of a trail that lead into a lovely valley where he could see the village where he had last seen his wife. This image was too painful for him to bear, so he returned it to the center where it disappeared. Then he went through a number of images and the one he was able to rest on was one of Wilma, who was holding a healthy baby boy. This made him happy. He had found a glimpse into the future. Finally, he came to a strand dark blue. It brought him the image of Tanya, who had made him promise to live.*

A female voice called him to come and have lunch. The smell of freshly baked bread and cake brought him back to the reality of this day at Hilde and Johann's house. The voice belonged to Hilde who sounded much more cheerful than she had earlier, when she was still full of dread about another day with the abusive behavior of her drunken husband. Hilde and Georg spoke quietly about plans for the next few days. Hilde reported that Johann had been able to sleep and that she had given him the second potion of his medicine. She was worried about being able to make him stay in bed.

"I will ask him to ride with me when we make deliveries. We keep him comfortable with his leg raised up like we did last night," Georg suggested. "Is he awake?"

"He was awake a few moments ago. Let me look." Hilde offered. "Hallo Hannes, doctor Georg wants to see you."

"Send him in," Johann answered.

"Let him finish his lunch. He will come in a few minutes. Do you want anything?"

"I want to get up and do things, that's what I want!" To Georg Hilde said: "Did I not tell you?"

"You were right. He has routines. Lying in bed is not one of them." Georg said with a smile. "First I want to taste your delicious smelling cake. Then I will examine our patient. I cannot remember how long it has been since I tasted freshly baked bread, and now cake. The last cake I ate was at my wedding when the bakers had gotten salt and sugar mixed up. It was terrible. We ate small bites. We ate them for luck." Georg laughed at the memory. The examination was done, and Georg concluded that Johann's dehydration was caused from alcohol. He suggested to Johann that they could do freight deliveries together. Keeping Johann's leg up like last night and Johann directing where to go, with Georg preventing the drinking binges at taverns. Then bed rest after deliveries. Johann agreed to most of this.

"Are you sure you want to do this?" Johann asked.

"I won the bet. I am sure. I would like to examine Hilde also. I noticed she has some pain in her stomach. She is holding her hand there when she gets up from the table and the small of her back then she makes coffee. I might be able to help her."

"She is not a complainer; you can examine her If she wants you to. We have not seen a doctor in years."

"When will we deliver the freight, you have on the wagon?"

"This evening. We travel mostly when it is dark. It is safer for us. Things have been quiet in our small town. I think Hitler is Austrian. He adopted us like second cousins." Johann said.

"I would like to keep you off your leg as much as possible. Can I have Hilde show me the livestock part of your business?"

"Yes of course. There is nothing she does not know and cannot do." Georg closed his medical bag. It was made of soft goat skin, a parting gift from Katya. It gave him a little Sting of pain every time he used it, but it reminded him of the vow to live he had made to Tanya.

"I will prepare a better seat for you on the wagon." Georg said as he left the room. He found Hilde in the kitchen changing aprons.

"Johann has decided to ride along on the wagon during deliveries and show me where to go and what to do. He has almost no pain if he stays off that leg." Hilde was close to tears but smiled bravely. She wiped the corners of her eyes with the apron and said:

"I am going to feed and water the horses. Tonight, we have to go to the docks to pick up freight after he delivers what he has on the wagon now. He is a gipsy freighter. There are not many freighters left. Horses and men were drafted to military service. We were lucky he was rejected. Please do not tell him I said that." Georg put his finger over his lips, then he said:

"I noticed you are holding your stomach and your back. Would you like me to have a look? "Georg asked, changing the subject. Hilde replied:

"You notice everything, no? Yes, I am having some women's issues. I am not used to anyone noticing things. Not since my mother passed last winter around Christmas." Hilde looked sad now.

"Will you let me take a look tomorrow morning?"

"Yes. Thank you, I have not seen a doctor in years."

"Can I follow you around to see the chores, Johann does?" Hilde smiled and nodded yes, then handed Georg an apron. They left the kitchen through a backdoor that lead to a wide hallway connecting two wings of the building. Georg observed living quarters and on the opposite side housing for animals and feed storage above, forming a u-shaped structure surrounding the courtyard, paved with cobblestones. The buildings were finely crafted post and beam structures with symmetrically curved braces and wide overhanging roofs, decked in red clay tiles, surrounding a courtyard large enough for horse drawn wagons to maneuver with ease.

"This looks very well established. I did not see the date sign. How old is your building?"

"It dates back to 1776. It is basically unrestored as it was originally built. It can become a museum one day. I have a feeling we are a dying breed." Hilde said.

"You have no children?" Georg looked at her. She looked very sad. "We have tried and tried." She said softly, then looked away.

"I am sorry." Georg answered. He opened the lid on one of several large bins which contained crushed oats for the horses.

"May I? "He noted the counterweight and pulleys to hold the lids open. Hilde and Georg groomed and fed the horses, watered chickens and ducks and collected eggs while Georg went upstairs into the hay loft to drop hay for the horses down a square shoot. Through an open hatch he could see a garden with a small pond and an orchard. There was a well with pulley, covered by a wide overhanging roof. There were large rainwater barrels fed from gutters. Yes, it is a museum, he thought, but one that shows a lot of smart ways of doing things. Now I better fix the seat for Johann. When he was back in the house, he asked Johann:

"What time do we have to leave?"

"In half an hour. We are going down to the docks tonight. That is not far. We will deliver the load we have on the wagon and pick up a new one that goes to Vienna tomorrow."

"Aha, so that is what Gypsy freighters do, drop one load and pick up one to be delivered elsewhere?"

"Yes. Just like that. We service Vienna and the surrounding towns. We operate in connection with the Donau river trade. Goods come down from Ulm and upriver from as far as Asia, Africa, Arabia and the Middle East. This has gone on for ages. We may be the ninth generation of gypsy freighters in my family. And maybe the last." Georg noticed that Hilde heard these words and that she looked sad again.

"It is all my fault," she whispered.

"Why don't we talk about that after we had a chance to examine you. Health is not something we are entirely responsible for. A lot of things are inherited. Some things are habits we are taught. Babies are born into an old world. They are not our invention."

Georg felt right at home at Hilde and Johann's house. He loved the smell of horses, hay and horse manure. The smell of leather Harnesses transported him back to his childhood. It saddened him to remember Tanja's horses and sled. Sweet and sad emotions.

Johann was seated comfortably on a reclining contraption Georg had improvised for him that was covered by a large lambskin blanket they used during the winter. Georg took the whip from Johann's hand.

"Let me, "he said, and Johann noticed the skill with which Georg backed the horses to make the turn out of the gate, where Hilde stood to close it after they left for the landing. The village was a cluster of houses arranged in a star pattern with a center that featured a fountain with six evenly spaced hitching posts for horses to stop and drink, while their owners went about their business. Now it was evening, and lanterns were being lit inside and outside. A fairytale town, in a fairytale world, in the midst of a war that was threatening to end this life forever. Georg saw the facades with soft colors of dusty blue to golden yellow and burnt orange. Some buildings had dark brown beams visible with tan to ochre colored infills, many had intricately crafted metal signs advertising businesses and taverns. Windows were adorned with flower boxes. All a reminder of a sane world, Georg had not seen in a while. Georg asked the horses to maintain forward motion when they attempted to slow for a tavern break.

Johann was breathing deep and heavy but did not say anything. They soon arrived in a section of town where the road was lined with warehouses on both sides, with elevated loading decks matching freight wagons. As they approached, Georg asked Johann where his load was going.

"The last warehouse on the right. They will unload what we have. Then we go down to the docks by the river. There we pick up a new load for Vienna. That will be tomorrow's delivery."

"You seem to be very busy. Do you ever think of adding another team for the second wagon you have at the house? Add a warehouse of your own?"

"I thought of that. Then I thought, what's the point. We don't have children. I was mad at Hilde, blaming her for being infertile and she was mad at me for drinking myself into impotence. No-one and everyone are at fault."

"We should look at one thing at a time and stop looking for blame and shame. We have to change a few things with your food and your habits. None of that calls for guilt. You did not invent the world. You inherited it. Your job is to get better and Hilde's job is to get better also."

"You sound like a preacher."

"I am the son of one. I grew up with a father who had all the questions and a mother who had all the answers. This war has thrown us into the middle of all this. No choice. Look!" The dockworkers were pointed at soldiers guarding a docked downriver barge.

Later at the house in his room, Georg composed this mental letter to Rose: It calmed him.

Today I would write to you: Are my thoughts and my feelings real? Should they be less real than what our eyes can see? What our hands can touch? Why the ears, eyes, hands do they not hear, see, feel as fast and as much as my heart does, as your heart does? In real life you and I have travelled, breathed, made love, laughed together, been more real, felt more joy, suffered more grief, felt more bliss than we deserve. I think we are the luckiest ones that have ever lived, and we are still the eyes, the ears, the senses and the hearts for all those who have been called back to the spirit world before us. It is our privilege to know about the magnitude of our experience and the privilege of bearing hearts that can feel and speak the truth, honor each other, love one another like no one has ever been loved before but as much as everyone surely deserves to be loved. Our ether bodies have bonded eternally. When our physical bodies meet again, we will realize that all that has already passed is as real as any story anyone can remember. You and I are as real as life can incarnate life. We have no limits to worry about. We are all love, heart and experience. That feeds our sense of gratitude. That makes our story real. I melt into you and we are one. Ask your heart. Do you fear death? Is life real? It is as you say: We are ready. When that time comes. The same Angel who guided us here will be waiting to guide us home. Will my meditation reach you without pen on paper? Or did you send me these thoughts?

Georg had not written home since he had gone underground. It was not safe for him to do so. Every letter was opened, and Georg and Rose had gotten used to writing in subtext without ever mentioning the regime. They were possibly still looking for him. On the periphery of this war there were people who did not know better but to report others to authority just in case. This had given 'brown nosing' a whole new meaning. There was time to get some more sleep before breakfasting this day. When Hilde called out to Georg, he asked her about the troops by the docks.

"They are protecting a shipment of war supplies, going by barge down the Donau" Hilde said." The contents of the barge are not known, but the signs say 'caution explosives. The river people think it is moving ammunition and ordnance to the south- eastern front near Baku. They are nervous about sabotage. So, are we? Tony, my sister in law's freight barge captain friend tells us that every day more voices are saying that the war is beginning to fall apart. Dictators, he says, are working for puppeteers, all fighting on a front too wide to manage, halfwit dictators dismissing real generals, replacing them with people who know only one word: Yes. If this barge blows up in our port, it would destroy our livelihood." She lowered her voice. "Someone at the bar, a know it all, has suggested that you might be a spy or a saboteur. They have not seen you before. He is an idiot but all the same, this type of talk makes me nervous. I had my sister in Law Gerda spread the rumor that you are a relative on leave, visiting while Johann is sick. That explains why he is not drinking. Don't say anything to Johann. He does not like women to talk war or politics or to have an opinion. Not even gossip. That is men's business he thinks. Women are bleeding too, I say." Georg nodded. Then he spoke:

"I think today is a good day for your physical examination. When we make the delivery into Vienna tonight, I will stop by the pharmacy to buy some of what we need."

After breakfast, Georg made sure Joann was bedded comfortably with his leg raised up, in the master bedroom. Then he asked Hilde:

"Can we use my bedroom for the examination? I made up the bed military style. I will need hot water in the pitcher, soap, small and large towels and a lemon." He washed his hands like a surgeon, then measured and recorded her vitals, checked lungs and heart, eyes and ears, nose and throat with Hilde sitting on one of the chairs by the window, using a beam of sunlight while he sat on the other chair to sit behind her, in front of her and at each side. With a very soft voice he inquired about her history and the pain in her lower abdomen and the small of her back. He told her about his observations. Then he asked her to move onto the bed and to remove her clothes. Soaping his hands again he said quietly:

"I need you to lie down face up. Place a small towel under your pelvis and with the large towel cover yourself from your breasts to your knees." When she was done, he explained: "I am going to examine your breasts. Inhale deep and exhale all the way. Good. Again…. Again…. Now I am going to apply some pressure when you have exhaled. I will feel your soft tissue and your organs. Cough for me. Again…. Again…. Good. Now I am going to examine your ovaries and your uterus. I will reach inside and feel the outside at the same time. I will move your legs and I want you to hold them still and relaxed. I need you to tell me what you feel. Keep breathing in and out deeply. I will be applying some pressure on the exhale." He asked her about her bodily functions, her menses, the regularity and timing. He asked about her water consumption. Her salt and spice intake. Her sugar usage. Her diet. He came back to her pain several times. Finally, once he had a good picture, he said:

"You have cysts on your ovaries. They may not be cancerous. They are restricting the swelling of your blood vessels during menstruation. The irregularity and varying duration you spoke of are caused by them. They cause your pain. These cysts can even explode and make your flow seem stronger. There is inflammation, which can make your body stop producing or releasing eggs, which is why you were not successful in getting pregnant. Johann's alcohol consumption has probably lowered his sperm count as well. You will have to learn how to manage this. There are several things you can do to reduce pain and inflammation. Fortunately, some of the things that are good for Johann will make you feel better too. Together you can improve your health and stop the blaming. I will make you a lemon compress which will reduce inflammation during menstrual pains. It reduces tension and brings circulation to the area. We will do this now."

Georg took a small towel and soaked it with hot water, wrung it out and dripped lemon juice liberally on the heated cloth, which he placed where he had observed her pain. Now he took the large towel, folded it and covered the lemon pack. He added a pillow and told her to breathe out deeply, focusing on relaxation and letting the pain dissipate.

"Out and out and out. Breathe the pain out. There. Very good. I will write down the food items for you and Johann. You will be getting better in time if you do as I say. You might even get pregnant before too long. Now relax. Breathe. I will be back in fifteen minutes."

Georg took pencil and paper and went into the kitchen, where he wrote:

No alcohol. Water. Lots of water. Make the vinegar baking powder honey drink Johann uses for both of you. Take it three times a day, with him. Use whole grains whenever possible. Whole grain flour for bread baking. Garlic. Lots of garlic on everything. Vegetables steamed. Red beets pickled and cut into your salad. Sauerkraut. No sauces made with lard or animal fat. Use olive oil. Eat fish instead of beef, chicken instead of pork. Eggs. Sour milk daily instead of raw milk.

Skim the cream off the milk for your coffee. One cup of coffee a day. Early breakfast and make it a big meal instead of crumpets with marmalade and white rolls. Honey instead of sugar. Cinnamon, half a teaspoon a day. Ginger freshly ground, a spoon a day. Use it on dishes and drink it as tea with honey. Peppermint tea. Chamomile tea. Dandelion blossom tea. Stinging nettle tea. Stinging nettle leaves cooked like spinach. Dry them for winter with your herbs. Cut dandelion leaves and roots into salads and sauces.

Nettle is important for your blood and for your blood vessels. Sweet potatoes instead of regular potatoes. Boiled and baked food instead of fried food. Very light on salt. Heavy on black pepper. No butter. Apple cider vinegar instead of wine vinegar.

Exercise: One half hour every day. A fast walk to the river and back. A fast walk along the brook into the forest. A long bath with four spoons of Epsom salt twice a week. More often during your period.

Georg left the paper on the kitchen counter and went back to his patient. She had fallen asleep. He re-read his instructions and added curcuma to the list. He added curry to go with whole grain rice and chicken meat. Georg checked on his patient she was asleep. Johann had fallen asleep also. He went to see the horses, took each out and gave them a good grooming. He liked the shading of their fur from brown to tan and the longer tan to blond hair covering their hooves. He liked the look of freshly groomed horses. He then looked after the poultry and brought in brown and white chicken eggs. He found some duck eggs. When he returned to the examination room, Hilde was getting dressed. Her hair was spilling over her shoulders. She looked softer. The strained expression of pain was gone. With a smile she said:

"How did you do that? The pain went away. I fell asleep." She followed him into the kitchen. Georg pointed to his list:

"Here is a list of food I suggest you and Johann eat. It is a choice list. Find the things that work best for you. "Two weeks later Georg spoke to Hilde after breakfast: Johann is getting better. Keep him from overdoing it with his leg. Keep up the diet. Georg finished his coffee. Then he added: "Thank you for taking such good care of him. And of yourself. I will have to leave as soon as river traffic resumes on the Donau. Promise to keep helping Johann with his leg. This change in diet will help both of you. You can make it work for yourself."

"I don't know how to thank you." Hilde said. "I wish there was something I could do for you."

"There is. Is your last name Huber? I saw a picture of an elder couple in my bedroom. It says Huber."

"Yes. These were my husband's parents. Father passed away the year after our wedding and mother passed last Christmas."

"I noticed one of the warehouses by the docks says Alex Huber, Logistics on it. Are these relatives?"

"Yes. Alex is my brother in law."

"Looks like he is doing well for himself."

"Not really. He was drafted to the German military and has not returned from Russia. Not a letter, not a word."

"Who is running the business?"

"His wife Gerda. She is the spunky one who keeps her hair in a modern wave with bleached tips of her locks and bright lipstick. She has a helper at the warehouse."

"Are you two friendlies?"

"Not at first. We got very close when Alex went missing. I looked after her like a sister. She opened right up, and we have been best friends ever since."

"You want to do something for me?"

"Yes. Anything."

"Take me to her. Introduce me. Tell her I am between assignments as a doctor in need of working my way up the Donau to reconnect with my medical command." Georg was observing her reaction. Then he decided to go out on a limb: He continued: "My entire field hospital has vanished in Russia, train and all. I have no papers. I am technically a deserter." In a very low voice, he continued: "Any member of any army on every side of this war can shoot me on the spot. When I get to my headquarters I will be reassigned." Georg turned to the present: "I need an introduction to a Donau skipper going upriver. Maybe I can work my way up. Can you do this?"

"Of course, nothing easier than that. I tell Johann we are going out. Then I take you to Gerda."

Hilde took Georg out the back door. They followed a narrow trail that went between gardens and fields at the edge of the village to a back entrance of the warehouse belonging to her relatives. From the office Georg could see the road up to the village and down to the docks by the river.

"Hello Gerda," Hilde said." This is Georg." She told Gerda the story of how they had met, what he had done for her and Johann. And what he had asked for. Hilde told Gerda about how lessening Johann's pain had already improved his drinking habit and his behavior towards her.

"You would not believe it, but Johann is actually at home resting with his leg up instead of getting drunk at the tavern." Said Hilde.

"That is a miracle". Gerda agreed then turned to Georg:

"My husband is missing in Russia. Having a drunk in the house, who turns abusive at any moment, is even worse." Georg looked straight at her eyes. "I know what you mean. I lost my entire hospital unit outside of Stalingrad. No word either. Do not give up hope. I am so sorry." Georg said softly, taking her hand. Gerda turned to the task at hand:

"I will send for Tony. He is a barge captain who is waiting for the army to clear out. He might be able to use an extra driver for his horses to tow an extra shift on a delivery which has just suffered another delay. He is a good friend of the family. This war stops business with no regard to people's lives. Let me send Frank to get Toni. She kicked the office door open and yelled into the warehouse: "Frank, please fetch Toni. I need to talk to him, it is urgent. It has to do with his shipment." The door fell shut and Georg could see the back of a very big man walk with long purposeful steps towards the docks.

"What kept him from being drafted, what is wrong with him?"

"Everything is wrong with him. He is illiterate. He is too big. He has flat feet. He has trouble talking."

"How do you manage with him?"

"Frank may not read or write. He has a heart of gold and a memory like an elephant. He is loyal like a Saint Bernard. I could not run my business without him. He will die for me and he will kill for me. No one has ever stepped out of line in this establishment. It makes no difference that the boss is not back from the war. Frank will not let a shadow fall over this house. You can trust him too. He knows who brought you here and he saw the way we were talking quietly and friendly. He includes Hilde and Johann and their friends under his protection. Nothing escapes his attention." Turning back to her visitors she said: "Would you like coffee?

There is a little kitchen and behind it there is a little bathroom. We call it Villeroy and Boch. This is the first warehouse on this block that was hooked up to town water. Very cozy and practical."

"Thank you. Coffee would be lovely" Said Georg. To Hilde he said: "You can have one too, if you like. How do you feel?"

"Amazing. Thank you." Hilde answered with a smile. To Gerda she said: "I have a cup too, thank you." With her eyes she pointed at Georg: "He is my doctor. I wish we could keep him here." Everyone laughed. There was a knock at the door.

"Come in", Gerda said aloud. A man in his mid-fifties with strong upper body and short cropped brown hair appeared from behind Frank. The newcomer was wearing a blue frock, a traditional shirt worn by Donau skippers. It had an embroidered round short collar and embroidered wrist cuffs. It had embroidered slits on the side seems for reaching into the pants pockets.

"Hello Gerda, Frank told me it is urgent."

"Hello Toni. How are you holding up? We have coffee on. Would you like a cup?"

"You know I would never say no to a good cup of coffee. Gerda knows good coffee." He said to Georg. "Hello, I am Toni. And you are?"

"I am Georg. I let Gerda explain." Before Frank left the room, Georg took him aside to thank him for his help and to tell him how important he was to Gerda and to the family. Frank shifted from one leg to the other and back, not being used to be praised like that. It was something he would not forget. His smile was one of gratitude and embarrassment. He went back into the warehouse. Gerda came in with a pot of coffee. To Georg she said: "You know coffee came right from Arabia to this very place outside Vienna, when the Ottoman empire tried to annex Austria."

"I did not know that. What happened?" Georg asked.

"We defeated them. They withdrew and left hundreds of bags full of brownish, greenish beans behind. No one knew what they were. A horse trader saw them and offered the Generals to buy them as horse feed at a very low price. He did not give away that he knew what they were. He had learned the art of roasting such beans into what is now known as coffee. He made a fortune on this trade." Tony chimed in: "He even knew the Arab definition of good coffee."

"What would that be?" asked Georg. Tony made a very serious face: "Good coffee, he quoted, has to be as hot as the kisses on the first date.

Has to be as sweet as the embraces on the second date and has to be as black as the curses of the mother when she finds out about it" With this, Gerda poured everyone a cup of her own best.

129

"Cheers" she saluted. Next she produced a tray of Viennese pastries." Take the one with Cinnamon" Georg said to Hilde. To Gerda he said:

"I cannot remember having seen such beautiful pastries since before the war. Thank you, Gerda. Everyone was glad about a lighthearted moment. Tony explained to Georg:

"This is a tense time for this village. We have not seen anything like this during the entire war. Resistance against the Nazis is beginning to grow. Rumors of atrocities committed against millions of Jews, mass murder in gas chambers, enslavement in concentration camps, minorities abused, disabled persons exterminated. Unbelievably, The Nazi claims that photos smuggled out of concentration camps are propaganda by the opposition. And people rather not believe the evidence. Now all this is beginning to get through the veil of the Nazi's complete news blackout. The cruelty of this regime is becoming visible as misinformed and mislead loyalists to the Nazi regime are becoming emboldened. Murdering unarmed civilians, public book burnings, breeding programs for a super race, murdering highly regarded officials inside their own ranks who disagree or ask questions. Even those who wanted to believe in a law-abiding society have begun to see it. The Nazi is getting jumpy and more dangerous than ever." In a low voice Toni continued: "The guards of the mysterious down river barge were assisted by special troops who arrived before the shipment was to move through. They stopped all up-river traffic. They came to clear resistance. This community is abuzz in speculation and frozen in fear. Innocent people are made an example of. The outrageous truth is, that some take pleasure in being snitches. You are the stranger in town. They might try to finger you too. They always finger someone to prove they are doing their fuehrer's work." He looked at Gerda. "Is it true that the furniture maker Jakob and his wife Rachel and their baby girl have disappeared? Were they taken or did they run? That is what they were talking about at the pub the last time I was there. Word was that Jakob and his wife Rachel were seen by the river three days ago. Ralf thought he saw them with one of the toy barges, Jakob was making for Christmas this year. He said they were trying to see how well it would float. Ralf starts drinking at nine in the morning. We were laughing at him, asking if he was sure he had not seen two of them in a twin river. He said no, but he said it was getting dark. He could not be sure."

"Sure is," Ralf had said, "the butcher's wife Anna had seen a large black unmarked car stop at Jakob's shop that evening. I am not sure. I was drunk. Forget I said anything. See nothing, hear nothing say nothing. I wash my hands of this whole thing."

Tony, Hilde and Gerda were now planning Georg's departure and part of this was his disguise as a deckhand on Toni's barge, working night shift, towing a freight barge with horses.

"Tomorrow before daylight, you come to the barge." Toni said to Georg. "Use the back way." To Gerda he said: "Have Frank pick up Georg's things and deliver them to me in his hand cart under some supplies. Have him walk right down the middle of the street. No one will look. Ciao." With these words he was gone.

"River keepers are this way." Gerda said. "They will be here long after the storms of politics have done their ugly work. We belong here and we stand by one another. That is the code we live by. The river codes.

"We have to get going with our delivery". Said Georg, pointing toward Hilde's place. They departed with thanks for the coffee. Gerda called Frank into her office and told him that she needed him to go to Hilde's House early next morning before sunrise with a hand wagon, to move Georgs luggage to Toni's barge at the landing without drawing attention. The hand wagon was going to show supplies for the trip up the Donau for anyone to see and she suggested he walk down main street, so no suspicion could be raised, or a connection made to Georg.

"I know. I'll be there." Frank promised.

"I want you to stick around and wait until we can be sure Georg is on the barge. "Gerda said.

"Will do," said Frank with a reassuring nod to Gerda. "I like Georg. He is a good man. He will make it to the barge." When Hilde and Georg came home, they found Johann in the kitchen with a stack of papers, organizing his delivery schedule.

"Looks like you feel better." Hilde went to the table and put her hand on his shoulder. Surprised by this touch, that felt almost like a caress to Johann, he smiled at her.

"I do. I feel better. I had less pain and more sleep than in time remembered. How did you make out with Toni and the barge?"

"It is all arranged. Gerda was helpful and so was Frank who brought

Toni to Gerda's office." Hilde said. Georg went to get the team ready. Hilde stepped in front of Johann. She took both of his hands.

"Look Johann. I promised Georg to help you make your leg get better. That means, I will take Georg's place driving our team and you ride until you can go back to work. Georg has made some changes to our diet. Feel your leg and tell me you rather lose your foot than follow the doctor's orders. You know I love you." Johann nodded silently. His look into Hilde's eyes was one of affection and gratitude.

"I love you too". They could hear the noises of the team backing into the wagon. Georg was ready.

Vienna emerged with its dim candle lit luster like an old painting. They made their deliveries and before picking up their next load for the docks, they stopped by the pharmacy. The smell reminded Georg of clinics, hospitals, and his operating station in Stalingrad. It was a mixture of mint, disinfectants, rubbing alcohol and herbs ground and spices mixed together to make medicine. Georg realized how much he missed Doctor von Wallenstein and his medical team and how worried he was about their fate. He felt selfish for focusing on his own survival. His heart came to his rescue when he heard Tanya's voice: I need you to live. And his promise: I will. He heard himself say out loud enough for Johann to hear him.

"Did you say something?"

"No. I was just talking to myself. I must be getting old. There is a lot going on and we have to try to keep it simple and to care for those we love. Survival takes all my attention. I have to remember the people I am in charge of. You are a lucky man Johann. Between Hilde and Gerda, you have two of the strongest women I have met by your side. If you do not drown it all in alcohol, you have a very good life ahead of you. Count your blessings, not your problems. I need you to make a promise to me."

"What is that?"

"Take care of Hilde when I am gone. She may become the mother of your child after all. You can do this. It takes both of you. Promise?"

"I promise. And I mean it. Thank you doctor Georg."

"There is one more thing. When you Christen your future son or daughter, ask Gerda and Frank to be the Godparents. They will never abandon your child."

"How do you know so much about Frank? You just met him."

"It takes three seconds to see it. Gerda feels the same way about him. She said so to me:

"He is as loyal as a Saint Bernard. He will die for us and he will kill for us."

"We could all use a little bit of this man's spirit. She only confirmed my feelings about him. I think he includes you under the umbrella he is holding over your family." The trip back to his yard was quiet and uneventful. The dog was as always snuggled up to Georg with his head resting on his thigh.

"I will miss you." Georg said to the dog. He saw Johann look at his dog's head.

"He will miss you as much as we will. You have become part of our family."

PART THREE
ALMOST HOME

CHAPTER FOURTEEN

DONAU

When they arrived at the house, they found Hilde serving coffee to Frank who had come to collect Georg's belongings. Breakfast was on the table and the mood was one that goes with saying goodbye to a dear friend.

Georg felt honored and part of him did not feel like he deserved this. Another part of him was filled with gratitude. He could see improvements with Hilde's pain and in Johann's walk.

"You are not well yet. Follow Hilde's directions and eat what she serves you. This food is also going to make her better. If we are lucky, she will be able to have a baby." After they had finished eating, Georg went to his room and completed packing. He handed his things to Frank, who placed them on the little hand wagon. Next to his enormous frame it looked like a toy version of Johann's freight wagon. Frank disappeared down main street towards the docks. Georg handed Hilde items he had brought from the pharmacy. He pointed with his eyes to the list of his instructions on the table. To Johann he made a gesture of a leg up in the air.

"You be good". He gave Hilde a short, tight embrace and whispered into her ear: "Take care of yourself. Good luck with him. Remember. He loves you more than he can say. God bless you. All the best to you. And I thank you." Nothing had escaped Frank's attention. He was on his way to the barge. Georg turned away, slipped out the back door and disappeared into the night.

It was pre-dawn when he arrived at the river. Georg smelled the water long before he could see it. The river was flat, and no ripples were visible on the surface. The gray sky matched the river in color. The reflection of the water merged with the sky creating a silent, milky bubble. The dark silhouette of Tony's barge was visible at the dock further down river. The army barge was gone. *I made it* Georg thought to himself. *I have come to the barge on the river that will take me home. I am in the care of a guide who knows this river as well as anyone alive. I do not have to board until just before sunrise.* Lonely hours by himself had taken their toll. He found himself talking to himself aloud and sometimes arguing with his inner voices. Check your scalpel, was one. He reached for his pocket and felt the knife in its leather sleeve. He looked around and noticed the reeds that were growing at his side of the shore. *I can cut a flute from these*, he thought. He could not resist. Without thinking, he took out his scalpel, cut off a suitable piece of reed just above the waterline. Holding the reed in his left hand, he dried the scalpel on his sleeve and returned it to its leather sleeve in his leg pocket. Suddenly Georg could feel the hair on his neck rise and his breath freeze. His pulse rate was rising. Heavy footsteps of several people were approaching. He slowly moved back towards the water and submerged himself to his neck, still holding the reed. The boots on the ground were coming closer and he could tell someone was slipping right to the water's edge.

"Shit," a voice said. "Shit, shit, shit, I hate this war!" Georg could make out the suction noise of a boot pulling out of the mud."

"Here, give me your gun, grab my hand. Now pull yourself out. I told you not to go so close to the water, there is no one here. I will bet you the guys on that barge would have sounded an alarm if they had seen any saboteurs. Now hang on. I will pull."

Georg lost the sound of the voices as he slipped silently below the surface, the reed in his mouth held up with his left hand, his right hand feeling the other stalks to be sure he did not touch or move them. He heard faint, muffled voices and tried to breathe shallow breaths, until the last of the voices had moved past. Georg's head reemerged slowly after a couple of minutes. In the distance he could hear the men talking more about how they hated the darkness of the night and the heavy weapons they were carrying. The soldiers were now moving past the barge and disappeared into the morning mist, rising from the river, leaving the world looking peaceful and serene, as it had been before. Georg's heart was still racing, and it took him another hour of sitting in the same place until his adrenaline had bled off and his knees stopped knocking on each other. Georg was soaking wet from head to toe and felt chilled. The first rays of the rising sun had tinted the fog from ultraviolet to bright red to bright white and finally burned it off altogether. Now he could see the riverbank and the reed, the dock and the barge.

A dog came running enthusiastically towards him, knocking him over on his back and licking his face. It was Johann's black sheep dog.

"Hello puppy, I am so glad you did not come earlier. They would have mistaken you for the enemy and shot you. Come here. Let me give you a hug." While he was holding the dog the large frame of Frank cast a shadow over the two. Georg looked up at Frank and said:

"Hello there again Frank, look who found me."

"I know, he followed me to the barge, and I took him on board. We had to put him in the Captain's quarters and give him milk to keep him from barking at the soldiers. We had to hide from them also, to keep them from snooping around. You are here. Good. I take you to Tony now."

The dog tore back and forth, in and out of the water, shaking himself once he was close to someone's pant leg, then running into the water again. This time he did not return. Georg could hear him give a short yelp. Frank saw him stalking something in the reeds. Both went to see what the dog was fussing about. It turned out to be a beautiful children's barge carrying a strange cargo: In it they saw a wicker basket. Large round cork blocks were mounted at each end of the barge for extra floatation. Inside the basket was a baby, swaddled in a blue wool blanket with a blue knit cap.

"Look what the dog found!" Frank was already in the water, breathing heavy, fishing up the line and the little anchor that had kept the barge from floating away.

"This is a sign from God" Frank said. "We have to bring it to someone. I have to ask Tony and Gerda what to do."

"You don't have to. Remember how much Hilde wants a baby?"

"Yes, I do." The baby began fussing, barely making a sound. "Is it hungry?" Said Frank, looking at Georg.

"This baby is breathing. Let me take a good look inside." They took barge, cradle and bundle to the barge and showed it to captain Tony. Georg said: "Get me soap, hot water and a few towels". He went through his luggage and found the medical kit. He took out his stethoscope and a salve he had found at the pharmacy in Vienna. 'Calendula' it said on the label. He went back to the infant and placed it on the table. He removed the diaper, collecting as much of the contents, while everyone took a step back." It's a girl." Georg said. "Let me have soap, water and washcloth, please." Tony handed him the items. Georg cleaned the baby carefully, observing early signs of starvation and dehydration and a diaper rash. He carefully cleaned the baby girl from head to toe. After listening to her heart and lungs from the front, he shaped Franks forearms as a cradle, covered them with the towel and placed the tiny baby face down on the towel. Seeing the baby against the huge frame of Frank made Georg think, she looks like a preemie.

"Hold still" he said. He was surprised that the baby had not begun to scream." She is a survivor. Strong little heart." He said to no one in particular. "We have to get her warm and get some liquid into her. Tony, do you have milk? Bring it to a boil and let it cool. Boil some water with a teaspoon in it. I need Everything to be very clean. Do you have salt? I need some salt." After applying calendula cream to the baby's sore spots, Georg placed the blanket into Franks arms which were still holding the cradle position, put the towel on top and wrapped the baby into a tiny swaddled bundle.

Frank began to hum a tune and gently swayed side to side while the liquids were cooking. Once the milk came to a boil, Georg mixed some boiling water into the milk and added a little salt into a tin cup.

"Tony, do you have honey?"

"No. but we do have sugar."

"I need a spoonful of sugar." Georg said. Tony handed him sugar. Georg mixed it into the milk and tested the temperature against his cheek. "Hold still." He said to Frank, felt the baby's cheeks and forehead. Everyone was holding their breath. With a pointing finger Georg felt under the right side of the baby's jaw. With his little finger he touched the baby's lips and opened them wide enough to gently reach for the roof of the baby's mouth. When he could feel the infant's sucking impulse, a smile formed on his face and breath escaped the bystanders. With the spoon he fed the baby little sips of milk. Frank was in his element, smiling a big smile.

"Temperature is important." Georg said to Frank.

"I know. I have raised my baby brother when we lost our mother." Frank replied. As the baby was being fed Tony investigated the contents of the crib hoping to find a clue. He found nothing. He took the crib out of the little barge and found an embroidered piece of black fabric. White images showed a menorah with five candles and tiny flames above each candle underneath a dove flying up to the right, holding a branch with oval leaves in opposite arrangement. Under the menorah they saw two rows of five waves one above the other.

"What is this?" One of the deck hands said:

"I don't know" Georg replied. Looking straight into Frank's eyes, he said with a subtle tilt to his head. "Keep this safe for the baby until she is eighteen years old. She will find out what it means."

Tony took pen and paper and drew up a document. He recorded day and time, location and circumstance of the finding of an abandoned infant girl in the river Donau. He recorded the witnesses and the name of the barge, the town, the landing and the country. Then he had everyone sign. Before handing the document to Frank, who was still swaying the infant Tony said to Frank:

"Ask Gerda to copy this and send it up to Vienna with Johann to file it with the Authorities. Not here. Too many snoops. Give the girl a name now. If you agree we can enter you as Godfather on the document. Without hesitation Frank said.

"Name her Maria Louise Huber." Frank said. "Hilde will adopt her. I am sure. If not, I will raise her myself. I raised my baby brother after our mother died. I know how to do it. Everybody knows. Put Gerda Huber as Godmother." He looked at Georg for approval. Georg smiled and nodded. To Tony Georg said.

"Add Rachel after Maria and put yourself as second Godfather. This way, she will come under the protection of your family as well. Fate did not place her next to your barge for nothing." Tony completed the document and with a candle melted a wax seal under the date and location line with his Captains name and signature. Then he impressed his captains seal in the wax. Everyone was very pleased when Tony brought out a bottle of rare brandy and poured everyone a snifter full in celebration. He raised his glass and said:

"Welcome Maria Louise Rachel Huber. Three cheers." Everyone

141

clinked glasses and cheered three times. The baby girl was cozily swaddled in her blanket had fallen asleep. Georg placed her in the basket inside the tiny barge which was carefully placed in Frank's hand cart. Before the ink of the signatures had dried and Toni had given it some thought, he had entered himself as the second Godfather besides Frank with Frank's approval. Tony was pleased. Goodbyes were said and with the dog in the lead, Frank left to see Gerda.

Georg's feelings were stirred by this event. Memories of Don Georg and the baptism rose sweet and sad. He was glad when Tony showed him his sleeping quarters, which looked very similar to the ones on the medical train, with bunks and seats. He had the luxury of not having to share this space with anyone. This made it possible for him to rest and to follow his own thoughts back to his journey and forward to his future. Tony had given him these instructions:

"You will be doing the night shift. Go with Basil now to look at the gear and see how we attach the tow rig from the barge to the harness on the horses. Then you can go to bed and get some sleep. Basil will shadow you on your first shift to get you off and running. For now, sleep well and welcome aboard." Georg had gone to the stables which were located at the opposite end of the barge and found Basil, introduced himself and helped him prepare the departure of the barge. Basil had explained:

"We have feeding stations and shelters for the horses where we normally spend the night. Now we do double shifts and they sleep at every other stop, usually when we go up on the locks where the river is dammed to keep it navigable. At one point near the cut, we put the horses on the barge and a steam powered tugboat pulls us through the narrows. That is when all hands come on deck with poles to keep the barge from hitting the rocks. You will see. It is one of the wonders of the world. Welcome to the team."
Once in his room, Georg tossed his pack into the corner and fell into a long deep sleep. The gentle movement of the barge lulled him into childhood memories of river outings on the rivers Rhine and Mosel. This helped him shed the weight of this moment. With his inner eye Georg saw cumulus clouds draw dramatic pictures into the skies of his childhood. Autumn was his favorite time to remember. It was turning green to red, yellow to gold and fruit was ripening everywhere. His favorite were the grapes. Heavy, sweet, and delicious. Even when he was very young, he could help with the

harvest. He could reach grapes from below the vines, cut them with his little bowed scissors and drop them into buckets. What he loved the best was the fact that he could command and get a new empty bucket every time his pail was full. Grownups gave him a grunt of approval with every bucket he filled. That was almost better than the meal they served picnic style by the side of the hill where some grownup always stood up and told jokes no one thought he would understand. His childhood dream was to find people who most resembled the generosity of nature in the things they were doing. His father represented the world of words and ideas. His mother represented the world of doing selfless deeds. Now he was sleeping on a barge that was gently rocking him into this dream and he felt that he was under the protection of such people as his mother. The sound of iron wheels rolling on steel tracks woke him. He needed a second to remember where he was. Outside it was getting dark. The air smelled of river water.

"Georg wake up. It's your shift." Someone called. He did not recognize the voice. Once he had placed himself on the barge and in the role of team driver, Georg dressed quickly, put on his Cossack boots and the blue blouse Tony had given him, went to the tack room, grabbed a pocket full of carrots and went to work. He nodded to the people who had lowered the gang plank to let him walk off the barge.

"Morning," he heard them say. No Nazis. His brain filed away. "Good morning" he replied, "glad to be here. See you after my shift."

He went to take the reins.

"Good evening Basil," Georg said. "Looks like a calm night."

"It is. Let's keep it that way. Welcome aboard Georg." Basil stayed with Georg. The horses pointed their ears forward when he offered them a carrot on the palm of his flat hand. It marked the halfway point of this team's shift and it did not take long before Georg and the horses were working together. Georg thought that maybe the horses could smell the lingering scent of the animals at the circus or of the animals at Johann's stables. He felt content and lucky to be moving towards home in this disguise. It felt natural and safe. Moving up a river at night felt meditative and healing. He was able to give into it without reservation or interference from memories or his circumstances. He was moving a barge upriver on the Donau from Vienna towards Germany leading horses. It felt Good. Basil interrupted his musings:

"At the bow of the barge we have a large rudder, designed to steer the craft away from shore like a standoff to prevent us from pulling it on shore and to steer it to the center when sandbars would threaten to ground us. There is another steering board mounted near the center on the river side of the ship's hull. This assists the rudder and gives it trim when we are towing."

"This is where river knowledge must be vital." Georg remarked. "It is in our blood" Basil answered.

"How many generations of river people came before you?" Georg asked.

"Untold generations. Far beyond memory. Before written history, even. This is the western end of the Silk Road that comes from Asia, India and China."

Georg was reflecting on this introduction and on the trust that skipper, crew and horse drivers had in each other. This was a large barge carrying a heavy load. Experiencing a skipper like Tony and his crew was the reassurance he needed, as he walked his horse team through the night. Georg knew that it would take a while for him to build a good relationship with the animals he was working with. It was especially important to him to have silent communications with them. He was working the night shift from nine o'clock to six in the morning. He had been given a head lamp adopted from a miner's light. He was concerned about being seen at night and decided to see how not to use this lamp and how much he could rely in the very keen senses of his horses. He attended to the horses by offering carrots and hands full of oats and a bucket of water during shift changes. He checked the hooves and cleaned out around the horseshoes. He greeted each horse by breathing into their noses, then he gave them a few carrots. During his first shift he made himself familiar with the harness again. He had the idea that walking between the horses would be safer for him, make it easier to talk to them and to reduce verbal communication in favor of touching them by the mane, neck and head. He was using signals he had learned in the circus.

"It will take a few times of practice to get this right." He said softly. He could see the ears turning back towards his voice. "Good. You hear me. And you have been here before. You show me" He whispered. The trail along the river was well trodden and curved in the wide sweeps of the Donau. Georg could not see the landscape in the dark. He knew that his trail was more level than the opposite side where the foothills of the Alps became visible in the moonlight and the horizon was showing alpine peaks standing as black silhouettes during starlit nights. He smelled the sweet scent of the horses and noticed the pace of their breathing, which was beginning to show puffs of smoke as the temperature was beginning to fall. The gentle counterpoint of the horse's footfall settled into a steady beat, enhanced by the muted sound of leather and hemp ropes chafing and rubbing, as the pull from the horses was transferred onto the barge. Once Georg had placed himself between the horses, this was the only thing he could hear. He became aware of how big these horses were compared to his own slender frame. It did not take long before the animals knew where he was and the language of his silent signals to the horses began to grow. He soon was able to move them right and left and change the pace with the slightest touch. He was aware of changes on the trail long before they became visible by listening to the horses breathing and by noticing how they were moving their ears or holding their heads. There also were guttural grunts and whinnies in the language of these gentle giants.

"When things get exciting, I want to be near you." Georg whispered to the horses.

During the fourth night shift the horses gave Georg an early warning about approaching persons. A grunt. A big inhale. Another grunt. A snort. "A patrol" he whispered. "Better disappear." During the shift change the horses were fed and watered while the barge was tethered to one of the evenly spaced markers along the towing trail. Georg had been reassured that patrols were not inspecting or harassing barge traffic. He was not ready to believe anyone on this count. He needed to avoid encounters. He considered the Nazis to be unpredictable, jumpy and more deadly than any other army involved in this war. To make his disappearing act possible, he had added short hemp rope loops to each towing harness, which he could use the way he had attached himself to galloping horses during circus performances. He could pull himself up on them and stay off the ground for any length of time. The horses were now raising their heads from their buckets. Georg slipped in between them, put his feet into the loops and pulled himself up to wrap the tow lines around his elbows. In this position he remained off the ground and undetected, even though flashlights of soldiers were sweeping under and in between the horse's legs. His heartbeat in his ears during such inspections.

"Don't touch that horse, you idiot" said one of the soldiers to his partner, who was about to pet one of the horses. "You spook them, and all hell breaks loose. The Sargent was clear about that. Barges and horses are taboo. You do not touch." Georg could hear the soldier back away from the horse's head. Once the patrol had passed, Georg was wondering about how come there was so much military presence in this sector.

"This is not an active war zone," Tony had said." But this Nazi is fighting many wars on many fronts. Internally and externally. We just got word about what was in the barge that said 'explosives' on it. Remember? They had us tied up for more than a week."

"I do. I thank this delay for being here with your team now. What was on that barge and how do you know?"

"I am a barge captain. We find out what is inside of barges. We load them. We drive them. If I have a question, I can get the answer."

Georg was trying to go to bed, but he wanted to know. The military escort was unusual and had left everyone guessing. Now Tony knew:

"Gold bars. Being shipped for safe keeping to an undisclosed location. Rumor has it that this load is part of the gold the Reich's Bank stole. The Nazi thinks he inherited this gold."

"What do you think is happening?" Georg had finished his meal. He was tired.

"I think the war is coming apart." Toni explained." Hitler has fired many of his best generals. He is directing the war himself. He is running pissing contests instead of strategic warfare with the objective of ending or winning war. I think it is all a distraction. People are dying. The people down here do not know anything and do not give a shit. That is why gold is being moved down here. The Nazi knows this war cannot be won. Now he is beginning to hide the treasure before the bill is presented. My guess is they were moving the gold to Albania. Albanians are as secretive as they are corrupt. All you must buy there is their leader. Everyone else is mute."

"Interesting. You might be right. I am turning in." Sometime later Georg said to Tony:

"I must have missed many of the locks while I was sleeping."

"Yes, you have. You sleep like a stone. How are you doing with the horses?"

"We are best friends. They hear me whisper. They understand my touch."

"I bet they do." Tony laughed with a deep belly laughter that was infectious to others and lifted everyone's spirit.

"You are our night owl. You sleep away day after day. Ciao ciao day, hello sweet night." Ever since Georg had to stop writing his daily letters to his love at home, his heart was getting heavier and his mood became unpredictable. He found it hard to stay positive and optimistic without encouraging words from his Rose.

'You are my compass and my anchor' he had written to her what seemed to him eons ago. Now he wanted to tell her: *Without your strength, I feel like a barge that has lost its tow line and its horse team. Its spirit and its soul.* Once Georg shut out the light, he fell into a deep sleep. He had dreams. In one dream he was sitting in his sleeping compartment on the hospital train. He was writing a letter on thin blue airmail paper. He remembered nothing more. He could not reconcile past, presence or future. He was feeling profoundly tired. Safety concerns for his pregnant wife and the promise he had made to Tanya kept him going. He had lost track of time. He was moving from Now to Now to Now. Loyalty was measured by loyalty he found in people he met. He was overwhelmed by this war and by his patient's generosity towards each other, when they offered their remaining blood to the person on the next stretcher, should they not survive their injuries. During dinner before one of his night shifts, he told Tony:

"I see them sit on their bunks with their remaining bodies and joke amongst each other, waving with ghost hands they have lost physically but can still feel. Sometimes they hold each other and the only way I know they are touching each other is the tears they shed, not for themselves but for their families and friends at home."

A hard bump stopped the barge from moving forward. Georg could feel a rebound like liquid moving back once again. He had heard someone use the word oil. He assumed that olive oil was in the hold. Through his window Georg could observe the walls of the lock moving slowly down as the upstream water was filling the huge trough, lifting the barge slowly and gently until the water level was even with the river above the dam. Locks made him nervous.

One never knows what is waiting up there. He thought. The closer to home he came the more nervous he felt. He did not sleep well anymore. This day was cold and brilliant sunlight made the emerging landscape blind him as the barge reached the top of the lock and the horses were reattached to pull it to the bollards where the barge was being tied up for a few hours to rest, water and feed the horses in one of the three sided shelters. Here they received deliveries of fresh food and meat for the ship's crew. Georg's night shifts gave him little interaction with other crew members, other than information about the animals or the next location and time for the shift change. The three am break was a short feeding, grooming and water. "River people are a quiet lot. I wonder when they will tell their story" Georg thought. When they reached Kelheim, Georg finally saw the wonder of the cut, he had anticipated. The horses were brought up on the barge and got a long break inside the stable, while their towing gear was being washed, treated with saddle soap and checked for signs of wear. A steam tugboat was placed in front of the barge. The smell of the exhaust from the firebox and the escaping steam from the pistons reminded Georg of his steam train travels. The mountain Georg had seen from the distance for days now had been cut in half by the river in a narrow canyon of pale gray limestone. Sheer cliffs, several hundred feet tall dropped straight into the water on both sides. All barges were towed here, and all hands were stationed on deck, rudders and poles in hand to stave off the rocks where currents were threatening to push the barge against the face of the canyon. Each successful canyon passage was celebrated with a rest day upriver from the Cut. Every barge captain anticipated the passage through the cut with an eye on the weather and the water level of the Donau. A meal was served at a pub located by the side of the river where the barge was tied up. The horses were sheltered, and captain and crew could rest after eating and drinking far more than they were used to on their river journey. Georg enjoyed seeing the smiling faces of the crew members, telling silly jokes and trading teasing remarks about the way they had handled their poles through the Cut. Georg could see concern on Tony's face.

"Anything the matter, Tony? You look like a frog has just crawled across your liver."

"The weather." Tony said. "A storm is brewing from across the Alps, causing severe downpours and flash floods that raise the river and make the locks dangerous if not impossible to navigate. You will not see any of this. You are lucky. We should make it to the lock at Ingolstadt." Toni gave Georg a long and friendly look into his eyes.

"I want you to get off the barge there and try to hop a freight train to Ulm. You know your way around trains. We will miss you. The horses will miss you. We never had a new guy who handled our team as well as you. That was a lucky break for us. We made the Cut. You made it possible. I pray you make it home." Georg looked around as if to remember every detail of the barge.

"It was good to have a break from emergencies, medical and otherwise. You kept me safe. You and your river team are very special to me. Steady as the river Donau herself. I will remember you with gratitude, always." Tony looked sad.

"It works both ways. You helped my friends Hilde, Gerda, Johann and Frank. They are my family away from home. You are part of that family, that makes you part of mine."

A quick hard embrace finished this conversation. The clouds Tony had mentioned were indeed pouring over the top of the Alps, making the peaks look like sugar cones. Georg saw rivers of white clouds stream down the folds. While he was getting ready for his last night shift, he observed lightning strikes further down the slopes indicating hail or rainstorms. The weather was still too far away for Georg to hear the thunder. It was a very slow-moving storm. The air had stopped moving. No sound." This will deliver masses of water." He thought. He pulled the barge into his final lock at Ingolstadt where he handed the reins to the next driver.

"Thank you, my friend" He said. "May God keep you."

Georg went on board and took his pack from his room. Rain began pouring in such quantities that he had trouble breathing. The railyard was only a quarter mile away. The heavy rain not only washed away debris and dust, it kept military patrols in the barracks in this otherwise heavily guarded rail depot and warehouse district that included chemical factories and a tank farm for a nearby air base. Once he reached the railyard, Georg approached the locomotive of the closest freight train. When he finally managed to get someone's attention, he raised two hands, one holding his stethoscope, the other holding the official pouch Hans had given him to present to other railroaders. He had chosen not to go to the station master because he was afraid of running into soldiers ducking under from the heavy rain.

"Hello, I am Georg. I have a message for you. May I come aboard?"

"Sure, come on out of the rain." Pointing at the stethoscope, "Are you a doctor or a medic?" The engineer opened the pouch and took out several sheets of paper. He held them under the small bow lamp above his little desk. After reading Hans's messages he turned to Georg and said:

"You are lucky you did not come here fifteen minutes earlier. They just scrubbed this train clean from any unauthorized train jumpers. They are on high alert right now. Industrial areas have come under attack from saboteurs of the resistance. They look with strong lights everywhere, even here on the locomotive and inside the tender. We are waiting for the green signal. This freight is going to Konstanz via Ulm. The storm has delivered this horrendous cloudburst just minutes after they cleared this train. They are especially nervous right now because a barge with jet fuel has arrived at the dock." Georg's arms were getting goosebumps. Was the engineer talking about Tony's barge? "You can see it from the train when we move out of the railyard. That barge is a target for all resistance fighters. It will keep the Planes of this air base flying through Christmas. They stopped adding tanker cars on freight trains in this region to keep the rails from getting damaged during air raids. You think a rail car makes a mess when it explodes. That barge has twenty times more fuel in it. If that goes off, it will not only sink the barge and block river traffic, it will demolish buildings in a radius of fifty meters. They lost a barge in January. Right here in the same port. Fortunately, that one had been moored in a side basin. Security and secrecy have been tightened to the highest level after that."

"What does that mean?" Asked Georg as a knot was forming in the pit of his stomach.

"It means that if anyone speaks a single word about content or destination of a shipment and gets caught, they are executed. Getting caught means a neighbor can rat out another neighbor." Georg knew exactly what the engineer was talking about.

"I had no idea. I was at the front in Russia. I am beginning to see that the quiet side of this war is just as deadly as the front. Only much more frightening. "He explained this to himself as much as to the engineer, adding: "There it is one army against another. Here it is one person against their neighbor and every armed person against the next armed person.

People seem to have begun switching sides." He decided to omit his river story from his narrative about how he made it to this railyard. Instead he only spoke about the urgency of getting back to his unit. The engineer stepped closer, speaking in a confidential tone: "I think this war is not going to last another four years. I feel things are coming unhinged one hinge at a time, even as we speak. Let me give you an official jacket and helmet. We are required to wear them all the time now because of snipers." He looked at Georg in his new outfit. "That is better. By the way, I am Otto. That fellow over there is Oliver. What was your name again? Georg?"

"Yes, it is Georg. Hello Oliver, good to make your acquaintance, Otto. Now you have a helper who knows very little about trains and a whole lot about medicine. Thank you for taking me in.

"You are one of us," Otto said, handing back Georg's pouch. At this moment the signal turned green and Otto moved the lever up to give steam to the pistons of his powerful locomotive.

"Thank God for family" Georg replied, more to himself than to Otto. The train began moving slowly through a maze of rails that began merging until finally there were just two pairs of parallels left, sweeping at the same wide curve as the river. First light was revealing a black and white picture of a rain soaked industrial park with docks, dim lights glistening on a maze of wet rails. Georg glanced out towards the river when Tony's barge came into view. Lights beyond the river were muted, reflected in the raindrops making a million little twinkles. Georg's eyes were focused on the barge to see if he could make out any movement of his friends on deck.

Suddenly, a bright white flash lit the barge and the dock, followed by a massive explosion which sent a mushroom cloud high into the sky. The sound caught up with the light like a thunderclap after the flash. Georg's breath stopped and his heart skipped a few beats. He could hear a scream escape his lungs and both Otto and Oliver turned to look at him. They could see the expression of abject horror on Georg's face which was now lit by an enormous fireball and more explosions detonated where the barge had disappeared a moment earlier. Without thinking, Otto accelerated the train under full power to pull away from the railyard as quickly and as far as he could.

The fire and the mushroom cloud above the barge faded into the distance like a silent horror movie. Georg felt his heart racing. He was breathing deep exhales to keep it from running out of control. His legs were no longer supporting him. He sank to the floor where he had been standing.

"Where did Georg go?" asked Oliver.

"I don't know, he was looking at the barge a second ago."

"I am here. I am sorry. I did not expect to have such a reaction. I have no idea what happened." Otto said:

"You must be shell shocked. Happens to many returnees from the front." Georg remained in his sitting position on the floor. He realized that at this moment he could not get up even if he wanted to.

I have to process this He said to himself.

"Give him time." Otto said to Oliver." Make him some breakfast. "Coffee?" Hearing neither yes nor no, he slipped his special long handled pan onto a rack he had mounted near the top inside the firebox. The pan contained water for coffee and six eggs for soft boiled eggs. Georg observed the movements of the men on the train as through a thick fog that muffled even the chugging of the locomotive and the grinding of its wheels.

"Breakfast, hey Georg, breakfast is served. Eat something. It will make you feel better."

"I am so sorry. I am so rude." Georg answered, turned onto hands and knees and crawled to a hand hold near the door to pull himself up. Oliver placed Georg's food tray onto a little fold down shelf that was mounted on the wall in front of a floor mounted stool. He took Georg under the arm and led him to his seat.

"There you go. Are you feeling better?" He spoke to Georg the way one would speak to one's grandfather. Georg was completely numb. He felt nothing and his hearing was shut out.

"I am fine, thanking you" mumbled Georg still disoriented.

"Take your time. You want a glass of water?"

"Yes, thank you. I'll have my water with whisky."

"That's the spirit" Otto said, relieved at Georg's return to humor. "Shellshock. Even a doctor. Food will be good for him. Who knows how long ago he had his last meal?" Otto said to Oliver and turned his attention to his own breakfast consisting of two soft boiled eggs, two rolls, butter and strawberry rhubarb jam.

"Thank you, Oliver. Perfect as always. Enjoy." Otto said." We have been lucky so far. Will our luck run out before this war ends?"

CHAPTER FIFTEEN

SNOW

Otto could see a red signal and the arrow that indicated to reduce speed for a turn to a side rail and a depot. These days water and coal were always refilled at every depot to keep trains in running condition. The engineers serviced their own locomotives. Otto stopped his train and went to see the stationmaster while Oliver attended to resupplies of coal and water with Georg's help. When Otto returned, he announced:

"We cannot go via Ulm. We were re-routed through Augsburg and Kempten." To Georg he said: "I can show you on a map. We are rerouted straight to Friedrichshafen at lake Konstanz. You can get off at Kempten. Go west from there. We should arrive at Kempten a little after dark. I will introduce you to the station master there. I have known him for a long time. You have met our international railroad brothers. Now you will meet the local team." Otto thought for a moment while Georg's mind drifted off. "We lost the railroad station in Ulm." Otto said." Airstrike. Heavy stuff. It will take months of repairs before trains can run there again. They spared the Muenster. Must have been the Americans. They were very efficient. They bypassed air defenses by the river and on top of the hill that were set to intercept aircraft using the Danube as a landmark. Word is that one plain after another came out of nowhere in low contour flight, circled the church steeple and began dropping bombs up main street to the Station. They succeeded in cutting the rail yard in half. Blowing up rail cars. Gutting the station, tracks destroyed and bent over deep craters. In, out and gone." Otto thought for a moment: "This was a strategic move. Ulm station and railyard destroyed has cut off the south-east side of the Axis war. Trains must be diverted now. Back through the most contested region where you were traveling to Moscow and Stalingrad, through Poland. That was the long way. The Orient Express is now closed." Otto was sounding hopeful. "I think the end of the war is near. Once the railroad is cut, no panzers can be used. They run out of gas. No gas, no tanks, no plains, no war. The Amis knew that. They are stopping the war."

Georg was not listening. In his mind he had already gotten off at Kempten. He was on his own home turf there. His mind was trying to wrap itself around the meaning of this. He had begun mapping a new route. His heart began beating faster in anticipation. 'Going south takes me close to Rose,' his inner voice was saying. His heart took a leap that was painful and joyful at once. 'I can see her and the baby now. I can go back to my unit after. I can return through Black forest. I know my way through there in the dark. First, I will have to survive the frost, then I will see Rose, even if it is just for a moment.' His head was spinning.

"Get off of me!" Georg yelled, jumped to his feet and reached for his scalpel in his leg pocket. Realizing where he was, he immediately tried to calm down and apologized. "Sorry Otto, I don't know what is happening to me. This has never happened before."

"No. I am sorry. I didn't mean to startle you. I thought you were listening." Otto put his hand protectively on Georg's shoulder. "You must be very exhausted. We are still hours away from Kempten. We will get there after dark at the earliest. Why don't you sleep for a few hours? We can discuss things then. I will wake you up for lunch. Try not to knock me out. Does one o'clock sound good? "He pulled out his pocket watch from a gold chain. It was his pride. His father had given it to him on his day of confirmation.

"Yes. I am sorry. I should be thanking you, not fighting you." With this Georg turned and laid down on the bunk Otto had folded down for him from the wall. He covered himself with a green wool army blanket and was asleep after a few more breaths.

"He must be shell shocked" Otto said to Oliver, who had taken the controls of the locomotive. "I have seen this before. They seem to drop way deep inside of themselves and when you touch them, they jump out of their skin. Poor Georg. He must have been through a lot." Oliver gazed into the mountains. White clouds were still pouring water, but big fluffy snowflakes were now getting mixed in. Otto stepped closer to Oliver.

"I have heard rumors about Stalingrad. That was supposed to be the end of the war. Too many lives lost there, too many mistakes made. He is one of the survivors. I don't think he will ever get over that experience."

The train was now headed straight into the storm as it approached the foothills of the Alps. The sky was gray, and water was washing over the hot locomotive popping in little bursts of steam. The two engineers looked over to Georg from time to time. He had not moved since he had fallen asleep.

"Why don't you make lunch now. When you are done, I will try to wake him up without getting myself killed." Otto said. Ahead, he could see the rain streaming like curtains in the breeze. The river next to the railbed was swelling rapidly, threatening bridges. "Some storm." He said to Oliver. "I have not seen anything like this since last Spring. If this is any indication of what lies ahead, we will have another winter with snow up to the upper floors and snowbound roads and villages."

"I think you are right. See the size of these snowflakes? Ten minutes to lunch" Oliver replied. Otto went over to Georg's bunk. From a safe distance he called out to him:

"Georg…. Georg. It's me Otto. You are on the train to Kempten. It is time for lunch. Lunch is served. Wake up." Before Georg opened his eyes, he did a quick self-examination. Heart rate had come almost back to normal. His breathing was steady, and adrenaline had bled off. He opened his eyes. He could see white out conditions outside the windows.

"I am hungry." He said. "Is there any food?"

"That's the spirit. Yes, Oliver has done his magic again in his firebox." Otto laughed. While they were eating a surprisingly good steak sandwich, the rain stopped, and it continued to snow in big, heavy flakes.

"There we go. Look at that storm. This may not stay. Not down here anyway. Further up the valley is a different story. The peaks have been white for several days already. I have been watching them." Otto announced. Georg looked at his Cossack boots.

"Still good for another hike," he said to Otto. "I better find my wool socks." Georg saw the world change from autumn foliage in bright colors to a white frosting. Visibility was shrinking. The tracks out front remained black, four glistening parallel lines disappearing into a white cloud. The wooden railroad ties turned white first, contrasting to the dark gray gravel of the railbed. The sight reminded Georg of a stairway to heaven. "One up, one down. I wonder who gets to stay up there." His homesick heart was beginning to ache again. He was getting closer to home and he could feel it.

The sound of the train's whistle and the screeching of the brakes startled Georg out of his musings. The train stopped. The tree men climbed down onto the gravel bed and went back to the back of the train. Georg saw the wreck about fifty feet away from the tracks. Snow was swirling, obstructing the view. A farmer had attempted to cross the tracks on an unsecured field way. The train had struck the wagon. The horses dragged the wreck another fifty feet. Then they had stopped, waiting. Georg, Otto and Oliver began searching for the wagon driver. No one was near the wreck. Finally, Georg found a lifeless body in a thicket of bushes near the gravel bed of the tracks. "Over here." Georg shouted. "The horses must have dragged the wreck away from the tracks." He felt for a pulse. He turned back and waved to Otto and Oliver to come and help him. "I need help!" he called out. Together they carefully pulled the body out from the bushes. Georg said:

"We need a couple of blankets and my pack. I want to start with life breaths right now." They gently moved the body to a grassy strip beside the field way. Otto was supporting the man's head. Georg said: "I think I saw a farmhouse right down there." He pointed to a cluster of buildings, just barely visible down the road from the accident. Otto sent Oliver to get Georg's Pack. Georg began to perform chest compressions, Otto went to the farmhouse for help. Georg had started to give life breaths to the driver of the wreck. After many repetitions, the man began breathing on his own. He was a powerful man in his late forties or early fifties with first strands of gray hair on his otherwise dark brown head. He was clean shaven. He wore traditional Bavarian clothes complete with knee long leather pants and a warm jacket with acorns embroidered on the lapel. Oliver arrived with Georg's pack and the two blankets. They placed the man on top of one folded over blanket and covered him with the other.

"Hello, I am doctor Hofmeister. Can you hear me?" Georg called out to the driver. He had put on his stethoscope to do an examination. The man nodded yes. Georg repeated: "I am doctor Georg Hofmeister. I want you to breathe for me and try to relax. We have sent for help. I will examine you to make sure you did not break anything. Just nod yes or no when I ask you questions. I tell you later what happened. I will be staying with you until you are stable. Then we talk." He repeated again: "Help is on the way. Did you hear what I have said?"

"Yes" the farmer nodded. Georg began to examine the patient and Oliver stood by to help manipulate his arms and legs. By the time Otto returned in the company of two women, who were pulling a hand wagon loaded with pillows and blankets, Georg had finished his first examination. He was glad to report to the women that nothing was broken. "Bruised ribs and a concussion." Was the first thing he said. After greeting the women and introducing himself, Georg thanked Otto: "I know you have to keep moving. I will stay here. We can handle it from here. If it is ok with the ladies I will stay overnight and keep an eye on the patient." The women both nodded yes through their tears and Oliver said:

"Liese, Jutta, take good care. I am glad this was not more serious. Doctor Hofmeister will take good care of him. It is not every day that you get run over by a freight train with a doctor on board the locomotive. Good luck." He said to Georg who had noticed a smile on everyone's face. Relieved by this, he said:

"Thank you, Otto and Oliver. Be safe. It was a privilege to be on board of your train. Godspeed." They shook hands, then loaded the farmer on the hand cart and parted ways.

"I am Georg." He said again to the ladies. Who is Liese and who is Jutta? Is one the mother and the other the daughter? I could not tell." Liese blushed and the patient grunted. "Let's not make him laugh, he has a very sore rib cage. What is his name?"

"Gustl. I am the mother of Jutta. Gustl is her father. We own this farm down there," said Liese. Fifteen minutes later, Gustl was resting on a daybed, eating soup, spoon fed by his daughter Jutta. To Gustl Georg said:

"The train you hit was not scheduled. It was supposed to go to Konstanz via Ulm. It had been diverted to Lindau because the train station of Ulm was destroyed in an airstrike. I was going to get off at Kempten. I am on my way to Tübingen. Now I have to go around to avoid Ulm. I can spend the night here and observe Gustl. He has a concussion. For now we have to keep him awake. He was unconscious when I found him. We can take turns sitting with him. I will do a thorough examination when he has finished his soup." To Gustl he said: "How do you feel now?" Gustl was looking around as though he could not remember where he was.

"Terrible. What happened? I cannot remember anything. My ribs hurt. I can't breathe."

"You are lucky to be alive. You even have a doctor in the house. I was on that locomotive you were trying to stop with your wagon. You are lucky to have two strong women by your side." Georg pointed with his eyes to Liese and Jutta. "You are in good hands. You will be better sooner than your carriage. First I will need to examine you one more time." They moved Gustl into a bedroom. Gustl said with shallow breath:

"Locomotive? What locomotive. I remember nothing." Gustl was still disoriented.

"Let me have another look at you" said Georg. He gave Gustl a thorough examination during which the two women were holding on to each other when they were not removing clothes from him. Now and then Georg asked them to help him move Gustl gently to other positions. He also asked them questions about his eating and drinking habits. He checked his motor skills and made him touch his own nose and Georgs fingers. He checked Gustl's eyes.

"You are a healthy and strong man. We are going to keep you awake to be sure you have no complications from your concussion. You will be better by four in the morning. Then we can let you go to sleep. Tell me why you are not in the army. Don't worry. I am only looking for medical reasons."

"I have high blood sugar." Gustl said. "When things go wrong my blood sugar goes way up."

"That was a good choice. At war everything goes wrong. I will talk to Liese and Jutta about food choices. You can do well and not go off the charts if you eat right. Rest will be a good start. You have to take it easy for the next couple of weeks. Concussion is very serious."

"I cannot stay in bed. Tomorrow we are expecting to have a cow give birth and we have no more veterinarians when something goes wrong. I have to be there." Gustl pulled his head up from the pillow and winced from pain. Georg saw this and said:

"Have you noticed what you just did with your head when you were thinking about your cow? That is exactly what I am talking about. Your whole body is trying to follow your head. Even your blood sugar is going up. I have an idea." Georg spoke to Gustl, Liese and Jutta now. He wanted all three to hear what he had to say:

"This storm is going to blow through hard for the next couple of days. I can do chores for Gustl to give him a break. I am sure Jutta knows everything you do. And she can do almost everything you do. She can show me where everything is and what to do with it. As a medical doctor, I have delivered human babies and assisted with many calves and fillies growing up. I can stay here; deliver you calve and keep an eye on you until the storm is over if you let me. I can even split firewood for you. This is a monster storm. The snow may or may not stay." To Gustl Georg continued: "Important is for you to stop worrying about things and to rest. While Liese keeps you comfortable, Jutta and I will deliver the calf. There is almost nothing we cannot do." He said this with a smile that only Jutta saw. She blushed. To Jutta he said: "Would you show me the stables so I can take a look at your mama cow? I want to have a look at your horses too. Georg laid one hand on Gustl's forehead and supported his neck with the other, lowering it into the pillow as Gustl exhaled. "There, now relax and exhale deep with every breath, but stay awake with Liese." To Liese he said: "Talk about something nice, like Christmas or harvest day. Or about when Jutta was born. Keep him relaxed and awake. Talk about how lucky you are. How lucky he is to be alive. Maybe pray together to Saint Peter for saving him". This was the first time he had a chance to look at Liese. She was a handsome brunette like her daughter, about five feet tall. Her hands looked like they were used to a lifetime of hard work. She wore a dusty blue Bavarian dirndl dress with a deep cut bodice that lifted her breasts and a white short- sleeve shirt with puffy sleeves. The wide cut skirt of her dress was protected by a green apron. Inside the house she wore a pair of wooden shoes. Her hair was gathered in a tight bun on back of her head. Her eyes were dark brown. They looked more like wanting to smile than to frown. She wore a discreet scent of lavender. Georg thought that her appearance was very much in harmony with her very tidy house. He was attracted by her orderly life in the midst of this horrendous war. It gave him a sense of pause from what was behind him and what he was anticipating beyond the driving snow ahead. When he followed Jutta into the stables, he noticed that she was about the same age as Rose and her figure was a perfect match, slightly taller than her mother. She wore a dirndl dress of a warm rose color and a forest green and tan checkered apron with a matching head scarf. A forest green felted wool cape protected her against the driving snow as they crossed the yard. To him she looked like a fashion model advertising rustic chic. This gave him an idea. He was going to consult with her to buy an outfit for Rose, which Jutta could model for him at a dress shop in Kempten. He told himself to focus on seeing the cow and after that the horses. He could feel his excitement about getting closer to Rose welling up like puffs of wind before a storm. The pain of missing her began washing over him like waves in a great ocean. He had kept these feelings in check as best he could. Feeling sorry for himself was not going to help him survive. The winds of war had thrown him in front of the mountains that had given his Rose and their child refuge. Now he was in walking distance of her and his heart was aching.

Georg followed Jutta to the horse stables, where he patted the horse's heads, then slipped into their box to examine their legs and hooves. Jutta noticed the way he slid his hand from the back down the legs to take up each leg in turn, feeling the joints. She was curious about how these hands would feel on her, so she stepped into his way as he ducked under the head of the horse he was examining. He took in the floral scent of her before he had reached his full standing height. When he did, he was touching her breasts with his chest and his arms reached under her arms to hold her shoulders so he would not lose his balance. Gently she took his head into both of her hands and pulled it to hers, giving his lips a tour of her features from ear to neck to ear to eyes to forehead to nose and finally to her mouth. Heat welled up in Georg when they connected in a long passionate exploration that was only interrupted by the need to breathe. Unable to resist, they both got lost in this moment and together they went through a wide range of pent up emotions and unmet needs. Unable to control his shaking, he drew her ever closer while his eyes were streaming tears. Her response was a combination of motherly care and unstoppable desire. The animal heat of the stable added an atmosphere that removed all restraints from them until they felt exhilarated and breathless into a pile of hay. Georg tried to speak but Jutta put her index finger over his lips and brought them back to hers. There was going to be no talk. Jutta found out everything his hands could do and her hunger was met by his need as they melted into each other. Two souls and two bodies giving and taking all there was to give and to take in deep, slow movements.

The lead cow was waking them from oblivion and brought them back to what they had come to do. They rearranged their clothing and went back to doing chores. She led him skillfully while he was following with all that he knew about livestock and humans, until they came to the cow expecting. He examined her and found that she was beginning to dilate.

"One or two more hours and we will get busy," Georg said." You must have Vaseline for milking?"

"Yes, we have Vaseline. What are you going to do with it?"

"I use it to lubricate the tissue that has already begun to swell. It will help our new calf slide out and prevents him from tearing up his mother."

"How do you know it is a 'he'?"

"The size of her belly. She has either twins or it is a mighty big bull calf. I felt her. There is only one of them in there." He pointed to the house. "Tell your parents that we are milking the cows after supper and that we will do the rest of the feeding and chores while we watch the cow and Liese watches Gustl. I will take another look at your Papa while you and your Mama prepare supper." Both Jutta and Georg were a little breathless and now they were glad they had something to keep them occupied and their big emotional wave had a chance to run up on the shores of alpine dairy farm reality. Now they went back to the house to see his patient and her mother. With Liese's help he examined Gustl and found him much improved. He told her to heat some milk and to serve it to him with honey. To Liese Georg said:

"Jutta will help you with supper. We will keep an eye on your mother cow while we do the milking. We will have a calf before bedtime. I know everything was crazy today. You are lucky you have a husband to take care of instead of a funeral. It was close. He is meant to be here with you. Not everyone survives a crash with a freight train. Your daughter is a gem. You are lucky she is here. I am sure you know that. After dinner we will deliver the next member of your household. We have about one hour and I predict the water will break any moment now. It will be hard work. The calve is huge. I believe it is a bull calf. Does that sound like a plan to you?"

"It sounds good and I want to thank you. We know we would have lost him without you. I will heat some milk and make supper." Jutta came in to help. Georg looked around. Dark solid wood armoires and display hutches were placed in an order that looked like everything had been there for generations. Chairs with embroidered cushions in muted colors, small side tables with pewter candlesticks on embroidered doilies were placed on small oriental rugs that gave the rooms the cozy feel of family tradition. Pewter cups, bowls, plates and pitchers were placed between family portraits on surrounding shelves that ran beneath beamed ceilings. "Everything is generations old. The wars have spared this family." He thought. This is what tradition looks like. Liese had begun to place a meal on the table when Jutta came in.

"How is father?"

"He is resting," Liese replied.

"Come. Eat." She said and took Georg by the arm and seated him at the place of honored guests. Jutta was seated opposite Georg. She looked flushed. To Georg Liese said:

"You said something about going to Kempten to buy things?"

"Yes, I would like to go to the pharmacy and get supplies. Also, I would like to go to a dress shop to look at some dirndls like you are wearing. I will need a present to bring home." To Jutta he said: "I was hoping you would help me with choices and model them for me. I like the way you dress very much." Georg paused and looked at the women.

"I was at the front in Stalingrad and did not know I was coming this close to home, before making my way back to my unit. It will be a surprise for Rose. I have had no word from home for months. How do you travel to Kempten from here?" Jutta answered:

"We take the Post bus. It is not very far. The post bus takes our big milk can into town and delivers it to the cheese factory. They make our famous butter cheese there. Much better than brie. Better than camembert or blue cheese. Ours is the best cheese in the land. The bus stop is at the other side of the tracks. Mother can take us there. We can use the landauer."

"I saw it in the shed next to the horses. It is a comfortable vehicle. Do you take it to church on Sundays?"

"Yes, but it is too far to take the landauer into town. We always take the Post Bus." Jutta said. Georg bent forward and looked out of the window. The world now looked like an old black and white photo. He said to Jutta:

"We have to wait for the storm to blow itself out. I want to stay with Gustl for a few more days. Tonight, we have a calf to deliver." He pointed to the cheese platter." You have no idea how good your food tastes. I feel lucky Gustl stopped the train. Even more that he is alive." Georg stepped to Gustl's bed and examined his ribcage. He looked at the bruises and touched them.

"How does that feel?"

"Sore, but not as bad as before. Is it broken?"

"I will tell you tomorrow. I am hoping that it is only bruised. The less you move now, the better. There is a lot of swelling. We are going to take care of the cows now. When we get back, you will have another calf." Gustl laid back more relaxed than the first time and said:

"You know Georg, I said to the Liese that my Guardian Angel has sent you. You have saved my life. Liese, Jutta and I will do anything we can to help you with your journey back to your unit. We will make sure you have everything you need for winter travel. Jutta will take you to Kempten and show you to our best outfitter for alpine clothing. I will not take no for an answer. You saved my life." Liese came in and took a seat next to the bed.

"I will stay with Gustl, so you and Jutta can milk the cows now." Gustl rolled his eyes in a mocking gesture.

"Yes mother," he said, "sure, I would disobey my doctor and go to sleep."

"Yes, you would. You do every night when we listen to war news. And that is without falling on your head first." Georg turned to Liese.

"Try not to make him laugh, his ribs are severely bruised." He left the room and followed Jutta to the stables. Heavy snow was falling, and Georg had to follow Jutta closely not to lose her in the dark. She waited for him and took his hand. Like a square-dance partner she slipped underneath his arm and snuggled into him.

"We get to go shopping together. I can't wait." Jutta said jubilantly.

Georg's mind was focused the task at hand. He asked:

"Do we have soap and a towel in your milking parlor?"

"I have soap, I better take a fresh towel." She turned back and he stood where she had left him.

"Make it a big one." He called after her. When they arrived at the stable, she put fresh hay in front of the cows and locked the ladder gate that kept them from stepping back and knocking over the milk pail. She took a one-legged stool from the hook and fastened it to herself with a belt that made her hands free to move around and sit with her pail in her hand. Georg noticed that she had changed into dark brown pants and a tan frock. Seeing that he was watching her, she performed a little dance featuring the adopted tail. When she saw his smile, she told him that there was one for him in the milk room also.

"I will look after our mother cow then I help you. What is the cow's name?"

"Luna" She replied while gently pushing the second cow out of the way to make room for milking the first. He noticed that she was wearing a light gray headscarf and was carrying a second bucket with a washcloth draped over the side. He paused to see what she was going to do. Jutta balanced herself, lowering the stool until it was supported by its leg, dipped the rag in what appeared to be sudsy water, wrung it out and gently cleaned the big odder before feeling the ends of the tits to see if the milk had begun to shoot in. Then he heard the steady rhythm of milk squirting into her bucket. She balanced herself, leaning her forehead against the side of the huge animal. *Good connection* Georg thought. To Jutta he said:

"I see how you do it. I will look after Luna, then I come and help you." He went into the milking parlor where he saw stools, buckets and rags on a drying rack. He took a handful of Vaseline and went to look at Luna, who was still standing up. The water had broken. Georg lubricated her again, then took a broom to clear away the liquid from behind Luna. He scattered a large fork of straw, found hay to make a softer bed for birthing. Back in the milking parlor he soaped his arms after rolling up his sleeves, returned to Luna and inserted his left arm deep into the cow to feel the position of the calf. He was impressed with the size of the calves' head.

"This, my friend, is going to be a big fight" he said to himself and to Luna. He went to the horse stable and found hemp rope, which he tied to a wooden dowel he had seen there earlier. It looked like the rung of a ladder. He left these items in the milking parlor, strapped on the chair and looked for his partner. When Jutta came out from behind a cow she had just finished, Georg did a little dance for her, then he disappeared between two cows down the row and followed her example to make the milk flow.

"We should play Mozart for these cows. They would give more milk. They like harmony. Mozart is perfect." Jutta chuckled. Then she asked:

"How is Luna?"

"Fully dilated and water has broken. The bed is made. I just saw her lay down. The calf is now in a good position. It has a huge head. Thank god for Vaseline. It will make it possible for us to get this big boy out without tearing her up. We might have to play the twilight of the Gods for this birth." He laughed, feeling just a slight sense of unease. Looking over at Jutta, he felt reassured about the combined power they could bring to the task. When they were done milking and everything was put away, they looked at the piece of wood and the rope he had found. Georg asked:

"Is it alright to use this?"

"Of course. What will you do with it? Teach the big boy manners?" They both laughed. Georg attached a piece of rope to each end of the dowel and let the two ends hang after tying a slip knot to each end, leaving an open loop.

"This is where we attach the calves front feet. You and I will help Luna. We pull and help maneuver head and shoulders through the birth canal. Follow my instructions. We will try to move the calves' shoulders sideways by pulling out first one foot, then the head, then the other foot. With the hip we do the same thing. I need the big towel and a bucket of hot water. Be a sweetheart and give me another two forks of hay behind Luna. Luna was now in labor and contractions were coming more frequently. Georg attached the front feet of the calf to the ropes and the two assisted by holding tension and releasing according to Georg's directions. The calf's big head was a major problem. Georg added a good lathering of soap to reduce friction. Two hours later, after an epic fight, the two were drenched in sweat. The calf finally slipped out, bringing the amniotic sack with him. Georg swiftly took it, cleaned it and shoved it back into the cow. Jutta cleared the calves' airway with her index and middle fingers. The cow and her two helpers were completely spent.

"We need to her to get up" Georg said.

"You tell her. I am just as exhausted as Luna."

"Watch," said Georg. He took the towel, dipped it in the water and swung it over Luna's back like a whip, smacking it on her spent mass where it made a loud bang which startled the cow. Luna was on her feet in the blink of an eye.

"Wow" exclaimed Jutta who had never seen such a spurt of energy from an exhausted cow. Together they pulled the calf in front of Luna after Georg had offered her the afterbirth to eat.

"Hormones" he explained to Jutta. "Give her a few minutes while we wash up and clean up the mess we have made. You can let the cows out of the rack now. I will spread their bedding later." Once in the milking parlor, the two helped each other clean up with wash cloths, soap and water, getting excited and intimately making good use of Vaseline following clues from their passionate natural instincts. Before returning to the house, they moved the newborn into a little stall, bedded softly with hay and promised him breakfast as soon as the mother could be milked in the morning. He was already trying to get up. They spread bedding for the other cows and moved another snack of hay forward into the trough. Georg now checked on the horses while Jutta went to see that chickens and ducks had water and kernels. When they entered the house, they found Liese nodding off on her chair while Gustl was still wide-awake, worrying about Luna.

"She is the most valuable cow of my herd." Gustl explained to Georg. "A bull calf out of Luna is worth a fortune. She was carrying the sperm from a State Champion in Oberstdorf. We had her on a mating vacation up there for weeks until she was pregnant. How is she doing?" Gustl asked.

"It is done." Beamed Georg. "You have a bull calf as good as they come. You should have seen your daughter. I have never seen such a powerhouse. She is tougher than Luna and myself put together. She makes complicated things look easy. You should be proud of her." Jutta came back downstairs and kissed her father on the forehead.

"How do you feel, Papa?"

"Much better, thanks to you and our veterinarian Georg. What do you think of his work at the birthing station?"

"He has performed a miracle and delivered a mega calf with ropes and a stick like I have never seen before. We almost killed ourselves, we worked so hard. I was sure the calf's head was going to tear Luna up. Our good doctor here prevented this in his own way. We owe him the life of the calf and the life of Luna. None of us could have done what he did." Looking at his badly worn travel clothes, that had been only superficially cleaned and smelled sour from his long journey in addition to smelling intensely like a dairy cow, she said to Gustl: "Papa, we must buy him a new wardrobe for his journey. I do not want to think something would ever happen to him because he was wearing these useless rags. Especially in this snow. We cannot let him die out there like our troops died in Moscow." Jutta pleaded.

"I already told Georg we would take care of him." Gustl answered. Jutta asked Georg:

"Can he go to sleep now, is it safe? I think he can relax now that we have our calf."

"Yes, he can. He is doing well. I will lead him to the chamber while you fluff his pillows. Then we say good night and we can all get some sleep." When Georg came back with Gustl the bed looked inviting and Gustl settled in as comfortably as was possible with his bruised ribs. Together they arranged pillows to prop up his knees so he would not try to roll over onto his side in his sleep.

"Focus on the exhale" Georg reminded Gustl. "Good night." Georg and Jutta went upstairs to the dressing room where Jutta found pajamas for Georg and a nightgown for herself.

"Where would you like me to sleep?" He whispered into her ear.

"I need you to help me warm up my bed," she answered softly and pointed to the second door down the hallway. They entered her room.

"Your mother?" He asked in a whisper.

"She knows. They both know. They have been praying to God to send someone to us. With all our young men gone and so many lost, taken prisoner and sent to Africa or Siberia. Mother and I fell in love with you when we saw you working on papa to save his life. We were sure God sent you. I want you to stay with me tonight. It is war. I know you must return to your Unit. You are needed to save more lives. And when it is all over, you will return home." She took his head in both hands and whispered: "Right now, you are mine." She stopped his reply with her lips and pulled him into the cloud of the softest feather bed he had ever touched. She kissed his hands and showed them where to touch her. Together they provided comfort and heat to one another as could only be matched in power, passion and urgency by the storm raging outside. After a very long time they fell into a blissful, dreamless sleep cradled in each other's arms. When they woke up, they dressed quickly to do the chores and to feed the new calf. Jutta was looking forward to this. Her intimacy with Georg had made motherly instincts wake up in her. After they finished with their work, she pointed to the pail she was carrying and explained to Georg what she was going to do with the leftover Milk from Luna:

"The first few days after birth this is a very rich substance." She explained. "It is better and richer than milk. We use it to make a slow cooked omelet. We spice it with salt, pepper and paprika. It rises like a sponge-cake. You will see, I think you will like it." She ran her hand over his shoulders and down his sleeve, looking at his worn clothes.

"The people we will see in Kempten are our relatives. Cousins of our family. Both the owners of the dress shop and the outfitters are." She looked deep into his eyes and standing on her toes leaned up into him to give him a long deep kiss which he returned with a sadness that he could not explain to himself. Gustl was slowly getting better. Georg's presence was helping him to relax, insistence on bed rest and hot lemon compresses on the ribcage speeded his healing. A relative came to rebuild his badly damaged wagon.

The storm was slow to move out. It took another two days before the post bus could make its run to Kempten. Several feet of snow had accumulated with snowdrifts reaching shoulder height. The snowfall ended, the mist lifted and revealed a winter wonderland that was enhanced by tree branches heavily laden with snow, accented by split rail fences around pastures and many large solitary trees that still had bright foliage beneath fluffy coats of snow, giving the landscape a fairy land touch. The hills leading up to the mountains looked like sugar-coated loaves of bread stacked one on top of the next. Streams ran out from between these hills, swollen by the heavy rains that had washed this watershed before the snow. They drew black meandering lines into this picture, rushing into the enormously swollen river of the main valley where the distance of water to bridges had shrunk to almost nothing and low-lying meadows had become large shallow lakes. Clear blue skies were meeting snow covered mountains. Sunlight during the day and moonlight during the night were enhancing the contours of these hills as temperatures were dropping. Georg offered to take over the splitting of a large pile of firewood while the women took care of the livestock. He worked the splitting tools tirelessly, sharpened cutting edges and stacked his work in rows of dry wood. Gustl's rest gave his bruises and the concussion a chance to heal.

Georg had explained to Liese how to make hot compresses for Gustl's ribcage with lemon juice which reduced inflammation and swelling, relieving pain and speeding recovery. During the nights, Georg kept warming the featherbed with Jutta in undiminished passion. The cocoon she created for him was like a dream of heaven in the midst of this nightmare of a war. Georg's exhaustion from the past was replaced by new energy from good food, vigorous exercise and better, deeper sleep after their intimate encounters. Georg had surrendered. His resistance to being taken care of had melted like butter in the sun. Jutta was in charge. He was telling himself to get ready to move on as soon as his patient was better. His survival instincts finally tore him away from her. While he was there, Georg insisted on taking care of the horses. These activities gave him pleasure. They reminded him of his beginnings as a child with his family.

Not being able to write to Rose broke his heart. Moving closer to a reunion brought the pain of separation to the surface. He knew that mailing letters to her was not an option if he were to survive. All this was on his mind when he attacked the last heap of firewood with increasing rage about his deadly predicament. Georg swung the axe hard in circular motion. He was reciting:

"This is not fair, this is not fair, this is not fair." The axe landing blow after blow on the word fair. He drove his axe into a knotty piece of wood so hard, that it got stuck deep in the chopping block. A splinter flew off and hit him in the face underneath his nose and cut off the tip of his upper lip. It did not break a tooth, but he felt a bleeding gap in his upper lip with his tongue. He stepped back. He saw the small triangular piece of his lip next to the axe, picked it up and rushed it into the house where he disinfected it and put it back. He made a patch with band aid and gauze, then wrapped gauze bandage around his head. When Jutta came into the room, she called out loudly:

"Georg, oh my God what happened to you?" He tried to show her with gestures but could not think of a motion that would say freak accident. Instead he gestured for pen and paper to write. In short sentences he explained that he was now unable to speak, laugh or eat with a fork.

He wrote that he could only eat cooked oatmeal with milk and honey and strained soup." I need to eat things I can put into my mouth with a teaspoon or a straw." He wrote. "Perhaps we can go to Kempten to the dress shop and the outfitter." He added one more note: "I look like a wounded soldier on sick leave now. What do you think? I have to skip milking and feeding for a few days. First I should lay down." Jutta read this and explained it to her parents. Georg stayed on his back for two days. Jutta gave her imagination free range whenever she had a chance to join him in his cozy refuge. When he re-dressed his bandage, the wound had begun to heal. "It's good," he said to Jutta who was trying to help him bandage his face." I will keep using this bandage until I am past Oberstdorf. The post bus is a public place. It will be best for me to hide right in plain sight." Jutta was getting excited about the outing to Kempten. Jutta was happy to take a break and go into town.

"Can you find me a triple chocolate milkshake?" Georg was beaming. On the third day Liese took Jutta and Georg to the Post bus. Jutta and Georg boarded the bus and their large milk container was mounted safely on the milk rack in back of the bus. The bus stopped at the cheese factory and dropped off the milk. They decided not to visit here but to start with the café and the milk shake treat with chocolate.

"I cannot try cheese with a straw," Georg had said, laughing out loud. To a returnee from the front, triple chocolate shake was a message and a gift from heaven. Next they went to the dress shop.

"This looks wonderful!" Georg exclaimed, when Jutta modeled the blue dirndl and white blouse, a dusty rose-colored triangle scarf with fringes, white panty hose and a dark blue apron. "The size is good. I could never have done this by myself. I make a terrible model for ladies' garments. Please have them packed in a tight bundle for travel." Seeing the outfit on Jutta helped him imagine it on Rose and his heart was aching. Jutta looked at him.

"You look a little sad. Do you really like it?"

"Yes, I do. It is perfect. What makes me sad is the fact that I am leaving. I have been leaving and leaving and leaving ever since I had to escape from the Front. Not leaving would have meant not living. I made a vow to live. That is what I have to do and right now it makes me very sad.

I want all of this to be over. My life is not safe until I get back to Tubingen and then there will be another deployment into yet another war zone."

They ate lunch at a guest house that was welcoming people with its brown, wine red and gold décor and a host who was talking up a storm.

Jutta told him that her companion could not speak. The smell of cigars and beer was stronger than the scent of the flowers that were placed next to the salt and pepper by the large ashtrays in the center of the round tables. The host was too curious about Georg.

"Here is one on the house for a wounded warrior." The host concluded his monologue and brought over a beer. Jutta said:

"Thank you. Do you have another straw? He really liked your soup. We have to go soon. He has an appointment with his doctor." She urged the host to hurry. Next came the outfitter named Alpine Sports. "Remember they are relatives of mine. I will answer their questions while we pick out everything new for you. I will tell them that you saved papa's life. All you have to do is nod yes when you like something and no if you don't." Jutta helped him with his outfit from undergarments to outer shells. Georg pretended it was his mother shopping for him. He used his extensive boy scout and alpine sports experience when it came to selecting lightweight, insulating wind- and waterproof outer clothing. He selected a white winter parka with removable liner. Wool socks and insulated felt lined boots completed his outfit. The only thing he was going to use from his present luggage was the pack and the Cossack wedding shirt. Finally, he decided to drop the army issue backpack as well and selected a high mountain expedition pack. He added a pair of long wooden skis with modern bear trap bindings and tie-on fir bottoms for climbing steep grades in the snow. A pair of long ski poles with large webbed plates at the bottom completed his snow gear. At the pharmacy he selected gauze, band aids, pain medication, cream against rashes, eye drops and small soap bars, toothpaste and a new toothbrush.

Now it was time to get on the return bus. They sat snuggled together feeling good about the day's accomplishments. Jutta came away with a pair of warm fur mitts, a fur hat and a wool stole in a floral design, matching the colorway of her dresses. Her relatives at the two stores had insisted she accept them as a gift.

Liese was waiting for Jutta and Georg with the Landauer to load the empty milk container and Georg's Packages. Georg patted the horses.

"How did it go?" Liese wanted to know. "Did you find everything you need?"

"It was easy. Georg simply bought the whole store", Jutta laughed.

Liese looked at the luggage. "Skis, do you know how to ski?"

"Basic Medical Corps training. Not reaching patients or getting stuck in snow are not an option for members of the medical corps." When they returned to the farm, Jutta and Georg quickly changed and went to do chores. They were met by the bleating of the bull calf.

"Remember to be meticulous about the temperature of his milk. He may be big, but he is still a baby."

"Yes papa." Jutta laughed. It was time to prepare for Georg's departure. A spell of sadness fell over the house. Georg decided to take the Post bus to Kempten and another one to Oberstdorf. He was dressed with bandage over his face looking like a wounded soldier on sick leave from the front. Last examination, last embraces, last kisses, last words, last tears, last thanks all around. Well wishes and prayers for God's protection. Then the bus pulled away.

Well-equipped and well disguised, Georg had an uneventful trip on the bus. It took two buses and one full day. He was testing his new outfit and found it to be the best he had ever owned. He sat in the back of the bus where he could keep an eye on his skis on the back rack. He was wearing his white winter hat from his unit with the red cross on the upturned visor, the ear flaps turned down with ties under his chin. Enough of the gauze bandage was showing to tell fellow travelers not to speak to him or to ask questions. Everyone seemed to be preoccupied with the snowstorm and road conditions. There were no patrols or inspections until he was busy untying his skis at his final destination of Oberstdorf. It was already getting dark. Georg had been the first off the bus with his pack strapped to his back. He could see some officers checking passenger's papers. He walked around the front of the bus and to the back where no passengers were lined up. Moving slowly, he took his skis from the rack and disappeared into the dark. He crossed a bridge to the opposite side of the river, away from the road and stepped into his skis. He was getting ready to approach the village where Rose was sheltered with their baby. He planned to arrive just before sunrise.

All he could hear was the steady swish of his skis on snow and the murmur of water in the swollen river. Moonlight was giving him enough visibility to avoid river debris and natural obstacles. He was deep in thought. The hoot of an owl made him almost jump out of his skin.

Nature had muffled all other sounds. His heart was aching to see Rose and the baby. He strapped on the climbing furs and started working his way into the ridgeline above the village. Here he expected to find the mountain cabin with Rose and the baby.

When Georg arrived at the cabin, the front door was covered in snow. The space beneath the overhang was filled with snow. Georg felt like a stone had dropped into his stomach. He looked for smoke from the chimney or other signs of life. He found none. He dropped his pack and went to the uphill side of the cabin to find a way in. He unstrapped his skis and opened the attic which was a drive-in hay loft. He stepped into the attic and left the door open for light. At the front gable he found a bulkhead with a stair entrance. The door was not locked. A steep set of stairs led him to the living quarters. Another door kept the cold out. He went inside and looked around. He found everything in place as expected, many objects he knew, books she was reading, the spinning wheel and the loom she used to weave blankets and fabrics. Everything was in order and the baby station looked like the mother had left with the baby, taking diapers and supplies with her.

Georg was heartbroken. Nothing had ever made him feel lonelier than the emptiness of this house. He walked around, touched the stove, picked up items of clothing and smelled them. The familiar scent of Rose made him cry and the scent of a baby he was yet to meet, made his heart pound. Everything looked like she would be returning soon. He suspected that the storm had something to do with this. He decided to ski down to talk to the Gmeiners, the owners of the cabin.

He and Rose had stayed with them for a ski vacation ten years earlier. This was where he had proposed to Rose. His thoughts were wandering for a brief moment into the sweet innocence of his youth. It seemed to have been a hundred years ago. First, he retrieved the package with the dress from his pack. He lovingly placed the items on her bed with a note explaining the circumstances of his visit, his disappointment of finding the house empty and the next steps he needed to take now. This done, he strapped on the skis, grabbed his pack and in one straight shot arrived at the owner's front door. The Gmeiners were watching his approach and his signature stop in a big white cloud of snow.

Introductions soon changed to "welcome home." The Gmeiners

wanted to know everything about the circumstances of his return and about his medical career. Georg wanted to know where Rose had gone and how long ago, she had left. They told him about warning her about the storm and their concern that she and the baby could be snow bound up there in the slope. They knew she had gone to Bolsterlang to her sister's house. They recalled her telling them about her older sister who lived further down the valley also with a baby and with an absentee husband who was serving as a doctor on the Russian front.

"We are so isolated here; we know only what people tell us when they come up the valley." They explained. "We are glad you came. We need you for a few days. Three women in our village expect to give birth within the next week. We have no doctor here. We would be grateful if you could make house calls and help our midwife with the birthing. You can stay here with us. We understand to keep quiet about the circumstances of your presence here."

Georg was happy to help and moved into a guest room. He and the midwife spent the following week making house calls to prepare the young mothers for birthing. He was eager to hear descriptions of his wife and child. He reminded his hosts and himself that he was not supposed to see her but to return to his unit. He explained:

"The war is not going well. I was going via Ulm to connect with my unit at Tübingen. Ulm main station was taken out by a precision airstrike by American bombers. The railyard was destroyed. The train I was travelling on was diverted from Augsburg to Konstanz via Kempten. This sent me too close to Rose not to try for a surprise visit. I was hoping to see her and meet my first-born child."

"Son." She corrected. "First born son." Georg was beaming. His hostess continued: "There are rumors you might be interested in. Stories about the different allied forces and the way they treat prisoners. The worst of course are the Nazi armies. They have no place to put prisoners. Austria's Nazi army is just as dangerous. British armed forces are in the same situation. They cannot even feed their own. The French have the foreign Legion. You do not want to fall into the hands of the French." She warned. Georg replied:

The Russians are out of food too. Everyone is starving, including their own troops."

"That leaves the Americans," she concluded.

"Americans are the only ones to have taken action towards ending the war." Georg said. She agreed:

"From what we hear, anyone taken prisoner by the United States Armed forces considers themselves lucky. Travel in their territory." She suggested. He refocused:

"This is a bizarre conversation. Not many people are on the run like I am. Everyone can shoot me on the spot." He paused. "My job is to protect life. Babies need delivery. I will do it. That is all I can think about right now."

"I will call the midwife. I will ask her over for coffee and cake. You two can set up your schedule of home visits. She will introduce you to the mothers. I think the first one will be Heide, the wife of the mayor.

Her husband is off to war. The other two are running summer and winter holiday homes like ours. All the husbands are with the army at war." To the delight of the entire village, three healthy baby boys arrived and Georg felt good about leaving them and the mothers in the competent hands of their midwife. Early the following day, he packed provisions and set off down a parallel valley to the one he had come up in. He followed a trail he remembered skiing during his ski vacation ten years back. It was a downhill run that went over a series of rounded hills connecting run after run with minor climbs. The distance to Bolsterlang could be covered in a day. His heart began to beat a little faster with every run he took down this series of hills. He was equipped with new state of the art ski gear and winter clothing. Nothing in his appearance was suggesting that he was a soldier. He was a doctor. He still wore his stethoscope around his neck and even carried a bundle of diapers the new mothers had given him. Truth was, he had just delivered three babies. He was on his way to see his wife and to meet his first-born son. No one had ever run down this mountain feeling as happy and excited as he felt right now.

The setting sun was tinting the mountain peaks rose and Georg said a prayer to ask God this one time, that someone would answer the door when he knocked. He did not know how to approach the house. He felt faint from exertion not only from running down the alpine trail on skis, something he had not done in a long time, but also from his time of silence and isolation from Rose. As he approached the house, he stuck his ski poles into the snow, dropped his pack and took off his skis. He felt restricted by his winter coat, so he dropped the gloves, the hat and the coat on the ground as he approached the front door.

Before he could reach the door, it opened and there stood the love of his life, holding a baby in her arms. She did not move. Perhaps this was a trick of her imagination? To the baby she said:

"Looks just like your dad. I am going to touch him. I have to try not to faint. Tears began running down her face. Georg sank to his knees. Slowly she moved closer to him and with her fingertips gently and carefully she touched his head and held it as he began sobbing and wrapping his arms around her knees. In this embrace they remained for a long time. "Is it really you?" She whispered. He nodded, far away from being able to speak. "Get up and come inside" she whispered, gently pulling him up to herself so that the baby was now part of this embrace. Like a pair of dancers, they moved through the door and into the house where she extracted the baby and placed him in his father's arms. "Christopher, this is your father Georg. I have to make sure. I am trying to breathe. My heart is beating so hard I am afraid it might break, but we cannot let that happen, can we? Not now, not ever. He came to see you. He came to see us. I have to put you into your crib now," she whispered. The baby had begun reaching for Georg's face, he was fascinated by his nose. Trying to realize that Georg had actually come home, she took her son from Georg's arms and gently placed him into his crib. Then she turned back to her lover and said through her tears: "I was expecting you. Day and night, I was expecting you. All these days, all these nights. Let me look at you. I have to be sure you are real. You came home. You are alive!" He interrupted her words with a long and desperate kiss. He whispered:

"Yes, I did, yes, I have, yes I am. Let me take you in. All of you, let me come in and hold you until we can speak again. Let me thank you, my angel, for bringing me here, because without you in my heart there would have been no way I could have made it back."

The Hours that followed were a celebration of life interrupted only by the need of feeding baby and parents and changing diapers, then by the grace of a higher power, the baby slept for a long time, allowing the parents to explore one another in a way they had only been able to dream about during countless long and lonely nights of missing one another. Finally, they lay exhausted. Holding each other and speaking very quietly not to wake the baby. Now they filled in the letters they had not been able to write in more than a year.

"I just delivered three babies at Gmeiner's village before I skied down our favorite ski run right into your arms. How great is that? How lucky can I be? How lucky can we be? Everything I have done; I did for you. It has saved my life every single day. It has saved the lives of others. Now I have to ask you, my heart: Turn around and look only to the future. We have not come to the end of this long road yet. The war is not over. I have to go back to my unit and get new marching orders. That is the condition of my survival. It will be over soon. One Year, two. No more than that. In the meantime, you and I must stay strong. We need to survive. This is the hardest part. We cannot become victims of this war. Our love is the life raft that will bring us on shore. Our love is the one great force in our power that we can count on. We have very important work to do, you and I and we must never give up." Georg and Rose spent one blissful night and the following day in each other's arms with their son Christopher. Georg gave the fate of his little family into Christopher's tiny hands and asked him to keep his mother safe:

"You are the man in this house now. Watch over your mother." He said to Christopher. Georg and Rose had resolved to treat this departure with the same stoicism doctors use to maintain standing while countless wounded soldiers keep arriving from the battlefield before them and there is no time for empathy, grief, self-pity or even self-reflection. "We stand and we fight. That is what we must do. We do it for each other. We do it for Christopher and we do it to make sure there is a future."

Georg left that night and chose side roads to ski towards Kempten where he hoped to board a train, using his special papers given him by his railroad friend Hans. Georg felt the temperature rise. In the distance he could hear the crack and thunderous rumbling of avalanches crashing down exposed mountain slopes. He saw the clouds as mist at first than as thick fog. He could hear water rushing wildly in a rapidly swelling river. It was pitch black dark now. It began to rain hard. Georg left his skis leaning on a trail marker. He could hear the rumbling of rushing water, tearing away the bridge he was about to cross. He was now forced to follow the stream, hoping to find another bridge. He cautiously made his way down a narrow foot trail used by fishermen. The ski poles came handy to find obstacles and to keep his balance on a trail that had now turned into a slippery slushy stream. The trail led Georg to an arched stone bridge. He strained his eyes in the dark to see signs of civilization, when he noticed a large building across the stream with windows lit on the inside by candlelight. Georg decided that his best chance to make it to the railyard in Kempten was to cross this bridge. He was hoping that whatever the event was that caused this large building to be brightly lit, was the distraction he needed to get to the railroad trestle on the other side of the valley. He stepped off the bridge. Suddenly two armed guards appeared and took him under arrest. They rushed him to the utility wing near the kitchen. They were about to remove his belongings when Georg could hear a call coming from the banquet room:

"Is there a doctor in the house?" Waiters were moving in and out of the kitchen in their tuxedos, their white starched napkins draped over their arms, balancing large silver platters and white china dishes steaming with delicious smelling food, pushing the swinging doors open with their backs. Candlelight streamed into the kitchen almost blinding Georg.

"I am a doctor" he said pointing to his stethoscope.

"Shut up and keep your hands where I can see them." Said one of the guards.

"I am a doctor!" Georg repeated very loud this time. He was going into command mode. The head chef heard him and stepped in, flanked by two of his cooks. He barked:

"Get out of the way you fool. Did you not hear him? He is a doctor." The Chef led Georg to the head of a long banquet table, where he saw a man slumped over his plate with his face turning blue. He was surrounded by excited bystanders who Did not know what to do.

"Give me room. I am a Doctor. Please step back." Georg commanded. He pulled the person up into sitting position, pulled his chair back, then turned the patient sideways on his chair, got behind him and performed the Heimlich Maneuver. The sudden upward motion Georg performed, pulling his arms hard into the diaphragm beneath the solar plexus, dislodged a morsel of food from his patient's airway. With a deep sucking inhale, he regained breathing and began coughing to clear his airway. Georg introduced himself:

"I am doctor Hofmeister. Let me listen to your heart and lungs. I will have to take your jacket off. Please stay seated as you are, I can reach your back from this position. I want to be sure your lungs are clear." He put on his stethoscope. At this moment the two guards came in and tried to arrest Georg again.

"You are coming with us!" They both said at the same moment. The Patient turned beet red in anger and to the guards he said in a menacing voice:

"Are you trying to arrest my doctor while he is examining me, you fools? Did you not see, that he has just saved my life?" To no one in particular he said loudly: "This is my doctor. He will finish his examination. Then he is free to go. Anyone interfering with Doctor Hofmeister will be court martialed for insubordination. I apologize Doctor Hofmeister. Please continue your examination."

The guards had left the room. There was complete silence for the next few minutes. Georg put his stethoscope back around his neck, nodded to his patient to continue the feast. The servers cleaned him up and helped him put his jacket back on. Everyone sprang back to life. The musicians picked up the tune that had been interrupted by the excitement and Georg collected his belongings from the kitchen. The cook thanked him for saving General Hagenbeck. He had been afraid that something in his food might have caused this distress. Georg told him that the General had taken a breath that moved a morsel of meat into his airway. The head chef quickly prepared a package of food with some of the best cuts of meat for Georg to take along. Georg left the building and disappeared into the rainstorm. He was dry and warm under his felted Bavarian hunter's cape. His gear had performed well. Georg reached the main road. There was a bus shelter. The post bus came. There were no passengers. Georg decided to ride the bus as far as the Kempten Railway Station. Once there, he left the bus, carrying his ski poles, his backpack and his food parcel. At the depot he spoke to the stationmaster who pointed him to a locomotive that was going to move the next freight train to Lake Konstanz.

"Good evening," he called to the engineers. "May I have a word?" Not saying Heil Hitler identified him to the railroaders as an independent. "Permission to board?"

"Come on up," the head engineer replied. Georg handed him his pouch of papers. He was made comfortable and after reading Hans' note, they invited him to join them and equipped him with the required jacked and helmet. Georg told his story of the lost train and the various legs he had traveled working on field hospital and medical evacuation trains. He unpacked the food package the chef at the resort had given him and shared the food with his new friends.

"It came from General Hagenbeck's banquet." He explained. "They live well. Enjoy."

"How did you manage to get him to send food? How come they let you go?"

"I crossed the swollen stream over a stone bridge to a resort. Guards arrested me and were beginning to search my belongings when a call for a doctor came from the dining room. I removed an airway obstruction from the General, who had turned blue from lack of oxygen. They tried to continue my arrest but the General was livid about someone trying to arrest his doctor. He ordered them to return my belongings and to let me go. The head chef prepared this food package for me. All I care now, is to get back to my unit. I must get new marching orders before some fool ends my life."

"You are safe with us. We will send you back to Tübingen. We are only a few hours away from Konstanz. You will be in Tübingen tomorrow before the day is over. We will check the freight train schedules. Meanwhile, you can try to sleep the rest of the night. You must be tired." In his half sleep, Georg could hear the locomotive start up and move onto a different rail, where the freight train was being hitched. He realized now how profoundly tired he was. The closer he got to reaching his unit, the harder it became for him to keep up his guard. Into his fitful sleep entered dreams, mixing events and images in confusing disarray. One theme came up again and again: He had survived and so many of his friends had gone missing or disappeared. He was still alive. Why, he kept asking himself? Also heavy on his mind was the burden of his unfinished grieving over the loss of friends and loved ones. He began having trouble to forgive himself for being alive while so many who deserved to live were dead. A black cloud surrounded his tragic breach of his compact with life as a doctor, when he saw no choice but to end lives to save others or himself. Georg kept hearing the promise he had made to Tanya and to himself time and again to survive and to return home. He felt good about his choices but was getting lost in the vacuum of relative safety. He was terrified about the uncertainty of what lay ahead. He was profoundly tired of this war.

Georg missed his wise, brave and beautiful wife Rose. He had been approaching her as a lifesaving goal and as a quest. Now there was his tiny family in his mind, and he was moving away from them again. Once again Georg felt adrift without his anchor or his compass. The heartbreak of this situation was overwhelming. He was having trouble raising the stoicism necessary to function with this pain. The look on Rose's face when he left stayed sharp and clear in his mind. She looked so very brave. It broke his heart.

A whistle sounded. "Tübingen." A stationmaster yelled. Georg jumped from his bunk with a start.

"Relax partner" said the head engineer, "this was the conductor for passenger trains.

We have to move into the railyard. That is where we part ways and you go home to your unit.

Have some breakfast first. After breakfast Georg repacked his travel gear and found his hidden pouch containing his wallet and identification papers. It was snowing again this morning and he was able to walk with his cape and hood covering his head and his backpack. He did not stand out and was able to make his way to the Guard house outside his unit headquarters, where he presented his papers and was admitted with a salute. A few minutes later he was admitted and greeted by his commanding officer.

FINAL FIGHT
A WORLD AT WAR

"AS MANY PEOPLE AS WERE
ENGAGED IN THIS WAR
AS MANY WARS
WERE FOUGHT"

James Mitchener.

NO
MORE
BORDERS

CHAPTER SIXTEEN
THE LAST FIGHT

"Doctor Hofmeister. We had you missing in action. Glad you made it back. Last time I saw you, I placed extra stripes on your lapel. You were loading a medivac train with supplies for the front. I can see you have no army issue or medical corps issue anything on you. Why don't you go to the quartermaster and have them get you geared up? I suggest we have dinner later and you report to me casually. No written report is needed. We are glad to have you back. Congratulations. Your new marching orders will be ready for you tomorrow morning. How does dinner at 18:00 hours sound to you? Meet me here."

"Thank you, Doctor Frank. Glad to be home."

The evening was spent in quiet conversation over a real meal in a real restaurant. Georg gave an account of his journey. It was informal and free of personal episodes and encounters with individuals he had met and gotten close to on the way. It was more of a travelogue with weather report. Georg appreciated home cooked items on the menu and tried more of them than he was hungry for. They ended up toasting each other and offered each other the personal address of Du as friends and colleagues now on a first name basis.

"Dieter."

"Georg."

"Cheers."

They talked about some personal things, how families and loved ones had fared. Georg was not comfortable talking about his family. He did not know enough, and it made him too upset. He steered the conversation to principle issues of the corps, the condition of the war and the population. He sprinkled in notes about the staff, excellence of medical personnel and avoided touching on the fate of the missing medical train. No information was volunteered to him and he did not feel comfortable to speculate. That would have pushed him over the edge at this moment. Georg thought to himself, *that will come up in good time.*

The conversation finally turned to Georg's next assignment. He was ordered to escort a supply train to the front in Italy. Monte Casino was a famous mountaintop monastery that had been converted into a hospital. "No moving target for you this time, Georg," Dr. Dieter Frank said. "Even though events have become more and more volatile and unpredictable in and around Cassino, we maintain our mission of saving lives. The red cross is now displayed again on all our medical facilities, tents, roofs, railcars and trucks. The Geneva convention rules, and the ban of the red cross and medical relief services is being challenged. With a low voice and as an aside, Dieter said to Georg: "I think it will be over soon. Monte Casino will likely be your last stop before you can return to civilian life. The army has been withdrawing from the southern part of Italy and the carnage of what they call the Italian Campaign is much greater than what anyone can comprehend. On both sides. On all sides. You will be staying there as part of the reinforcement for the Monte Cassino field hospital. You will bring with you much needed supplies, food and medicine. You will find the medical staff there to be completely exhausted. The operating rooms are in the center buildings of the badly damaged abbey. No one knows the present condition of the hospital or the surrounding area.

Cassino, the town, is completely destroyed." He changed the subject.

"I know you are interested in archeology and anthropology. The damage done to the architecture and to all artwork will break your heart. It might make you feel better to know, that treasures and the ancient foliants of the monastery library have been rescued and transported to the Vatican by an educated commander when they first set up the hospital there." Georg had a hard time pulling his thoughts away from Rose. He was startled by the next words he heard:

"Cassino is a rubble field. The tracks were destroyed. You will be transferred to trucks approaching the monastery from the inland side. Americans do not leave infrastructure in place. It was destroyed during the last three battles in this region. There is military mayhem on the ground. You will find wounded from many nations there and everyone will have begun to question their affiliation and responsibility to their commanders or to their country of origin, which may not be the same."

"I have come across this on my way here." Georg agreed.

"The monastery was never used for military purposes. The army left a rear guard in the slope below the ruins surrounding the main building. We were informed that the slope was spiked with land mines before our army withdrew. You will be bringing mine sniffing dogs. But you must warn your team to be cautious. The hospital is being maintained for remaining troops and for civilians who have suffered three assaults by different armies and allied forces trying to dislodge our defenders. There is no more military significance to this region, or to this mountain. This is a humanitarian mission you are going on."

"I understand," Georg said trying to appear friendly. He was tired enough to fall asleep with his fork in his mouth. The evening was concluded with a four handed handshake among friends.

Georg returned to his quarters, wishing that someone had more information of what lay ahead. All he had been able to learn was the fact that now there was the wildest mix of soldiers and armies involved in the defense and liberation of Italy and other Mediterranean countries. It was a nightmare of destruction and rearrangement of small religious, ethnic and social population groups occupying areas for many thousand years to some who arrived just a few decades or months ago. Many were relocated by the generals of the feuding parties after World War one. People were being armed and thrown into battle against each other for no understandable reason other than that they happened to be under someone's control and command. That created victims on all sides and emboldened a great number of opportunists who thrived under this violent confusion and vacuum. People who had lived in their villages were not prepared for confrontations with foreigners who had lost their roots a generation ago.

A doctor who had lost his left arm during his deployment and was now serving as a clerk, spoke freely to Georg:

"Be prepared. Both offense and the defense are designed to inflict maximum damage to civilians and soldiers on all sides. The population has suffered unimaginably. They have been raped, pillaged, misused and the absence of resemblance of military order has left zero accountability or command structure. We are now boldly marking doctors and medics with red crosses. A safeguard that is being too often ignored. The myth of legal, just, or defensive wars only exists in the minds of war profiteers and is used for fresh recruitment. These ideals have long died in anyone who was actually out there and has seen personally what war does to the human spirit. I suspect that the same people are supplying all sides of this conflict with weapons, money and propaganda. I believe it is about getting control over natural resources including the only thing that can really create value: People. Beat them hard enough, rile them up against each other and they are willing to agree to do anything as long as they can vent their hatred. Just wait and see for yourself." This was the pep talk of a wounded military surgeon, who lost his life in more ways than one. Worst of all for him, he was still alive.

Georg was taken to the Red Cross train at the rail yard. He was back in Army issue clothing and his pack was carefully loaded with the essentials a doctor and surgeon needs. His first lieutenant rank from his recent promotion afforded him an assistant, a second lieutenant and authority that comes with the extra stripe. Befriending and caring for the locomotive crew were something Georg did as a matter of principle. He was careful to carry the pouch with the letter from Hans with his personal papers. After he finished moving into his compartment, he began meeting the personnel on the train. Then he went forward to meet the drive team. Now that he was finally safe with new marching orders, he began to feel his deep fatigue more intensely.. He gave in to the motions and familiar sounds of the moving train. Being on this train made him feel safe. He was once again part of a team chartered to save lives. He finally went to sleep, able to let his guard down. In his sleep, images of his journey to Russia and back began pouring in. When he woke up, he had no idea where he was and how long he had been asleep. He felt the stubble on his cheeks to get a sense how long it must have been. His stomach was growling from hunger and thirst. The sliding door to his compartment opened slowly and quietly and a face appeared. Seeing that Georg was awake, his new assistant Dr. Ruediger Benning, who was his second lieutenant, greeted him and offered to bring him coffee and food. For a moment Georg did not remember who this caller was.

"I am Ruediger Benning. Doctor Ruediger Benning. Just got my doctorate. I am still getting used to my title. I was assigned to be your assistant. I was ordered to shadow and assist you any way I can until I know what I am doing."

"I Hope you never have to get used to what it is we have to be doing soon. There are skills we practice until we find our special talent and discover our passion in the medical profession. I am indebted to Doctor Wilhelm von Wallenstein my first lieutenant who is a superb surgeon. He was my mentor and guide. Lucky to serve under him in Russia. And I am starving. Did you mention food?"

"Yes, Doctor Hofmeister." Benning said, drew up the black-out blind to let the brightness of a snow-covered alpine world shine into the compartment. "It may be lunch rather than breakfast. I will bring you a sampling of what we have available for this trip. Permission to leave?" Georg nodded yes. Dr. Benning went to the canteen. Once alone, Georg stretched all his muscles, one at a time and looked into the small mirror above the tiny sink. He touched the tip on his upper lip and mused why Rose never asked about the scar that was still visible from close up.

Not a bad job, if I say so myself. She never asked about my hand either. She was more interested in me than in the wounds on my body. That's my Rose. Sweet as nectar, sharp as a thorn and tough as nails. She will get around to the details once we see the end of all this. The thought of Rose and baby Christopher made him weep. When food arrived, Georg wiped hands and face with a towel.

"Thank you, doctor Benning. What have I missed? Where are we now?"

"You have slept for almost twenty hours. We went to Konstanz, Friedrichshafen, Kempten and Innsbruck. We are now approaching Bolzano. We were beginning to be concerned. They say you have just returned from Stalingrad?"

"It was a long journey. I would rather not talk about it right now. I feel more fatigued than tired if you know what I mean. We must stay in the present. We must move forward. We must survive. More importantly we must see how many lives we can save. That is why I am still here. I will only say this: I made a vow to live. The secret was not to save my own life but to save other people's lives. Do we have sugar?"

"Yes, we do." While Dr. Benning went to get sugar. The train pulled into a railyard. Georg looked out of the window and saw swirling snowflakes. Memories of snowstorms swirled in his mind with the effect of blocking his mental view, just as this snow was now obstructing his view of the alpine landscape. He had no choice but to withdraw into this internal fog. His mind shut down and he sank onto his bunk and went to sleep again. When he woke up, several doctors were in his compartment and before he was fully awake, Georg heard his team discussing his long sleep and exhaustion. He opened his eyes.

"I appreciate your concern gentlemen." Georg said. "You are right. I am exhausted.

I have had no time to process what has happened since I left Stalingrad without marching orders. I was technically a deserter on the run. I went underground. My mind is still on the run. I have to try to let it calm down. I appreciate it if you do not ask me questions about my return from Stalingrad. It needs to rest. I was debriefed at Tübingen headquarters. I should have been given recovery time. Our fearless leader believes in getting up and dusting oneself off. I keep waking up every few minutes. No rem-sleep. Nightmares, not dreams. Trying to sleep has made me more exhausted. Trying not to sleep was also unsuccessful. Do we have oxygen on board? Perhaps you could set me up with supplemental oxygen. What do you think, Doctor Benning?"

"I agree. And please drink plenty of water." He went to get oxygen.

When Benning returned, Georg asked: "Where are we now?"

"We have gone past Trento and Verona and are now close to Milan. We are going to be briefed on conditions at the front. The army is in retreat. It looks like we are going to be stationed south of the new winter front." Benning was Georg's personal physician now.

"I should have asked for a break," Georg said. Spending more than a year to return from Stalingrad is considered a vacation in some people's mind. They have not been out there much. Let me have some of the oxygen now. I might sleep again. Wake me in time for the briefing. I will go to see the locomotive crew at the first stop after Milan." With this he put the oxygen breather over his nose and mouth, closed his eyes and took deep breaths and exhales. The oxygen improved his sleep and his outlook on the next moment. He no longer had one on life. He woke up when the train stopped at the Milan rail yard. "Where are we now?" Georg asked Dr. Benning.

"This is Milan". Dr Benning was sitting on his bunk, writing on blue letter stationary. Georg gave him a smile and said:

"I used to do that. Letters to my wife Rose. We had to interrupt writing when I went underground. I cannot bring myself to writing yet. I get too upset. I create her in my mind and now I have a son to invent as well. I have lost my ability to focus. In my mind's eye I see too much. I will come out of it. I treated a nurse who had saved her Sargent's life after an ambush on their medevac train. She was completely shut down. I will have to treat myself one step at a time. I will need your help to do so. You will be the only one I will talk to about this. Let me say thank you in advance. I will be your patient for the next few weeks. I will see the locomotive crew tomorrow. Either at Bologna or Florence. They must be picking up the next engine right now." Georg could feel the knock of the bumpers when the locomotive backed into the train to connect. It made him wince to remember how painful this moment was for his patients on the medevac train. He observed that this had put him into a heightened state of alertness, as close to pain as he could get without physical injury. I am not well, he said to himself. The next day he shaved, dressed and went to the dining car where doctors and staff were to be briefed on the status of the war. Several army officers had come to the train to deliver short speeches about affairs on the other side of Rome and south of the new winter line. They described the landscape around Cassino and the hospital at the center of the Abbey. They declared that Cassino had been the scene of fierce fighting and that the allies had suffered losses of a scale five times greater than the defending German forces. Georg noticed that no one mentioned the civilian population of the region. They were treated as traitors by everyone.

"This is now an emotional fight. The Americans will retaliate. Everyone will retaliate. Militarily there is no significant defense left in those hills. Just enough to give the army time until our winter defenses are established. You will be there to keep defenders and civilians alive and to move the wounded to evacuation points. We have no intelligence about the plans of the enemy. We have seen what American warfare looks like. They are all about fire power. They have been sparing churches and hospitals. Life and treasure have been poured into winning. You will not be able to go all the way to Cassino by train. We will provide trucks and escorts. You are not to interact with the civilian population."

Georg formulated a response but kept it to himself:

> *We will see about that. Five minutes ago, they were our allies,*
> *now they are suspect and not to be trusted. All along every one*
> *of them was and is someone's child, parent or grandparent.*

Georg mused on this while some technical details were being discussed. As soon as the speakers had finished, they disappeared and left the medics to their own thoughts.

The train pulled out of the railyard and moved towards Florence where another locomotive was waiting to move them to Rome. Georg was on oxygen treatment which invigorated and relaxed him. He used talk therapy with his assistant Benning both for his own benefit and for the development and preparation of this talented doctor. Rome was the last resupply stop for the hospital supply train. Masses of military movement could be observed, which gave the train crew time off and Georg had opportunity to spend some hours with the engineers, who seemed more nervous than the train crews in Poland and Russia. Mark Yanatschek, the head engineer, welcomed Georg, who's reference papers from Hans he had read when they first met. Yanatschek felt comfortable enough to share some of his thoughts: He was very agitated.

"This war is going in the toilet" he opened the subject.

"How long have you been doing medical runs?" Georg asked. "Time or kilometers?" Mark asked.

"Both" Georg suggested.

"I started one week after the war began and about 35000 kilometers"

"Did you ever take time off?"

"You are joking, right? I have not seen my family except for one day, when we stopped at Darmstadt and my wife was almost shot, because they thought she was a saboteur trying to blow up our locomotive."

"I am sorry. I am from Alzey, we are almost neighbors, in normal times."

"What normal times? What normal times!" This had set Mark off: "There have been no normal times since 1900. My father was a railroader before me. The most ridiculous time was, when the army thought they could run trains. They cannot even run wars. They think that tanks and aircraft can perform miracles. They run tanks into tight valleys, one behind another. You can see a panzer division stuck behind one tank that lost a chain. The enemy takes the front runner out with a grenade launcher. Their ordnance pierces armor now. Stop one and they all have to stop. Sink one and they all cannot move. That, my friend is sitting duck warfare. Then comes the need of resupply with food, ammunition, fuel and grease. Every six hours these jokes stop running. You have to build roads behind them to keep them moving. There are no service stations and grease shops in the Italian mountains like on the parade grounds where they are being sold. This is all bullshit. Deadly, fatal bullshit. Tanks are designed to scare civilians. Nothing else. To make them feel insecure. So they will agree to finance more tanks."

"You seem upset" Georg was concerned.

"Of course, I'm upset." Yanatschek replied his voice getting louder. His eyes shooting arrows. "I could explode! I have been transporting doctors and casualties all over Europe. You have seen the wounds. Never mind what we are doing to the locals. Civilians, women, children and old people being raped and pillaged by out of control soldiers. From out of control armies. Do you know how many nationalities are fighting each other? Do you realize how confused they are? Some actually believe that the Nazis will free them. So, they turn on the Socialists. They did not notice that it's all the same thing: A few at the top control everything. They collect the rewards for everyone's labor. The fascists buy cheap goods from the communists. That frees up capacity to make more weapons. The weapons are used to fight everyone and to scare the crap out of everyone. Look out of this window. You see the United Nations of armed victims. These boys have no beef with one another. They cannot even speak each other's language. They all look alike. "He looked out of his locomotive window and at the olive trees beyond the railyard. "In the beginning we were sharing technology of tank building with Russia. Then we attacked them.

Now they shoot at us with gear we sold them. They called it an economic miracle. I say Bullshit. It was fraud from the beginning. Fraud that destroys people's moral fiber. Fraud that leaves them orphaned and widowed." He took a long look at his grease stained hands. "Do you have any idea how I feel about shipping you boys to this front of all fronts? These bastards are shooting to do maximal damage to humans now. All of them do it. I am waiting to see where they have shut down the railway tracks. Then we all have to run for our lives, because no one trusts anyone out there and we have no place to hide. I pray to God they figure out a way to end this war. To end all these totalitarian regimes. Tito, Franko, Mussolini all sellouts to Hitler and his paymasters. Someone is making money hand over fist. Germany had no money. Comes Adolf Hitler and suddenly they can use the Reichsmark and he can buy things everywhere, as long as he buys arms or makes weapons. The same is true with the socialists and the communists or whatever label you want to print on their flag. This is no propaganda. These are facts." There was a long silence. Finally Georg said:

"This was the pep talk I needed. I have to go to my compartment now. I need to rest. I am sure that like myself you have seen too much of what you are talking about. I still have lives to save. I cannot give up. Never. That is my mission. Good night."

The train reached the end of the line, at the last depot with a functioning service carousel, where locomotives could be serviced, reloaded, turned around and attached to the front of a train going back. A long line of trucks had been assembled to move doctors, nurses supplies and food away from the coast onto back roads and up through the mountains. To Georg this all seemed unreal, like the quiet before a storm. No more army present except for some rear guards like highway robbers in strategic positions to slow the pursuit of allied troops, which they knew were sure to show up sooner rather than later.

By the end of the week they had reached their destination in a landscape that was destroyed by several waves of artillery attacks from the sea off the shore of Cassino. Some signs of life were still stirring here and there. On the way they had stopped for old people and very young starving children with their mothers holding out their hands in hopes of gifts of water, milk powder, cheese, bread or flour. Images that would stare forever at Georg in the middle of the night, when they broke into his restless sleep. Remote valleys, where they had been routed with their convoy were devastated. What they were witnessing was a humanitarian crisis. This war had caused total destruction, and no one was reporting it, because there were no news reporters or newspapers. The witnesses were also the victims and no one in less affected areas of the planet would believe what he and his doctors had witnessed here. Georg also could not stand the loss of world heritage in works of art and architectural treasures he saw broken and strewn throughout this region. What struck him the deepest was the destruction of a population that had no stake or interest in this worldwide conflagration.

Just as they arrived at the Abbey of monte Cassino, Georg felt the onset of joint pain, headaches and a rise in temperature. He felt chilled and hot at the same time. He asked his assistant to measure his temperature and to keep an eye on him. Boosting oxygen was no longer doing the job.

"I feel profoundly exhausted". He told his assistant. "Make sure I do not get dehydrated." He was asleep as soon as his head touched his pillow in a small meditation room facing the slope overlooking what was once Cassino and the Mediterranean. He noted the absence of books and artifacts, noted his inability to focus. He did not remember that he had not taken command of this Lazarett, as they referred to it here. He had not been able to introduce himself to those who were stationed here. At the moment of his arrival, Georg was disabled and unable to care.

A familiar scent was the first thing that entered Georg's consciousness. Before he opened his eyes, his mind was roaming to place the scent. It contained one specific ingredient which he needed to find a name for. Suddenly it came to him: Jasmine. There was a second scent, which he could not find a name for. Then his body was responding to an emotion which lead him to feel his way through memories until he felt a hand touch his forehead. Before he could formulate a thought, he heard himself say:

"Anne? Sister Anne, is that you?" His eyes were still closed. The hand left his forehead and placed a small object in his hand. When he opened his eyes, he saw the tiger eye stone he had given to the nurse on the way to the front. Then he saw her. She opened his right hand and examined the scar.

"I am thirsty." Georg said. She felt the scar on his lip. looked into his eyes. "I have tea for you, and we have time." She said and after giving him long, deep kiss she added: "Welcome back".

They spent the next few days of his recovery making time to catch up on their journeys of rescue and survival. Georg recovered and eventually took command of the hospital. Seeing Sister Anne in action, Georg felt it natural to promote her to head of nursing staff. Together they organized the supplies Georg's unit had delivered. Together they spent hours gazing over the ocean, speaking quietly about visions for the future and dreams for their personal lives.

All their thoughts were on expanding their mission from saving lives to saving the future.

Suddenly the present felt like the ash from a volcanic eruption had fallen on the hospital of Monte Casino when a group of women from a remote valley arrived very early one morning. Georg was called by the doctors on night shift. He did not have to wait for words but saw in the doctor's eyes that a very serious event had taken place that needed everyone's attention. Before he arrived at the operating room, he saw in the waiting room scattered torn clothing and undergarments mixed with ragged blankets and scarves left behind as the patients were led into the examination room.

"How many" Georg asked. "Fourteen. All from one village."

"Is Sister Anne here? Is our interpreter here?" Feverish at first, the patients were prepared for examination by the nurses. Bleeding needed to be stopped and time needed to be won to give each arrival a place in the order of urgency. Then the doctors started to go to work.

"The physical injuries are the easy part," said Sister Anne to Georg as they scrubbed side by side in preparation for surgery. "They will heal. The emotional injuries will take a lifetime. I am afraid these are all rape victims. From what I can understand, a group of soldiers has fallen over their small settlement about forty-eight hours ago. They had no choice but to let these animals have their way if they wanted a chance to live. Those who resisted were mutilated and died of their wounds. One of the women took the lead and organized a feast during which they made the soldiers drunk. The soldiers perished by their own bayonets, handled by women who were used to butcher animals for meat. Last night, they left the village about three hours away from here in the hills. These are the survivors who got away. Some are barely alive. We are still doing intake right now. All are in shock. We are preparing the operating station for several lines, depending on the severity of the injuries. Are you up to it? This will be a long day."

"Yes Sister. Thank you. I am ready."

Fourteen tables were now occupied with patients in green gowns, surrounded by orderlies and nurses. The doctors began the assessment process and sedation was given. Patients were moved to different operating stations where work began in the hushed silence of complete concentration interrupted only by occasional requests for items needed to be handed to the surgeons. Further talking and questioning would have to wait for later, after patients had spent a few hours in the recovery room. Nature and severity of the injuries cast a cloud over the entire team. Actions that had caused these injuries were far beyond anyone's imagination. They had to be banned from the caregiver's mind and focus had to stay on one task at a time. During a short break, Sister Anne and Georg exchanged a few words. Anne said:

"I want to schedule a debriefing for every caregiver who is present and was working here today. These are mothers, sisters and grandmothers we are treating. There is no war justification to the crimes that were committed here. These are victims of the most heinous crimes. We understand that similar events have taken place all over this region by marauding splinter troops of various nationalities who were lost or forgotten and had no more leadership. I will offer private counselling for our caregivers. I would like to offer private consultations to the victims over the next few days with our interpreter present. I want to intercept guilt as soon as possible. I believe we can use the same energy towards healing in these victims and turn them towards recovery. I know it will take a lifetime of work for these women to heal. What do you think, Georg?"

"I think you are correct and wise. You have my support and my gratitude. History will have to write what happened to these women. You and I will have the rest of our lives to try and forget what we have seen here today. I pray that this is not the fate of all who were left behind. We should finish surgery in about four hours. Do you have the stamina?" He looked at her.

"I will do what it takes. We have a very dedicated team." They returned to work.

ASSAULT NUMBER FOUR
MONTE CASSINO

One morning battleships with canon could be seen from the Abbey of Monte Cassino maneuvering into position. Fear rose in everyone's heart as one could observe landing craft being deployed. Masses of foot soldiers in combat gear were pouring over the beach and struggled through the rubble fields of Cassino. Georg called Anne to join him at his tower room.

"They are coming for us", Georg observed. "But there is nothing here." Anne protested.

"This is the fourth assault on Cassino. Three times leveled the town. Now they want to put a flag on this building."

"But there are no soldiers here to capture!" Anne was exasperated.

Georg replied patiently:

"They do not know that. What I have seen are just a dozen or so hidden machine gunners and I was told that this slope is heavily mined. We brought dog teams to sweep for mines before we can even rescue anyone during and after this assault."

"Are you sure there is nothing we can do? Raise a white flag and surrender?" She said pleadingly.

"No, my heart. We are flying the red cross. Nothing can be done to argue with these few machine gunners. They have their orders. I can only hope the ships gunners know how to aim their cannons. Look. You can see them adjust their aim right now. I do not want to continue this war and I do not want it to end our lives here in these ruins. I think you are right about surrender. I am ordering you and your team to prepare white sheets to hang out of windows to surrender. Hang them alternating with red cross banners."

Georg felt exhausted, sad and lost. He did not know if he could recover from this feeling. He was searching for the drive to live he had felt when he crossed the Don. He was now hoping for anger to be a motivator, the way the locomotive driver was fired up, ready to stand up against this war. At the end of the day Georg assembled the Hospital staff and brought in the patients, who could be moved to attend a prayer meeting.

He asked God for strength, patience, forgiveness and absolution for trespasses and sins and for the safety of loved ones of all who were assembled. He included the foreign soldiers in his prayers, knowing that their mission was to end this war. He thanked everyone for their service and dedication to saving and preserving life.

"We must prepare to see our maker. God bless you." Georg concluded and returned everyone to their stations. It was eerily quiet all night. Georg woke up before first light when Sister Anne joined him by the window overlooking the ocean and Cassino. They saw no signs of life in the slope beneath the abbey. A puff of white smoke appeared along the flanks of the battle ships out at sea and a delayed thunderclap followed by a series of impact explosions and plumes of smoke on the ground. The view from the window on the top floor of the abbey revealed to Georg and Anne a pattern of bomb blasts ahead of an endless stream of foot soldiers who were beginning to storm the slopes of Monte Cassino. Progress of these infantry forces was steady and went up about halfway, when the first landmines in the slope were set off by falling debris from bomb explosions. The advance of the attack slowed but did not stop. There was no way anyone could turn around and escape. More and more soldiers were pushing up the slope, carrying heavy combat gear, hundreds and hundreds of their comrades following, making retreat impossible. Shortly thereafter, concealed machine gunners opened fire on the attacking forces. Smoke from bomb explosions from the ship artillery and from land mines made it impossible for anyone to see where the machine gunners were firing from. "These soldiers are doomed", Georg whispered under his breath." The ones who escape machinegun fire are tripping land mines." He could feel his pulse rate rising, adrenalin almost disabling him.

"We have to get ready to collect the wounded" Anne shouted, left Georg and went to the ground floor to inspect readiness of stretchers and personnel. Georg followed her to caution everyone to stay calm and to wait for the gun fire and the bombardment to cease.

"They are not bombing the abbey. If they wanted to, we would no longer be standing here. Hold your places. I do not want anyone to be sacrificed. No one goes out without a dog team clearing a path through the land mines.!" Georg ran back upstairs to await the secession of the cannon fire from the battleships. He was devastated by the sight of countless soldier's dead and dying. His mouth went completely dry. His hatred for war had now reached its peak and he was in a state of hypervigilance when the cannon fire came to a halt. Georg ran back downstairs and ordered rescue operations.

"Only behind the dogs. They will be detecting mines and trip wires. Only after the specialists have disarmed them." Georg shouted for everyone to hear.

At this moment he saw Sister Anne leading a couple of medics with a stretcher ahead of everyone else. Georg saw them disappear in a powerful explosion of a land mine. A scream escaped his throat. Georg was unable to breathe. For a few moments his legs gave out and he sank to his knees. With the greatest effort, he picked himself up, turned to the rescuers and with a gesture of both arms indicated slow, slow, slow and caution. He went to his station and prepared to receive the first wounded. What happened during the next twelve hours did not register in his memory. Georg saw the ward fill up with very young, severely wounded soldiers, barely twenty years old. He was stoically operating, ordering surgical tools, ether, gauze and serum. He had lost track of time. Finally, a nurse took him by the hand and led him outside. He was trying to breathe.

"Doctor Hofmeister. You are on break now please rest. You have not stopped for the last twelve hours. You need to eat something. You need water." Someone handed him a flask of water. These were the pleading words of his assistant, Dr. Benning.

"I have to find Sister Anne. She was right over there. I have to find her." Georg ran to the place where he had seen her disappear in the blast. He searched and found a few of her remains after he discovered her severed hand still clasping the tiger eye rock he had given her for a keep sake and safe travel. He collected as many parts of his dear friend, colleague and companion as his operating apron would hold. Then he collapsed. When Georg came to, he was in a room with people who spoke English. "Where am I? "He asked. "And who are you?"

CHAPTER SEVENTEEN
POW

"**D**octor you are under arrest. You are in the custody of the United States armed forces. Your hospital staff are also under arrest. We have given them orders to continue the rescue work which they have done in an outstanding way. You will all be given special consideration as members of the Red Cross."

The voice faded. Georg was physically and emotionally completely spent. He could barely see, and the world had gone silent behind the sound of rushing water in the center of his skull. His assistant had not left his side. Georg had pictures in his mind from before the attack. Just two days ago from the top floor of the Abbey, where he and Anne had observed the bottom of the hill. It looked like a rubble field in front of a quarry. At the hospital which was occupying the main floor, the medics treated a trickle of wounded and sick people from all corners of Europe and west Africa, both military and civilian. Georg had begun turning the soil in the garden to somehow stay connected to life. He transplanted some perennials and collected seeds from dry stalks, wondering what might sprout and grow. The archeologist in him unearthed some Roman marble artifacts that were buried in the soil of the cloister garden. He kept seeing the face of Sister Anne and could feel the jump his heart had made when he realized that she was still alive the day after he had arrived at the Abbey.

These were images he was clinging to as he was taken back to Germany. He had no capacity to record new information or to understand what was going on. He was unable to formulate thoughts. He smiled at people who fed him and slept for many hours without caring where he was or where he was going. Georg could not recall how he had gotten back to Stuttgart. His mind was like a tape recorder that worked but did not have a tape in it to record. Georg spent weeks in a hospital that was part of the POW encampment of Stuttgart and slowly recovered from a state of global amnesia and exhaustion. He was considered a low risk prisoner. After a while Georg became acquainted with the commander of the camp. The state of his health was improving but the past month eluded his recall. Dr. Benning, his assistant, was still nearby and saw himself as the guardian of his superior officer. His accounts of events and the actual events Georg was able to remember were getting mixed up. He remembered the American officer saying that he had ordered his staff to continue rescue efforts. He remembered wanting to say that it would be harder to stop them from saving lives than to make them continue. His desire to forget was greater than that to recall events. He began thinking of contacting his friends in Stuttgart, his hometown. He knew that his war would not end until he could get away from here and make his way to the mountains, to Rose and to their son Christopher. His desire to return home became an obsession that was informed by the experience of his escape from Stalingrad. He began visualizing the route, the weather, the landscape and the obstacles he needed to overcome. He began by being a model prisoner serving as a doctor anyone who needed his help.

The POW camp was located on a former track and field sports complex. Inmates were separated by levels of risk and guarded accordingly. Georg was held in the company of physicians, teachers and scholars, who were considered low risk. He was still in the care of his assistant Doctor Benning. Both had permission to receive visitors and be supplied with literature and to exchange books regularly. With friends and family who were residing in Stuttgart Georg developed an active book exchange. His exhaustion wore off and he was able to add exercise into his daily routine. Doctors in Camp were looking after one another and as they were given permission to look after other inmates and the US Armed Forces prison staff. Positive relationships and acquaintances were soon forming.

"I do not have an issue with you" was a sentence heard often from doctors. Georg was able to consult with his friends during visits and they felt secure enough to be able to talk in private. One idea that sprang up was to obtain permission to leave camp for medical visits to relatives at first and to other patients later on.

Georg became the personal physician for the camp commander and his family. To make this easier, he studied English to freshen up his language skills. He began wearing formal clothes, beginning with dark pants, then jackets and white shirts, black shoes and socks. He was holding a pass that gave him movement to the camp commanders residence. To build his image as a physician and for his comfort, he accepted the offer of a friend to collect his laundry and to return it washed and pressed. Being meticulously groomed was his habit throughout his time as a doctor, no matter where he was. Most of his time Georg spent in intense studies on medical subjects. He was interested in expanding his view and knowledge of the functioning of nature and the relationship between substance, energy and the phenomena of life in the bloodstream and in each living cell. His daily routine was predictable and repetitive. People stopped watching Georg.

It was an early morning late October 1945. The sky was overcast, and Georg had a visitor who had been coming to supply and exchange books for him regularly. Today he did not bring new books, but an empty book bag, to collect Georg's books and notes. Then he left with a nod to the guard who had seen this visitor many times before.

Georg had a doctor's appointment to see the children of the camp commander at 9:00 o'clock at their residence. When he was done examining the children, he spent some time with the children's mother to reassure her that they were developing fine, followed by some dietary suggestions. "I am very grateful to you, Doctor Hofmeister. You have taken away my fear of raising my children during these extended deployments. Especially the fact that you seem to have improved your English from visit to visit. What is even more remarkable is the way you connect with my children.

They talk about you like of a family friend, not like a physician or an authority figure. Let me know if you need anything at all."

"Thank you. You have remarkable children. Being their doctor has given me a chance to feel normal. It has taken away my uncertainty about the future, even though it was just for moments. You must know how lucky I feel to be in the custody of the American Armed Forces and especially under the command of your husband." She felt like giving him a hug but remembered just in time that Georg was still a prisoner of war. They exchanged courteous goodbyes instead and Georg called out to the children:

"Bye-bye Julia, By James, watch over your mom!"

Two days later Georg was climbing a steep trail of a mountain in Black Forest. He was carrying his medical supply bag over one shoulder and a large wreath of Norwegian spruce with a black bow over the other. His friends had given him a black minister's shirt, a white minister's collar, a pair of black boots that could be worn in bad weather or even snow. He had a map that gave him the names of villages and little towns he was going to come near. In his mind and heart, he was now on the final leg of his journey. He had seen his Rose more than a Year ago just before his departure for Monte Cassino. He had seen her only for one brief moment. He remembered the passionate encounter that ended in a sleepless night and a long talk about their role in a post war world and about the way they would prevent the past years from turning toxic in their minds: Georg remembered these words, little did he know how important they seemed after the events of Monte Cassino.

"We will never talk about the horrors we have seen during this war. We will point our eyes towards the future and try to focus on the heritage we own and wish to preserve. What we will be asked to do is not as important as how we support the people who share our desire for freedom and social justice. I owe my life to this pledge. Giving up and dying would have been the easy way out. Staying committed to our future and the future of the children of this world was hard but it kept me in fighting mode."

"Good morning, father!" A young soldier in peacetime dress uniform startled Georg and he almost dropped his wreath. By the shade of green of his coat and the emblem on his beret Georg guessed that this was someone from the British Armed Forces.

"Good morning, son." Georg answered. Are you familiar with this area?"

"No sir. I am sorry. Unfortunately, I am a bit lost myself."

"I am on my way to Horb. I am sure that once I reach the river, I cannot miss it. I should be able to get there in about an hour or two. I am

standing in for a fellow minister who has fallen ill to officiate at a funeral.
I will turn left towards the river when we reach the top. And You?"

"I was thinking I must turn right to get back to my base," his companion
said. They talked about the good fortune that peace was finally achieved.
And how much they would have liked to talk more. Georg reached out to
shake the soldier's hand when they reached the fork in the road.

"God bless you my son." Georg heard himself say. *I sound just like
my father.* He thought to himself. *Good thing they call me Father* Georg
chuckled at the thought. The first encounter with a soldier had made him
very nervous. He was slowly realizing that he was once again an escapee.
A P. O. W. from an internment camp of the United States of America,
an outlaw on the run. He remembered Mrs. Gmeiner's words: "Try not
to get caught by the French, the English or the Russians." This thought
made him almost jump out of his skin. *I have to let this all go.* He reminded
himself. After he had walked through a small forest, farm fields opened
up before him and he recognized a linden tree with a bench where he had
spent time during his cavalry training. He and his companions were using
this bench regularly to rest and have meals during training rides. He had
always considered old linden trees to be holy places. Now he offered a
prayer of thanks worthy of a real minister of the church of his ancestors.
Then another thought came to him: Not five minutes from here was the
farm of a family named Singer. He knew them because he had assisted in
the delivery of the first-born child of their oldest daughter. He was about
to visit and see the baby. He was hoping to get some rest here and some
provisions for the next leg of his journey. Then he remembered what his
friend who brought him the wreath had said: "Do not interact with people
who know you socially until you get home. You have come a long way. Do
not let your success get to your head. It might be your downfall."

Georg turned the opposite direction and walked right into Horb
instead. Here he hid his wreath and went to a small bakery to buy supplies
which he crammed into his medical bag. A chocolate treat turned into
space saving energy supply, so he included six bars of dark chocolate to be
consumed with the fresh rolls he had compressed into flat discs for extra
space. He came across the letters Hans the railroad engineer had given him.
This reminded him to see the railroad people at the local depot. He spoke
to the station master after presenting his letter, inquiring about a freight

train going towards Augsburg via Kempten. After reading the message the stationmaster said:

"The freight train on the third rail to the left is scheduled to leave in half an hour. It will be stopping at Kempten for resupply. Show the drivers your letter. I am sure they will help you out. We should be able to end this war one of these days. I suppose it is not over, until everyone has made it home. Good luck doctor." Half an hour later Georg was on his way to Kempten. Seeing how tired Georg was, the engineer flipped down a bunk for him. After he had slept for a few hours, he looked out of the window of the locomotive with new eyes, even the conversation had changed. Now it was about the forty million returnees who came home to ruins or who had lost their countries altogether and were looking to start a new life at a new place. Georg and the other refugees had in common that local people were treating homeless families as outcasts.

"I will have the same problem", Georg said to himself as much as to the train crew. "First step is to get home. I appreciate the lift and wish you all the very best as we rebuild our world." The freight train had moved into the railyard of Kempten to switch engines. After goodbyes and good wishes Georg left the train and hiked along the main road until he reached the road that crossed the rails and lead to Gustl's farm. He noticed the ongoing preparations for winter. His excitement rose, when he saw a woman crossing the yard, carrying a child. She could hear his footsteps, turned towards Georg and paused just long enough to make sure it was not her imagination running wild.

"Georg, it is Georg! He is alive!" Jutta shouted loud enough for her parents to hear. Her face lit up in a broad smile, laughing she part skipped and part walked towards Georg. She presented her baby." Look! This is Georgl, your namesake!"

"Namesake"… Georg took a second to let this sink in. He took the baby from her hands and kissed her across the baby's belly." I would have preferred patron saint," they laughed.

"He looks wonderful and he smells like you. Congratulations. How are grandma and grandpa?" He looked around, as he returned the strapping baby boy to his mother.

"He looks just like you. He has your eyes. That is even better than a patron saint." The proud mother said to Georg. The farm was once again in winter preparation. "Please come in, papa and mama will be so happy to see you alive. You know how it is."

"Was" Georg corrected." A few more days and this will be all over."

"Is there anything you need?" Georg looked down his ministers' suit and his worn black hiking boots, then at his outstretched arms and said: "I think I need everything one more time. You might have to take me to your relative's shops again. Everything." he repeated. With this, they entered the kitchen, where Georg was received like the long-lost son. Everyone spoke at the same time and every time he tried to speak there were more questions than answers. "How about some coffee so I can catch my breath," he said with a broad smile. His hand on the baby, he said: "Look at what you have grown while I was running all over creation. He is beautiful. Are you proud yet? And how is my patient? Everything back to normal? Have you finished cleaning up your farm after me? "He joked. "Do you need any wood cut?" He covered his mouth with his hand.

"Here is coffee and forgive us, but we have absolutely nothing in the house. Just a few pastries and fresh Christmas cookies no one is permitted to touch." He touched them. He was very emotional about this moment and tears were streaming down his face "You need some real food? You must be starving. Where did you come from today?"

"From north of Horb in the Black Forest. Via Kempten by freight train. I wanted to stay with friends in Horb, but I was afraid that they might be too excited to see me and perhaps tell too many people. I did escape from the Americans in Stuttgart and now I would like to return to my wife and see my child in Hirschegg. There I will be in a different Country under different occupation. I was a low risk prisoner as it was. I am curious how the French are behaving?"

"We hear they have been carrying young men off to North Africa to the Foreign Legion in Algiers. Maybe it would be safe for you now because you might be the only doctor of medicine up there."

"Yes. Last time I was there I delivered several babies. I am not sure this small village can support their own doctor. For me the war is not over until we are settled somewhere."

"How about your relatives? Where do they live?"

"My older brother is somewhere between the Caucasus mountains in Russia and Munich. He is also a doctor. I have no final report. His wife lives with her children here at Bolsterlang. That is where my wife was escaping to, during some wild snowstorms." Georg looked out the window. He could see clouds amassing near the mountain peaks." Looks like even the weather remembers me. What do you think? Will we get snowed in again?" He had directed these words towards Gustl, who walked over to him to look out of the same window.

"In one day or two this will unload. The temperatures are dropping already. The slopes are still wet from the last rain. If that freezes and then snows, there will be avalanches. Did Jutta say, you need to go shopping again?" He looked with some amusement in his face at Georgs minister outfit. "Your Grace." Gustl added and gave one of his infectious belly laughs.

"Yes. I told her. I need everything. Again" Georg laughed. They all laughed happily.

"Will you tell us about your journey back and about what else happened since we last saw you?"

"How about after you finish with the animals. If you don't mind, I could use a nap after this wonderful meal with absolutely nothing in the house, as you called it."

"Use your old bedroom. We kept it for you to help us wish for your safe return. We are superstitious about things like this and", crossing herself, "we were right. You came back alive." Liese said. Georg took her into his arms and held her until he could whisper:

"Thank you, grandmother." He followed Jutta to the room he had slept in before. He could see that she had used it as a nursery for her baby with a changing table and extra bowls and pitchers to bathe her child. "This looks nice. You are sure you don't mind if I sleep a little? I will sleep so deep; you can put the baby in bed with me and I will not wake up."

"All I have to do is to feed him and change diapers and then we will leave you to rest."

Georg took off his boots, jacket, vest and pants and slipped under the cover. He was asleep as soon as his head touched the pillow and he had inhaled two breaths of her scent lingering in this room. He woke up from the nap disoriented and confused about his whereabouts. He could not remember if it was the Cossack baby, the infant from the tiny barge at the Danube near Vienna or Rose's baby…. then he heard the voice that went with the scent: Jutta.

"Shhhh" she said. Georgl you must be quiet; Georg is still sleeping."

"No, he is not," Georg chimed in" but I think both Georgs are hungry."

"Yes, this one is always ready for a meal. He also likes mashed carrots and he hates spinach."

When Georg appeared at the family table, he had to pinch himself to bring time and place together into the present. His black attire reminded him as did a shirt belonging to Gustl which Liesl had laid out for him telling him that his black shirt needed a wash. He told his hosts that he could only tell them about the return to his unit at Tubingen. That his last deployment was so horrific, he could not remember most of it and never wanted to speak about it again.

"I became very sick with influenza and ill with global exhaustion. What is most important to me now is that you saved my life with the outfit and provisions you gave me on my way."

"No, no Georg, that was nothing. Georg you have done more for us than you will ever know." Liese said. "Look at Gustl. He is sitting, breathing smiling and a proud grandfather. He has not even tried to crash a train once. What is most important is that you are alive, that you are here and that you know we will do anything in our power to see that you make it safely home to your family." Liese looked Gustl, Jutta, and at the baby and smiled. Jutta nodded agreement and added:

"Georg needs everything, just like last time. If grandmother watches Georgl, I will take Georg back to the shops and we will fit him an outfit to get him home." Together they spent another hour and Gustl took Georg into the stables to show him the pride of the breeder, a strapping young bull in his own stall.

"Remember him?" His eyes were shining. "We have shown him twice at different breeder's events in the region. He has taken two first prizes. That is what you have done for us." He took Georg's hand with both of his and shook it for a long time. Then he looked at Georg's upper lip to see if he could tell the scar from the chopping accident." That accident might have saved my life" Georg said. "Having my head bandaged was a disguise most people prefer to look away from."

After another restful night and tearful goodbyes, Jutta took Georg into town and once again they found everything Georg needed. This time he removed the labels and put everything on, right at the shops. The black garments of the minister's outfit went into the wastebasket. It had begun to snow heavily, which reminded them to pick out skis, poles and climbing furs as well. Looking like a Bavarian mountaineer, Georg took Jutta to the bus and waved until she had disappeared. Tears were streaming down her face when they said goodbye. Both happy and sad. Now he turned up the valley with his eyes on the mountain peaks, where snow had begun to accumulate in massive amounts. Georg remembered the storm the last time he was in this area with avalanches at the opposite side of the mountain. The snow was now accumulating fast, all sounds were muffled, and visibility became that of heavy fog. Suddenly someone stepped in front of him and in an official voice said:

"Passport and papers please."

"Passport and papers? Georg asked.

"Yes sir, you are leaving Germany and entering Austria. This section of Germany is under American administration and Austria is under French control."

"You do not sound American."

"The Administrator hired us to man the border. There are many former military personnel from many different armies still on the loose and America is looking to sort them out."

"I am a doctor" Georg pointed to the medical bag he had slung over his shoulder. "I have patients to see in Klein Walsertal and this barrier was not up the last time I came this way."

"Which village are you going to visit?"

"Hirschegg."

"You have to speak to my colleague at the other side of this building. He works for the French." Georg began taking off his skis after dropping his pack. He was about to pick up his skis and gear when he heard the signature crack and bang of an avalanche right behind and above the little building with the customs office. This put him in a state of hypervigilance. His time perception changed, giving him the impression that everything was happening in slow motion. The roar of the avalanche increased, as Georg flung his things to the wall of the building. At the instant when snow started pouring over the top of the roof, Georg grabbed the border guard and tackled him sideways to bring him down next to the wall, covering him with his own body. They remained in this position for several minutes. After the stream of snow had stopped and the wall of snow became visible right where they had stood a moment ago, the guard relaxed and said:

"Thank you." Then he began to shake.

"Show me where the door is. Do you have shovels? We have to find the other border guards. Time to shake is later after we have found everyone. You tell me who else is here." Georg used command tone in his voice and the guard snapped to and pointed to the door. They went inside, took two shovels and went looking for survivors. They saw a boot of the French border guard who had not reacted in time. Now they dug him out and took him into the building. He had not been able to breathe and had begun to turn blue. Now he began to recover.

"Is there anyone else?" The Guard from the German side asked. "No, they left half an hour ago. I was alone."

"Good. You are lucky. Look at your desk." Half the building was filled with snow and debris, the desks and chairs of the guards were buried where the avalanche had taken out the windows on the uphill side of the building. "Do you have blankets?" Georg asked. "It is important that you stay warm. How do you feel?" Georg had directed this question to both men.

"Fine," said the Guard Georg had covered.

"Better," said the guard from the French side, his knees were shaking so hard he had to grab the sides of his chair. "I thought I was dead." He giggled involuntarily. To the first guard, Georg said.

"Make no fire. Your chimney may not draw. Do you have a thermos bottle with something hot? Give him sips of coffee or tea. Water will do too." Then he felt both guard's pulse at the wrist and neck. When he found good circulation in both border guards, he said:

"I have to go. God keep you safe."

Georg picked up his gear, dusted the snow and debris off, stepped into his skis and disappeared into the snowstorm. Now he began to breathe hard and his entire body was vibrating from adrenaline. He could hear the snap and thunder of several more avalanches on the opposite side of the valley. Georg's energy was now concentrated on getting home before it was dark. Two more hours to climb. No more borders to cross. He had taken one of the snow shovels with him in anticipation of finding the entrance of the building covered again. By habit, he left the road and took to the side of the hill where he could approach the cottage crossing the slope almost level. Georg reached the chalet; his heart made a jump into his throat when he saw smoke from the chimney. He put down his backpack, dropped his doctor's bag and took off his skis, then began digging out the entrance. When he was almost done, the upper half of the door began to move, and the beloved face of Rose appeared. Surrounded by the weathered wood of the door frame, her arms resting on the lower half of the door, she looked like the ikon he had visualized, an image which had given him the will to make it all the way back.

"My heart, I am home. He whispered through his tears. The war is over."

"Wait," she said, disappeared for a moment and came back holding out a bouquet of red roses. "I grew these for you. I want to give you these roses, my children, my world and myself. All of it. It is all yours now.

The embrace and the kisses that followed were making time stand still. The only sign left at the threshold were the petals of red roses, a few green leaves and some long stems. They remained untouched until Spring, while inside in the warmth of the cottage a feast began that left nothing untouched, unspoken, uncherished, uncelebrated or uneaten. His son Christopher pointed to another baby. A beautiful girl named Sophia. Georg decided that he was the happiest man on this planet and that now finally together he and Rose could cross all the borders they ever wanted to cross.

GRATITUDE
POSTSCRIPT

The French occupation administration made everyone leave the valley, who had not lived here for at least twenty years. Young men were sent to the French Foreign Legion in North West Africa. The guard from the French side of the border to Austria made sure that Georg did not have to go to Algiers.

"He is my doctor and I owe him my life," he told the French official. Even though Georg had delivered several babies in this village, one of them being the child of the mayor himself and Georg was the only doctor in the valley, he, Rose and their two children had to leave this valley before the following winter. Rose was with child again. They returned to Germany where they found temporary employment caring for children with disabilities.

The POW Camp at Stuttgart had been closed and prisoners were sent to the United States of America. Prior to the closing of the camp the Commander had removed Georg's file at the request of his wife.

Georg pursued a career as a physician and educator, founder of schools, protective workshops and housing for disabled adults. He wrote books for teachers, taught and lectured extensively on education and social justice issues.

It took another seven years before Rose and Georg were able to build a home and move together as a family in walking distance to the school where he worked and taught.

There was a part of Georg that went to war but never returned. Georg died many years later of heart failure, while doing work on a new edition of one of his books. The latest had been a collection of poetry about Nature. He was eighty years old.

His love of art and music created a special life for Rose and her family. The trauma of the war cast a shadow over his family's life but never defeated him. He would rather go without shoes than not buy musical instruments or pay for music instruction for his children.

*   *   *

Rose had a baby every other year until she had given Georg five girls and five boys. She began writing and lecturing on social issues into very high age even though at first, she did not think that anyone wanted to hear from a housewife with ten children. She removed this glass ceiling by founding her own publishing company. She published her work under a writer's name. Later she became the rock star in her assisted living facility, where she lived with Alzheimer's Dementia.

She needed only a chord, a few notes or a description of a song and could accompany them with her guitar. She sang with her fellow seniors, bringing joy to all. She knew how to celebrate.

She went missing in a four hundred square mile forest. Her body was found untouched after fifty days.

Rose is remembered with love and admiration by everyone who knew her. Her life was celebrated with poetry she had written thirty-three years earlier. Her poems revealed a deep spirituality as well as her struggle with the mysteries of PTSD. She was looking to muster the strength and spiritual fortitude to be an adequate partner for Georg. She did not find answers in religion or philosophy. She did not know that Georg had PTSD and that she too had inherited benefits from PTSD from her own father, who had returned from service in World War One with malaria and PTSD. Trauma was the norm of her time and the extra challenge of her generation.

THE END

Printed in the United States
By Bookmasters